A Division of the Light
Christopher Burns

Quercus

First published in Great Britain in 2012 by

Quercus
55 Baker Street
7th Floor, South Block
London
W1U 8EW

A CIP catalogue record for this book is available
from the British Library

ISBN 978 0 85738 635 9 (HB)
ISBN 978 1 78087 211 7 (TPB)

10 9 8 7 6 5 4 3 2 1

Typeset by Ellipsis Digital Limited, Glasgow

Printed and bound in Great Britain by Clays Ltd, St Ives plc

Christopher Burns is the author of five previous novels and a collection of short stories. He lives with his wife near the western edge of the English Lake District.

for Iain Burns
1974–2010

I

It begins with a sudden blow, a young woman hurled onto a pavement, a waiting motorbike being revved in a quiet city street. A
simple but efficient robbery is carried out on a stranger, and this
takes place twenty paces in front of a man with a camera. The man
is there only by chance, but he immediately takes his opportunity.

He does not focus on the riders in their beetle-black helmets
as they speed past in a clamour of acceleration. Instead his concentration is on how the hard-edged shadow of a tall building bisects
the woman's body. She is sprawled face down but has broken her
fall with hands that are folded up beneath her. One leg is stuck
out at an ungainly angle and a shoe hangs from the foot as if she
has pitched forward whilst trying it on. Just beyond her grasp a
pair of dark glasses gleam on the brightly sunlit paving.

It is not the crime that excites the photographer's attention,
but a chance configuration of shape and texture – the smooth
opacity of the lenses, the knotty tension in the victim's hands,
the summer clothing rubbed along the ground. These, and the
dishevelled hair that screens a face he cannot quite see and that
could so easily have smashed into the pavement.

Only after he has taken several rapid photographs does the man turn to look down the gently sloping street and focus on the thieves. In that instant the stolen bag is lobbed from the pillion as if it were an empty carton, and then with a brief flash of red the bike tilts and swings out dangerously into traffic. Squealing brakes and angrily punched horns momentarily clash with the clatter of its exhaust and then everything disperses into a rumbling hum.

The narrow side street has become eerily quiet now that the thieves have gone. Both victim and photographer are motionless for a few seconds. Sultry heat slides down between the tall office blocks in an invisible layer and presses on the scene.

Later, Gregory will consider what might have happened if someone else had been present. If they had been, then they could have made sure that the woman was unharmed. They might even have contacted the police. If there had been another witness – anyone – then his own life would not have been changed so unalterably. Gregory's natural instinct was for avoidance and observation, not involvement. He had taken his few sly photographs and that was enough. The chances were that the sprawled woman did not even know he had done this. But there was no one else nearby; at the mouth of the street the indifferent traffic moved along the broad embankment, and no witnesses could be seen peering from the mirrored windows in the high buildings.

Conscience took hold of Gregory. The victim was struggling to her knees and reaching forward for her glasses with arms that seemed too loosely articulated. The building shadow fell across her like a burden. Only now could he hear the shocked, convulsive sound of her breathing.

He studied the woman with a professional eye. The lightweight olive trousers, ripped across one knee, had been dragged down a couple of extra inches to expose the pale skin at the base of her spine and the scalloped upper edge of white underwear. The woman was slender, a little taller than average, probably in her early thirties. Gregory considered it his job to notice such things. Just as he had noticed that beneath the open lightweight jacket her white T-shirt had been scuffed across the bust by contact with the unswept pavement.

He bent closer, holding his camera bag close to his hip. The Canon swung in front of him like a sensor. The woman pushed her hair back with her left hand. It had been lightened to a reddish blonde but was darker red at the roots. She wore no wedding ring.

'Are you all right?' he asked. 'Are you able to stand?'

She pushed the glasses high up on a slightly prominent nose so that her eyes were shielded. Behind the large obscuring lenses her face was a pale oval. As if she were a child on the verge of tears, her lower jaw quivered noticeably.

He stretched out a hand. 'It's all right, you can trust me.'

But Gregory knew that although some women would claim that he had many admirable qualities, he had never inspired trust.

She did not take his hand but remained kneeling, as if the ground were a penance and she a supplicant. Gregory knew the pavement must be hot. He could feel sweat gather on his forehead. Perhaps it made him look menacing.

'I—' the woman began, and then stopped, her lungs still robbed of air. After a few seconds she put the shoe back on her foot in an odd, almost absent-minded gesture.

Gregory reached out a little further, this time with both hands. The camera was a barrier between their two bodies.

'They threw away your bag further down the street.'

She did not react.

'We can go and find it, but they'll have taken whatever was valuable.'

The woman accepted his grasp and got to her feet with her weight pressing on his hands. The skin of her palms was roughened and he realized she must have scraped them along the ground. As soon as she was steady the woman pushed at the bridge of the dark glasses with one finger so that they rested even closer to her eyes. Then she tugged at the waistband of her trousers to adjust them on her hips. Gregory could see the outline of a white bra beneath her cotton T-shirt.

'You took a hard fall. Are you hurt?'

'Did you see them? How many were there?'

Her voice was classless, educated, a little stunned.

'Just two. The pillion passenger was the one who hit you and lifted the bag. It was all in one movement. His friend was the escape rider. They must have singled you out. You're probably not the only victim they'll get today. I know that won't make you feel any better.'

'What about your camera? Did you photograph them?'

He did not trouble himself by debating how he should answer.

'I only had time for one shot. It won't help identify them. Listen, if you can walk all right, then we can go down there and try to find your bag. But if you're still shaky then just stay here, I'll go, and if I can find it I'll bring it back.'

The woman said nothing.

'I won't steal it again. Promise. One theft is more than enough.'

'I can walk. Thank you.'

'Do you want to lean on me?'

4

'No. No, I'll manage.'

They set off together along the pavement and through the motionless air. A set of spiked black railings in front of blank walls gave way to a second office block with smoky glass. The woman walked unevenly as if a stone had lodged in one shoe. Gregory feared that without warning she could topple to one side and he would have to catch her as she fell. If she did then he would have to be careful not to touch her breasts.

'Are you sure you're OK?'

'I'll survive. Could you recognize them again?'

'Not with those helmets. They're no fools. They make a living out of this.'

The woman shook her head and he registered the way that her hair moved.

Two men in business suits walked towards them, deep in loud conversation, jackets slung over their shoulders, and did not look up. Gregory realized that the men had probably walked past the stolen bag and simply ignored it.

'I feel so *stupid*,' the woman said. 'I always carry that bag across my shoulder on the inside, away from the traffic, and yet today I didn't. I don't know why. And *this* is what happens. I didn't even plan to be walking down this street. Usually I take the busy one, just a block along.'

'You were unlucky, that's all.'

'Maybe not.'

'You shouldn't think that. You were just in the wrong place at the wrong time.'

'But maybe it was meant to happen.'

This, Gregory thought, was an irrational comment made under stress. He ignored it because he had no reason to believe in fate.

A little further on they came to an entrance to the building. There was a broad, shallow flight of half a dozen steps beside a disabled ramp with a metal handrail. Two women were standing on the ramp in the shade. The taller one had taken the higher position so that she appeared even taller than her colleague, and they were both smoking cigarettes that were almost finished. The taller one also held the missing bag at the end of two fingers of her free hand, delicately, as though aware that she should not presume to hold it any closer.

'Is this yours?' she asked as they approached.

'It's mine,' the woman said.

'We came out here on a smoking break and those bikers threw it away. We usually stand leaning on that rail but it would burn your arms off in this heat so we stood back here. We thought something bad must have gone on. Same thing once happened to a cousin of mine. But with her they ran away on foot.'

'Some of those young bastards would steal from their own mother,' her smaller colleague announced.

'I picked this up from where they threw it – just down here. Almost at our feet. I haven't looked inside. Sorry, love, but whatever's missing, they took.'

The shorter woman quickly confirmed that neither of them had looked inside. And as the victim took the bag and examined it, the smokers began to ask for detail on exactly what had happened.

As Gregory had expected, the woman's wallet and mobile phone were missing, but all the other items were untouched.

'I'll ring the police,' he said, producing his own phone, 'although they probably won't be all that interested.'

He was right. To the police it was just another street robbery, the kind that happened several times a day. Gregory handed his phone across for the woman to speak to an officer whom he imagined to be filling in a form at a desk and concerned that he get the details correct. She gave her name as Alice Fell and quoted an address. The smokers each lit another cigarette. In the still air a nicotine smell wreathed around everyone.

After the report Alice turned back to him. 'They say I have to get in touch with my bank straight away about any credit cards.'

'Of course. Do you know their numbers?'

She shook her head. Sunlight smeared the dark lenses. Gregory wondered what colour her eyes were.

'They'll take you for whatever they can,' he warned. 'Tell me which bank you use and we'll do what we can to limit any damage.'

The smokers brought tea in plastic cups from a dispensing machine and would not take payment; meanwhile Alice used Gregory's phone again. As she talked, he began to wonder what would happen if his own daughter were attacked and robbed and there was no one there to help. At the end of the street an unbroken stream of traffic moved past.

'I owe you for these,' Alice said when the last call was finished.

'It's all right. You owe me nothing.'

At this moment she appeared to become disoriented again.

'I'm at work,' she said. 'I should get back there.'

'Go on home,' the tall smoker said, collecting the empty cups. 'You can't go back to work in the state you're in. Besides, look – those nice trousers are all torn at the knee.'

'She's right,' Gregory agreed.

Alice looked unsure. 'They'll be expecting me back. This is my lunch-break and . . .' The sentence tailed away.

The smokers were ever eager with advice.

'Report in sick, love, that's what you should do.' The tall one turned to Gregory. 'Give her back your phone so she can do it – *go on.*'

Alice did not need further persuasion. She dialled a number and told whoever answered that she had been attacked and robbed but would be all right soon. When she handed the mobile back to Gregory she told him that her employers had advised her to take the rest of the day off.

'What did I tell you?' the tall smoker said. 'You should get a taxi back home. It's not right you standing around like this. It'll make you feel better to get those dirty clothes off and have a shower and relax.'

'Besides, you could go into shock real easy,' her friend added.

'She's right. You could start to shake all over and not stop. That wouldn't do you any good.'

'I'll walk,' Alice announced.

'You should do no such thing.'

'I have to. All my money's gone.'

'Your friend here will lend you some cash – won't you, darling?'

The smokers fixed Gregory with challenging stares while Alice hid behind her dark lenses.

'Don't say you're going to say no,' the tall smoker accused him.

'We can get a taxi easily at the end of the street,' Gregory said.

Alice moved her head like a blind person reacting to noise. 'Thank you. I can pay the driver when I get home.'

They walked to the end of the street and were surprised to find that the smokers accompanied them. Evidently they were not yet prepared to relinquish their part in the drama of the robbery. Gregory was sure that within a few short minutes they would be back in the office eagerly telling their colleagues what had happened.

In the distance a taxi with an illuminated sign appeared and he hailed it.

'Give her the fare,' the tall smoker said. 'Go on.'

Alice shook her head. 'There's no need.'

'Course there is. *You* don't mind, do you?'

'I don't mind,' Gregory said. There was little choice. He asked the driver approximately how much the fare would be. There were lots of hold-ups on that route, the driver said, and a few diversions; it all depended.

Gregory took a twenty-pound note from his wallet.

'It could be a bit more,' the driver said.

'I don't think so,' Gregory answered. He passed the note to Alice. She folded it several times and then closed her fist round it.

'I'll pay you back. Give me your address and I'll send the money. Honestly.'

As she settled into the back of the cab Gregory handed over one of his business cards. In the dim interior Alice had to lift her glasses slightly to read the print. For just a second he saw that her eyes were puffed up with weeping. She had not cried since he had helped her up from the pavement. It must have been happening just before the attack.

Alice lowered her glasses again.

'Should I know you?' she asked. 'It's an unusual surname.'

'Maybe you've seen it in print. When you get home will there be someone to look after you?'

She hesitated for longer than he expected before she answered. 'Yes, there will be.'

Gregory closed the door and nodded at the driver. He expected Alice to say something else, or at least look at him as she was driven away, but instead she looked down, like a mourner at a funeral.

The smokers surveyed him with the satisfaction of match-makers.

'Lovely woman, that,' the tall one said.

'Lovely,' the shorter one echoed.

Gregory nodded, said thanks, and began to walk away.

'You won't have seen the last of her,' the tall one added. 'I know.'

'We can tell,' the shorter one said.

But Gregory did not expect to see the woman again. His life was filled with brief meetings and casual encounters. He believed that Alice Fell had been one of those. And besides, if he wanted, there were always other women.

From across the city there was the sudden noiseless flash of summer lightning.

Alice topples like a felled tree, her arms flung out like spreading branches, the lost shoe parted from her like a root left in the ground by the stroke of an axe. Gregory's photographs testify to the force that propelled her body forward with a single blow. He studies them on a monitor, weighing their virtues and failings, and it is not long before he begins to manipulate them. Because of the high contrast between sunlight and shade they have unintended limitations. However, adjustments that are merely necessary soon become creative.

Gregory drains the images of colour. He contracts the margins. He enlarges sections until their texture becomes granular. One of the frames he crops so severely that all it contains is Alice's tumbled hair parted into shadowy roots and the fallen sunglasses that have darkened to jet. Her body is abstracted into balances of shape and texture. When he has finished, Gregory puts his visual rearrangements on a slideshow program and assesses them even more critically.

He does not put his shot of the escaping thieves on the slideshow, although unexpectedly he has come to regret that there are no means of identification to be found within it. Indeed, the picture contains so little information that no arrest could ever be achieved from its content. Gregory understands that it is impossible that he should become an agent for justice, and yet to him it is also inexplicable that he should fantasize about being thought of as a kind of saviour.

In almost a week he has not heard from Alice. Although at first he assumes that she has merely been delayed in returning his money, he soon begins to believe that she has never intended to. This does not prevent him from thinking more and more about her.

After seven days he was due to leave on his next assignment and still he had heard nothing. Her silence was disappointing but perhaps inevitable. Gregory told himself that he, too, had been robbed of cash, but only of twenty pounds, and not by opportunist thieves but by a woman who had probably simply decided that there was no moral need to return a stranger's kindness.

Nevertheless he wanted to hear from Alice. The money was not important. He was willing to forget that. At one point he checked the call log of his mobile and discovered her work number. When he rang it an unfamiliar voice answered and quoted a company name. Although he had intended to ask if Alice Fell was there, he immediately closed the connection when she did not answer.

He told himself he should think no more about the robbery. And besides, he was leaving within the next few hours. And yet when his daughter Cassie rang on the landline Gregory realized that he had wanted the call to be from Alice. Disappointment hit him as a sudden ache across the lower line of his ribcage. This was both irrational and reprehensible; he had, after all, been expecting Cassie to phone.

After the call was over Gregory felt guilty about his crazy hope that it could have been Alice. He was also uneasy that Cassie might have registered the evident deflation in his tone. Perhaps she could have learned more than he had wanted to reveal.

For three days each week his daughter worked as his assistant, secretary and unofficial manager, and on the other two days she worked for a national cancer charity. Gregory had grown dependent on her abilities. She organized his contracts, diary, correspondence, and accounts, and often she helped out in the studio. On occasion she had even taken photographs instead of him.

Although he had told her what had happened Gregory had not confessed that he had given money to Alice Fell. Instead he used the robbery as a cautionary tale of how easily one could be attacked on a city street in broad daylight. Cassie's reaction had been so offhand that he felt it necessary to repeat how risks could be minimized. He recognized that she and Alice were about the same age, and he could easily imagine Cassie being struck between the shoulder blades in the same callous manner. Furthermore, Gregory could picture how his daughter would look if she were unable to break her fall and instead smashed her head against the pavement. He did not want to have to photograph those injuries. As always, Cassie had allayed his fears with a breezy confidence.

Twenty minutes later he had just picked up his bag and was about to leave when the landline rang again. Gregory paused by the door. His own voice rasped from the answerphone. The caller hung up without saying anything.

He wondered if he should go back and check the incoming number, but then decided that this would be madness. If the call had been important then either a message would have been left or he would have been phoned on his mobile. Gregory closed the door and tried to put the incident out of his mind, but all the way to the airport he wondered if he had done the right thing.

The flight was delayed and made unpleasant by turbulence. By the time it landed Gregory could feel the tensions of the journey in the muscles at the back of his legs. He was jaded and cynical and felt that he was getting old. Around him the airport was featureless and unwelcoming, with armed security guards in ill-fitting uniforms and a luggage carousel that creaked and squealed as if about to seize up completely.

Carla from the agency was waiting in Arrivals. Her name was all that he had been told about her. She was in her early forties, had angular features and an unwavering stare, and spoke English as if she had spent time in the States. An ignition key was held in her hand like a valued possession.

A shower of heavy rain passed across the airport before they reached the car. Droplets pocked the grey dust on its surfaces so that they resembled NASA studies of lunar plains. Gregory sat with one camera on his lap and the equipment lodged behind the passenger seat. He was already telephoning his journalist contact as Carla drove away from the airport.

Within a few minutes Gregory knew that they would spend most of their long journey in a silence that both he and Carla understood, just as he was confident that she would offer him the opportunity to sleep with her that night. He was not sure that he wanted to. Even if he did, he wondered if he would be doing so just because it was expected of him. Perhaps it would be wiser to remain alone in his hotel room and hunt through the satellite channels.

In this part of the world even the best roads were narrow. Military vehicles moved along them in short convoys, but so did overloaded lorries that left a smell of burned diesel in the air and tiny cars that looked as if they would fold up under the slightest impact. In litter-strewn lay-bys alongside spruce forests prostitutes stood at intervals of two or three hundred yards. They ignored Carla and, as if under a conditioned reflex, lifted their skirts as the car passed. One stood at the corner of a fenced area, as immobile as a mannequin, her heavy coat left open to show a pale body wearing black knickers and nothing else. Dark glasses covered her eyes like shields, like targets. Momentarily Gregory thought again about Alice and the way she had scrabbled on the pavement for the camouflage of smoky lenses.

They drove to a tiny village that was two hours away along potholed zigzag roads and so high above the central plain that the air was permanently cold and damp. Tall conifers dripped rain. Below the village a few tents had been pitched on a level band of earth sheltered by a thin line of broadleaf trees. At the edge of the houses a tall cross of raw pine had been erected. The heads of nails gleamed like silver against the wood. A tractor's rusty hulk stood nearby, stripped of all usable parts. Just beyond it a series of cars had been parked on a stretch of mud. One had its window open, and behind its wheel the driver was talking excitedly into his phone. In another a woman in a fur coat snoozed with her chin sunk on her chest.

It was here that they met the journalist. He guided Gregory and Carla up through the village while its people gazed at them as if they could not quite decide whether they should be welcomed. When the journalist asked if he made a speciality of recording such cases Gregory told him that he did not, and that neither had he any religious belief. It was possible, he added wryly, that his editor thought he would be interested merely because he had recently photographed a controversial bishop and turned him into something monolithically baroque. He did not say that it had been on his return from this assignment that he had witnessed a woman being thrown to the ground and robbed.

A small group of visitors waited near the home of the girl who had seen the vision. Most were silent, but some prayed quietly and continuously. Others knelt on the stony soil with their hands clasped. Some were evidently poor, but one woman had brought a plush velvet cushion to kneel on; another wore clothes for a skiing holiday, the manufacturer's logo bold across her back. Carla asked if they minded having their photographs taken. No one objected. One woman even asked which newspaper Gregory worked for. He lied and said the English *Sunday Times*.

'They all want to be part of this,' Carla said as they walked away.

'They always do,' the journalist said.

A few chickens scratched around their feet and a goat ate a sparse shrub at the end of its tether.

'You must have covered other stories like this,' Gregory said.

'I've read the files on dozens of cases,' the journalist answered. 'They're all similar. You'll see what I mean when you meet the family. Miraculous visitations are the product of marginal communities with deep religious beliefs, and the person who sees the vision is always a lonely pubescent girl. Mostly the visions fade when she grows up.'

'You think that will happen here?'

'Maybe, but there's a force behind this. You can feel the pressure. This girl fascinates believers, but the rest of the world is fascinated too. If she didn't have that quality then you and I wouldn't be here, and neither would anyone else. There's another TV crew arriving tomorrow because the world wants to know about Little Maria. And a few weeks ago she wasn't ever called that; she was Anamaria until a newspaper rechristened her. Now even the villagers call her by her new name. Her family does, too.'

'Everyone believes it is better to call her that,' Carla told them.

'And do you?' Gregory asked.

'Perhaps. If she saw what she tells us she saw.'

'What she saw,' the journalist said, 'was what these disturbed young women always see – an apparition that resembled a naïve painting. Little Maria saw a Virgin Mary who was just like an illustration in an instructional book for children. Adults in advanced societies don't ever see visions like that.'

'A vision can come to anyone,' Carla said.

'We don't have visions; we hallucinate,' the journalist answered. 'We hear voices inside our heads, or get blinded by non-existent lights, or lose ourselves in the numinous. We don't get visited by images from picture books. Look around us: we're at the very edge of subsistence here. It's like stepping back into feudal Europe. People see what they've been taught they will see at the moment of death.'

The family was what Gregory expected. A few weeks ago the parents might have been credulous, but now they had become used to media attention. He photographed them against a scabbed and whitewashed wall to show off their frayed clothing and lined faces. He asked them to make sure their hands were on display so that readers would be able to study the stumpy fingers and broken nails.

An ambitious local priest asked to be photographed, too; after all, he was the only one able to provide spiritual guidance to these people. They were, he confided, simple, good-hearted, and unable to understand why their daughter should be so honoured by Our Lady. Why, Little Maria herself was perplexed that she had been chosen. Although he doubted if the photographs would be required, Gregory allowed the priest to pose alongside the crucifix that hung above the deeply recessed window.

The girl he photographed standing outside the broken-roofed cowshed where the Virgin Mary had appeared and promised to return. Her brothers and sisters looked on with a mixture of puzzlement and envy.

Gregory was certain that the priest had advised the family that Little Maria should be dressed as if for a communion. Probably he had also supplied the dress: it was slightly too large and its frills were out of place in such bleak surroundings. Little Maria's face was bony and pale, as if she had lost blood, and she stared into the lens with a stubborn unearthly superiority. Throughout the short session she said nothing. There was animal shit on her boots and the hem of her white dress was spotted with mud.

As soon as Gregory indicated that he had finished she spoke. It was a sentence of only a few words, delivered in a monotone. Her expression did not change. Then she walked back into the house and the door was closed behind her.

'What did she say?' he asked.

'She said,' Carla began, and then seemed to consider her translation for a moment before she continued in a quieter voice. 'She said that you do not need to live your life like this.'

Gregory smiled. 'If I'd known that, I would have asked you to tell her that I live the kind of life that I want, and that I'm happy with it.'

Carla nodded, but said nothing else.

The priest had remained outside the house, his face expectant. The journalist suggested an amount of cash Gregory should hand over. 'For the upkeep of the church,' he explained drily. Gregory paid up and received a cursory blessing. The priest made a little speech that Carla translated.

'He said that we are all instruments of God. He said that we do not understand what is really happening to us, just as musical instruments are not conscious of the tune that is played on them.'

'Right,' Gregory said. They thanked the priest and walked away.

'You'll not have got as much as that from the famous Little Maria,' the journalist said wryly. 'She's laconic at the best of times.'

'She told me that I needn't live in the way that I do. Not that she knows anything at all about how I live. But that's what they call faith, I suppose.'

'The girl only says what you expect her to say. None of it is thought-provoking. She doesn't know why she was chosen and she has no idea what will happen next. But the Virgin says that one of these days she will pass on a great secret. That kind of thing.'

'These people believe it is certain that the Virgin will return,' Carla added.

'When she does I bet she won't be visible on film,' Gregory told her.

'But the visual isn't everything,' Carla responded. 'Neither are words. Some things are beyond photography just as they are beyond description.'

The journalist shrugged. He had seen so much of the world that he could no longer be bothered to argue such points. When Carla turned away he raised his eyebrows at Gregory, who gave a wry complicit smile in return.

By early evening Gregory had uploaded the photographs to his laptop, judged and selected them, and then transmitted his choice to the picture desk. Later, he ate with Carla from a hotel menu that exhibited only the faintest trace of national cuisine, and immediately afterwards they went to bed together.

Gregory felt no guilt about this. He was merely choosing to take something that was being made available. He was neither excited nor intrigued by Carla, and he viewed their sexual union as a purely technical exercise, one that he would perform and then forget. It had happened often enough before. And even though he obtained a certain amount of pleasure from it, a part of his mind remained aloof. For Carla, it was different. Like a castaway, she strove for something that seemed to have drifted forever out of her grasp.

In the morning their farewells were perfunctory and slightly embarrassed. They both knew the night had been a failure. Gregory was certain that he would never return to that part of the world. Why, he had not even bothered to take a photograph of Carla.

As he walked to the plane across the windy tarmac, and as he unexpectedly began to examine the way in which he had lived his life, he became convinced that a change was about to come. But he shook the feeling off because he knew it was irrational. Gregory prided himself on a clear-eyed perspective of the world. He thought that perhaps tiredness, or the rarefied air of the village, or its barely suppressed hysteria, had begun to seep unwanted into his dreams.

3

Even before he opened the envelope he guessed the sender. Inside was a twenty-pound note fastened to a postcard by a red paper-clip. The picture on the card was an Edward Weston photograph of a seashell. Silver and pearl-grey, the shell folded in on itself like a swan asleep.

Knowing that Cassie was watching, Gregory looked across the room to where she sat at the desk with her papers and computer screen. She inclined her head in a wry, questioning manner that always reminded him of his wife. His daughter had inherited her strong features and yet she, too, disliked being photographed.

'They say you should never send cash through the post.'

'So they do,' Gregory said drily, unclipping the note to find the message written on the card's reverse. The first thing he did was look at the signature, even though he was certain whose it would be. He was unable to suppress a tiny smile of pleasure even though Cassie kept watching.

'You're keen to find out about this, aren't you?' he asked.

'It looked personal so I didn't open it. You know I never—'

'Yes, I know. You're very discreet for a daughter. Or so you often tell me.'

'I'm discreet about all kinds of things. You should know – you've tested me several times. Officially *and* without my knowing.'

The note was short and to the point.

Dear Mr Pharaoh
Thank you so much for looking after me and for being so
trusting. Here is the money that you kindly lent me.
Disappointingly, the police tell me it is unlikely that anyone will
be charged with the theft. Best wishes and thanks again.
Alice Fell.

Beneath the message she had written the number of a mobile phone.

Gregory looked across to his daughter.

'I lent her twenty pounds. It was for a taxi.'

'The woman who had her bag stolen? You didn't say you'd given her money.'

'It must have slipped my mind.'

'I see. Maybe you're lucky that you got it back.'

'Maybe. But if it had happened to you I would have wanted a good Samaritan to give you the taxi fare back home.'

'Dad, I've been surviving on my own for a long time now. And do you know what? I've never been robbed. You needn't worry about me.'

Gregory thought about confessing that in some ways he had never stopped worrying, and that it would be comforting if his daughter could find someone to live with. Cassie had had a few casual relationships and then an extended but unsatisfactory one, after which she had given up on matters of the heart. She remained determinedly alone, unattached, and, as far as Gregory knew, celibate. His behaviour and his needs were utterly different to hers. And yet, paradoxically, he envied his daughter's resolve, and could understand her contentment at being free of the tightening coils of intimacy and romance.

'There's a phone number,' he said.

'Ah.'

'Do you think she wants me to call?'

Gregory wondered why he should ask Cassie for approval. When she was not present he did not need her opinion. Often he did not even consider what she might think, however sensible her advice. It was only when they were together in the same room, or talking on the phone, that he felt compelled to ask his daughter what she thought. He had continued to do this despite his intermittent decisions to stop. Gregory was sure this had something to do with Ruth's early death. His wife had left guilt behind her as well as memories; it coloured her wake like a dark stain.

'You must realize that it's an invitation,' Cassie answered, reaching up to touch the beads on the necklace that she had inherited from her mother.

Gregory looked again at the message and then reversed the card to study the Weston photograph. It had been taken almost ninety years ago. The curved shell chambers looked like barriers engineered to protect an invisible centre.

'Why not ring her now, and get it over with?'

Gregory nodded but faltered.

'Dad, would you rather make that call when I wasn't here?'

'Of course not.'

For the moment, at least, he had nothing to hide.

Alice answered after a few rings. Usually Gregory began speaking as soon as he could, but for an unexpected moment, no more than a second or two, he was silent. He could hear a background of amorphous murmur, as if a hand had been cupped to his ear.

'It's Gregory Pharaoh.'

After a pause, Alice spoke. 'Yes.'

'I just thought I'd let you know that the money arrived safely. Thanks.'

This time the pause was slightly longer. 'It seemed easier to send cash and not a cheque. Was that all right?'

'Yes. Yes, of course. How are you feeling? I mean, after what happened?'

'Not bad. You saw how shaken up I was.'

'Right. Maybe there are people with you. Can you tell me anything else?'

'I'm still bruised but I'll get over it. It was upsetting and embarrassing but it wasn't a disaster.'

'The credit cards?'

'The bank people blocked them before they could be used, so things could have been worse. Now I have replacements. And a new mobile that I'm talking on now. There were store cards as well. I'd forgotten about those.'

'I didn't think about them, either.'

For a few moments Alice did not speak. Silence vibrated between them.

'Are you at work?' Gregory asked.

'Yes, I'm here now.'

'Good,' he said lamely.

'I know why you rang.'

'I told you why.'

'That was just an excuse.'

'You think so?'

'Yes. You rang because you want to see me again.'

As if by reflex Gregory looked across at Cassie, but she was pretending not to listen. Her face was pallid in the glow from the computer screen.

'You were badly shaken up,' Gregory said. 'I'd be interested to find out what you remember.' He cleared his throat and went on. 'Maybe we could meet up sometime?'

The response was immediate, as if Alice had been poised to make it.

'I live with someone. I've lived with him for a while.'

Gregory had not expected to be told that. In the background the office conversations were fragmentary and indistinct, like noises through an adjoining wall.

'Right,' he answered, 'OK.'

'I just wanted to make that clear.'

'It's clear. But it doesn't change things.'

Another slight delay; again Gregory detected a sense of calculation. He was not certain if he had been refused.

'I have to go now,' Alice said; 'I'm busy.'

'I understand.'

'I was right, wasn't I? About why you called?'

Unexpectedly Gregory felt that he should rush out a confession. If Cassie had not been present then he could have been foolish enough to do it, even if he was unsure if it would be true.

Passion, Gregory thought, was no guarantor of truth. Like a younger and more impulsive man, he could have told Alice that he could not stop thinking of her. If he had told her such things, then maybe she would have ridiculed his fixation. It was even possible that he could ridicule it himself. Gregory was puzzled by his own feelings. He felt suspended, unequal, and faced with choices he was strangely cautious about making.

There was only one certain way of tempting Alice to meet him, and that was to admit that he had taken photographs as she lay sprawled on the ground. And yet he could not tell her that in a telephone conversation. Only if they were face to face would he be able to persuade her of his good faith. Over a telephone he would come across as exploitative and sinister.

'You were right,' he agreed.

He believed he heard a small exhalation of breath. What she said next took him by surprise.

'I could meet you by the river. On my lunch-break, near to where I work. But not until Friday.'

Gregory was already consulting his diary. He was free. If he had not been, he would have made sure that he was.

'I could get there by about ten past one,' Alice said. 'I couldn't stay for very long. I have to be back by two.'

'Tell me where exactly and I'll be there.'

It took less than half a minute to agree a place. As soon as they had done so, Alice repeated that she was busy and hung up.

Gregory leaned back in his chair. The postcard was still in his hand. Now that he had gone to the trouble of arranging a rendezvous, he wondered if he should keep it.

'Well,' said Cassie, not looking up, '*something* must be happening.'

'She doesn't know I took photographs while she was on the ground.'

'You didn't tell her?'

Gregory stared into the seashell whorls and was silent.

'You'll have to confess,' Cassie advised.

'I know how to do the right thing.'

'That hasn't always been true.'

'It will be this time.'

To close the subject Gregory handed over some prints he had made of the girl who saw visions, her family and the priest. He liked the photographs of Little Maria. Posed in her soiled confirmation dress, her imagination seized by the miraculous, she stared numbly into his camera.

Cassie examined the prints with an expert eye and asked several questions. Gregory answered truthfully, even repeating with a laugh what Little Maria had told him, but he made no mention of having slept with Carla.

Picture editors had already selected the images they wanted, but these were not the ones that Gregory would have chosen for a planned second exhibition of his work. In the newspaper his portraits from the visitation site would be embedded in a journalist's text and printed with explanatory captions. But for his gallery exhibition Gregory would strip personal and social contexts from each of the prints. They would be hung as pure images. The intense young girl with the bony features and the white confirmation dress with a dirty hem would stare out at the viewer in a challenge to interpretation. She would be neither visionary nor pawn, but just an arrangement of gradations in tone, abstracted and mysterious, her meanings kept hidden from the inquiring eye.

Gregory liked that. He wanted his work to be lifted free from its origins and valued for its compositional qualities alone. If ever he chose to include images of Alice, no one would know who she was or how and why they were taken. Viewers would not even be sure what had happened or what would have happened afterwards; they would be denied a narrative. Such uncertainties would give a mysterious edge to his other work, too.

Gregory kept photographs of all his lovers, photographs that Cassie had often seen. Their bodies were of as much aesthetic interest to him as their faces. For one particular session, with one particular lover, he had paid homage to the 1950s work of Bill Brandt and posed her nude against a bank of pebbles, so that her form and texture became as abstracted, sculpted and inert as an object worn smooth by an ocean. All that was some years ago, and the woman in question had liked the results. She had especially liked walking round Gregory's first exhibition and overhearing comments by visitors who stood in admiration before the huge prints without realizing that the owner of such smooth flesh was standing beside them. Another lover had eagerly posed naked and with her legs apart, head and limbs cropped from the shot so that her torso replicated Stieglitz's 1918 study of Georgia O'Keeffe. Gregory was no longer surprised at what some women would do when asked.

Not all of his lovers had been like this. Some had been repulsed by the thought of appearing so nakedly and for the eyes of others. One had consented only to having those parts of her body photographed that would normally be visible on a public beach. But whatever their choices, and however he had portrayed them, all of Gregory's women had been fascinated by the pictorial traces left by their predecessors.

They were still there in his files, all of them, but when he turned to the records Gregory seldom thought of the times they had shared. His women had become their own representations. Their lives had been frozen into motionless and unchanging moments; those brief instances were all that was required. He had given each of his lovers their instant, and in doing so he had also given them eternity. And that was something that he believed he could also give to Alice Fell.

At first it seemed that she intended they should progress side by side along the busy embankment like court officials discussing a case. Gregory realized that if they continued walking like this then Alice would always be looking ahead and he would have to turn intermittently to study her profile, so he was relieved when she agreed that they should stop at the nearest riverside café. Until that moment they had done little but self-consciously exchange small talk, as if their first encounter had been so unusually dramatic that it was difficult to adjust to the everyday.

They sat opposite each other. Gregory studied the contours of her face, the shape of her neck, the cut of her hair. Within a few minutes he was an expert in the way that Alice turned her head, the angle of her gaze, the way she sometimes composed herself by linking her hands together on the tabletop. Everything about her was discreet. The fact that she lived with someone else, and apparently had done so for some time, was only a minor irritant to his intention.

'Pharaoh,' she said after a while, 'that can't be your real name.'

'You think it's unusual?' he asked.

It was the first time he had clearly seen her eyes. Now there was no indication of distress; instead they were guarded. The irises were dark with a hint of gold. He wanted to photograph her with a sudden flash to catch those eyes when they had widened in a dusky light.

Aware of the intensity of his appraisal, Alice turned away to look across the grey river to the far bank. Boats moved along the

water and yellow cranes straddled a building whose metallic outer shell glinted like mercury.

'It sounds artificial,' she said. 'As if you chose it for effect.'

'I didn't have to make a choice,' Gregory lied. 'I was born with it.'

She did not ask more, but he repeated a story he had told many times to others.

'Pharaoh's a name passed down from the mystery plays. The same person acted the same character year after year, and after that his son took over, and then his son after him. The name of the character became attached to the family.'

Alice did not admit that she knew a little about mystery plays; she had once been in love with a man who was an expert in theatrical history.

'And your ancestors always played the Pharaoh – aloof, sensual and cruel. Is that something to be pleased about?'

'Why not? The public must have been satisfied that they acted that part better than others could.'

'But the people who acted Jesus and God can't have inherited their names. Those must have been *far* too holy.'

'I suppose so,' Gregory agreed.

He could see no circumstance in which he would ever confess to Alice that her suspicion was correct. The name Gregory Pharaoh was on all his documents, but in more than thirty years he had never revealed the truth to anyone other than his wife and daughter. Even his former business partner had not known.

Gregory had not been born with the names he used. As a child and as a youth, he had answered to George Farrar. In adolescence he had become convinced that those names were like shackles, and that they had to be transmuted into something distinctive, unforgettable, even grandiose. Soon after becoming a photographer he had discarded his birth names, and now they lay broken and unused in the abandoned museum of his past. For decades he had never thought of himself as a Farrar; he was always a Pharaoh.

'In your line of business it must be an advantage to have an unusual name,' Alice suggested.

'So they say.'

'And are you an unusual person?'

She looked hard at him across the scuffed table with its coffee cups. Even in a setting such as this her face called out for a lens to be focused on it.

'Of course I am,' he answered. 'And so are you.'

She dismissed the compliment with a smile. 'You must use flattery as easily as you use focal lengths.'

Gregory refused to be nettled. 'Tell me what happened after you got home,' he asked.

She ignored this. 'I telephoned your office last week. A woman answered.'

'That would have been Cassie – my daughter Cassandra. She works for me.'

'You're married?'

'I used to be.'

'I would have felt better if you still were.'

'I couldn't be. She died. It was quite a long time ago.'

Alice nodded, but did not offer any sympathy for his loss.

Gregory thought again of Ruth, of the way he had obsessively, meticulously recorded her decline, so much so that she had eventually cried out in humiliation and despair, so much so that an adolescent Cassie had become furious and tried to slap him and he had let her. None of that had stopped him. Despite her distress he had photographed his wife's last moments, and he had photographed her corpse. If he could have, he would have followed her coffin into the furnace.

'After you got home,' he repeated.

In some detail Alice described the protocols she had followed for the credit card and store card companies. Gregory hardly listened, but never looked away.

'And your partner?' he asked. 'What did he say?'

'Did I tell you it was a he?'

'You did. Why, would you prefer to remain *that* mysterious?'

'I don't like to give too much away. Not on a first meeting.'

'I'm pleased we both agree that we should meet again.'

'You know I didn't mean that.'

'You won't tell me what he said?'

Alice looked across the river again. 'Thomas was very concerned. He thought I should see a doctor just in case.'

'And did you? See a doctor?'

'No.'

Gregory wanted to put his fingers to the side of her neck and lift her hair. He thought of the feel of her skin beneath his fingers.

'No lasting harm done, then,' he said quietly.

'I recover well. It's a gift.'

A haughty dark-haired woman paraded along the path with a small groomed terrier on the end of a lead. The sound of her heels clicked across their meeting like a stitch. Suddenly Gregory imagined the woman naked, aloof and unconcerned, still holding the lead, the dog still trotting beside her as in a Helmut Newton composition.

'You're thinking about a complete stranger,' Alice said.

'I was thinking about pictorial values, that was all,' he replied with a light touch of protest, but he thought it would be unwise to study the woman as she walked away. 'I think about pictures most of the time,' he added, as if this were an intriguing confession.

'So you have your camera with you now – in that bag?'

'Not the one I had that day. That was a second-generation EOS 5D: a favourite, even though it's a few years old. But I always carry something, just in case.'

'And you were thinking of pictures when I was robbed?'

Gregory wondered if this was the moment to be truthful. Alice's eyes were wide and unblinking. He suddenly became aware of the drop in temperature that happens near water.

'It's like a reflex. It's built into me.'

'So you took photographs as I was hit?'

'I took photographs as you were falling. My reactions were as quick as that.'

The seconds dragged by as if held back by weights.

'You didn't mention that before.'

'I wasn't sure what they would look like. The 5D is built for portrait work and not action shots. And there was high contrast because of the building shadow. And the depth of field was shallow.'

'I think, Mr Pharaoh, that someone like you would always be very sure what your photographs would look like.'

'If I were a paparazzo, maybe. But I'm studio, not street.'

Although Alice appeared resentful, Gregory believed that it must disguise an interest, possibly even a fascination.

'How many did you take?'

'A few,' he answered, although he had taken a dozen. 'Five or six. I'm not a Cartier-Bresson who walks round with a Leica in the crook of his arm so that he can work surreptitiously. Although by chance I did photograph what he would have called a decisive moment.'

Gregory waited to see if she showed signs of recognition of the phrase. She did not. He became convinced that Alice must have chosen the Weston postcard purely because it had pleased her, and that her knowledge of photography was not as great as he had at first hoped. She had not failed a test, but he had found out a little more about her.

'Are you pleased with the ones that you took?'

'I like some of them, yes.'

'And where are they now?'

'In my studio.' Gregory cleared his throat, not because he needed to, but because he believed that if he signalled a kind of hesitancy then Alice might find that more persuasive than a show of confidence. 'You're welcome to see them – if you wouldn't find it unsettling.'

For a few moments Alice appeared to be wondering how the images would look. Three youths walked past, swearing loudly, and a horn blared on one of the boats on the river. At last she spoke.

'Is there anything *unusual* about them?'

'What do you mean – unusual?'

Alice moved one hand through the air as if it were some kind of signal. 'I don't know . . . any effects you hadn't expected. Distortions of light; something like that. Anomalies in the emulsion.'

'They're digital. And they all look perfectly normal. Why shouldn't they?'

The shake of the head was made too quickly, as if Alice had recognized too late that her question had almost revealed something she wished to keep hidden.

Sensing a need that he could not yet identify, Gregory encouraged her.

'Did you feel anything when that thief pushed you?'

'Just shock. And fright. I didn't know what was happening.'

'I mean, did it seem that you were falling in an extraordinary way, or that an observer might have misjudged what had actually happened?'

Her eyes seemed to want to reach deep into him, but he stared back without giving way.

When Alice next spoke it was with careful determination. 'There *is* something unusual, isn't there.' It was not a question. 'You have to tell me,' she said.

Gregory shook his head. 'I don't know what you want to find in those shots, but you'll be disappointed. In one of them you seem to be lifting from the ground rather than dropping to it, but that's an illusion. Perspective and body posture and the fall of light just make it seem that way. There's nothing unusual or bizarre or inexplicable about it. Take it from me. If you photograph divers from the side of a swimming pool, without a horizontal in the frame, then often they appear to be rising and not falling. It's an optical illusion. All cameramen know it. Riefenstahl used it in her Olympics film. Something similar happened on one of your photos.'

Alice continued to stare at Gregory as if testing him out for an untruth.

He repeated the invitation. 'Check them out for yourself, if you want.'

'If they're digital then you could email them to me.'

'I could. Except that I won't.'

'Why not?'

'It goes against commercial principle. And the images are better in large prints. By the way, they don't show that you'd been crying.'

'I didn't cry until I got home. That's when the shock got to me.'

'You'd been crying beforehand. We both know it. You'd been so distressed that your eyes had puffed up.'

Alice looked down at the table, across to the cranes, and then back down again. Her fingers toyed with the handle of her empty cup.

'Thomas likes rivers,' she said unexpectedly. 'They make him think of the flow of time. He used to walk me along here and talk about axe heads and stone tools that have been found in the sediment. They've even found hippopotamus bones – did you know that?'

But Gregory would not relent. 'You were conscious of how you looked and you tried to hide the signs behind those dark glasses.'

'You don't want to give up on this, do you, Mr Pharaoh?'

'Not when I'm looking at someone who has a face that was made to be photographed.'

Alice wondered if this was the kind of statement that all photographers were likely to make. She waited before speaking again.

'How bad was it?'

He shrugged. 'Not bad. But noticeable.'

'I was in a tearful mood, that's all. The time of the month.'

'You don't expect me to believe that.'

'I don't care if you believe it or you don't. It has nothing to do with you.'

'In the short term that may be correct,' Gregory said. He waited for a heartbeat and went on. 'And did it have anything to do with the man you live with?'

36

Alice brought her arms closer to her body. Her voice had a raw edge. 'Why should it have anything to do with Thomas? Are you my father or my brother, that you think you have the right to ask such questions?'

'I don't have any right. All I have is a professional duty. I need to be able to assess how a subject will present herself.'

'I'm not your *subject*.'

'There are photographs at my studio that prove that you should be. Don't get me wrong – I've photographed people at their most vulnerable and injured. I could photograph you looking as if you were going through hell. But I don't want to do that. I don't want any problem to get between you and the lens.'

'You talk as if we'd made an agreement. But we haven't.'

'No, I'm talking as if we're going to *reach* an agreement.'

'And yet you won't let me see the pictures you've already taken, and which you took without permission and without my knowledge. Fate played a trick on me and you made use of it.'

'But if there had been no robbery, if the street had been empty except for the two of us, then maybe I would have stopped you and told you who I am and what I do. If I'd been able to see the whole of your face I would have done that. Any photographer worth his salt would have.'

'It wouldn't have worked. I'd have walked away. Any woman would have.'

'I wouldn't be so sure.'

'Look, if you took photographs of me then I have a right to see them.'

'You seem to be keen on rights. Those photographs are my property. You have no right at all.'

Alice hesitated. Gregory believed that he could see her sway.

'You could still let me see them.'

'You have an invitation.'

'I could give you my email address. You could make an exception and send them. Don't you owe me that?'

'I owe you nothing. I rescued you. It's you who are in debt. The images belong to me.'

A breeze blew up the river and ruffled her hair.

'Did you want to meet me again just to torment me?' she asked.

'No,' Gregory insisted, 'I wanted to meet you again because I want to take more photographs of you. I could tell that you were my kind of subject. I still think that.'

'Am I just an object to be seen through a viewfinder?'

'Of course you're not.'

'You talk as if I am. You even said that my face was made to be photographed – as if that would flatter me; as if that was the point and purpose of my life. What are you going to say next? That you only have an artist's eye for my looks? That you're like some kind of disinterested judge?'

'I wouldn't claim that, no. But what I do claim is that there is something in you that responds to a lens. Some people have that quality but most don't. Men can have it as well as women. You must have seen portraits where the subject's personality seems to be radiating out from the frame. A skilled photographer has caught their spirit; an amateur couldn't. It has nothing to do with exploitation. The subject's life hasn't been disrupted. In fact they're usually delighted they agreed to sit.'

'But not everyone.'

'Nothing pleases everyone. An honest photograph will never appeal to someone deluded. But an honest photograph will enlighten anyone who truly wants to know more about themselves.'

'I don't know if that's true.'

'Believe me,' Gregory said, sitting back, 'it is.'

He had been so persuasive he had almost convinced himself. He just could not be certain whether eventually he would also be able to convince Alice.

4

She had not known quite what to expect – something efficiently clinical, perhaps, with work carried out by tousle-haired unshaven youths in a white room with intense lights and skeletal tripods. In the event she found Gregory Pharaoh's top-floor studio to be a converted loft with tall windows, large skylights and an uneven floor of varnished wood. A rack of industrial shelving had been filled with lenses, filters, boxes, files, books, lengths of cable and other items that were mostly unidentifiable. Propped in one corner of the room were tall polystyrene boards with crumbled edges and a fathomless purpose; next to them, folded flat, was what appeared to be a Victorian or Edwardian screen bought from a junk shop. Two or three wraps hung from an office hatstand. Nearby there was a noticeboard with letters, magazine cuttings and a few glossy prints, the size of a human hand, fastened to it by tacks. Alice looked quickly to see if her own image was there. It was not.

The area where the sitters must pose was proportionately small. Two straight-backed chairs and a couch draped in Moroccan fabric were pushed against one wall. A circular object that could have been a reflector was leaning against one arm of the couch, and alongside this were two lightweight wooden frames, like painters' canvases, one with a grey covering, the other with red. An aluminium stepladder had been closed and pushed up against a wall of ochre-painted brick.

'I hope you weren't expecting anything glamorous,' Gregory said.

'More spacious, maybe. And less crowded.'

'It would have been even more crowded a hundred years ago. This was a sweatshop for the rag trade. You can see that the walls, the floorboards and the windows are all original. The temperature varies a lot. It's like living in a caravan.'

Alice nodded. Men always talked too much when they wanted something.

'When I first set up a business here I could only afford to rent this floor; I didn't have the space downstairs. There was an old watchman — I took his portrait — but he wasn't too reliable and there was always the chance of a break-in, so I kept my Hasselblad and my OM up there.'

Gregory pointed up to the rafters. They were gloomy enough to appear unclean. A grey electric cable ran along the upper wall and connected some ceiling lights with fluorescent tubes.

'I hid the cameras on top of that crossbeam so they couldn't be seen from the floor. You needed a ladder to reach them. In those days most of the property round here was nearly derelict; nowadays everything is gentrified and this entire building is split up into little offices and studios. My immediate neighbour is a painter. I've seen his work loaded into vans by professional art transporters.'

'You work on your own?'

'These days, yes. To begin with there were two of us in business together. We used to do whatever we could get – fashion catalogues, holiday brochures, factories, boardrooms. I still do some work for a chain of expensive hotels. After a few years the partnership split and he followed his own path. I'm happier like this. If I'm exceptionally busy my daughter helps me – she can take a good shot if need be. Mostly the demand has grown in ways that mean that I often work far away from here. I prefer solitary work, anyway. I'm not one of those who are happy with a dozen people fussing around my feet all the time. Cassie's official job is to deal with the bureaucracy; it's an arrangement that suits both of us.'

Gregory folded his arms and looked hard at Alice. She wanted to stare him out but instead had to turn away.

'I thought you would have my photographs on show,' she said. 'That's what we arranged.'

'They're on the next level.'

On her arrival Alice had pressed the intercom to be admitted and Gregory had met her as soon as she stepped inside. He had indicated his office on the ground floor and then led her up the stairs to the second. Now she realized that he must have deliberately taken her past the room where his work was stored.

As if he could read her mind, he spoke again.

'We used to have the floor below as a darkroom, but not any more. Most of us have had to go digital whether we like it or not, so these days everything is kept in picture files. For print copies there are a couple of professional inkjets downstairs that will do large format. For even larger copies or special papers I have an arrangement with two other studios. It makes economic sense.'

'Why did you bring me all the way up here?'

'I thought it would be worthwhile to let you see where I work.'

He took a single step forward, and for a moment Alice believed that he was about to reach out and touch her face. Instinctively she moved back an inch.

'What made you think I would want to see it? Do you think that all women want to be photographed?'

'Yes, and men too. Most of us are vain in some way or another. But most don't have a face made for a camera.' Gregory paused only for a second before going on. 'Maybe your partner hasn't got the insight to recognize that you have.'

When Alice did not answer, he spoke again.

'Sometimes it's difficult to see the obvious.'

Still she did not reply.

'I know you told me his name,' he said. 'I'm sorry but I've forgotten it.'

She wondered if this were true; Gregory had easily memorized other things about her.

'He's called Thomas.'

'And his surname?'

Partly as an avoidance tactic, Alice crossed to the shelves. In front of her were boxes with coded labels, a plastic tray overflowing with what looked like random objects, and a row of large-format photography books along with some on painting.

'Laidlaw,' she said.

Gregory's speech ceased to be discursive. They had reached the point he had wanted to reach.

'And if this partner of yours doesn't realize the potential of your looks, will he object to me photographing you? Do you need his agreement?'

'I make my own decisions,' she said.

'Of course you do,' Gregory said calmly, as if he had always known that for a fact. 'The Weston is on the far right, after Stieglitz,' he added, 'they're alphabetical.'

Momentarily Alice did not know what he meant, but then she read the name on a dust jacket spine and quickly realized that this was the man who had photographed the seashell. That was another thing that Gregory had remembered without effort – the postcard she had sent.

She had not deliberately sought it out; instead it had seemed fortuitous that she should chance upon a card that a professional photographer would find pleasing. She had not consciously intended the card to carry any message other than the few words that she had written. But now she wondered if Gregory believed that she had chosen it to demonstrate her taste and, by inference, an interest in him.

Alice took the book from the shelf and leafed through its pages. Here were shells that gleamed like silver, trees with bark furrowed as deep as a field, pebbles speckled like eggs, landscapes infused by dawn light, and discreet middle-distance nudes whose bodies had the cool texture of marble. And here, too, were unashamedly graphic shots of a thin young woman stretched out naked on grainy sand with her arms and legs apart to show dense black stars of pubic and axillary hair.

She closed the book and returned it.

'I thought you liked Weston,' Gregory said, and she wondered if the studied neutrality of his voice was in itself a kind of challenge. 'Or maybe you know all the contents,' he added.

'Tell me, Mr Pharaoh: is it just my face that you're interested in?'

'Of course it's not just your face. But whatever we did, and however you posed, it would be by agreement.'

Alice looked up through the skylight. High above the city a plane cut a thin white line across the sky, the vapour widening and dispersing behind it.

'Maybe your friend Thomas doesn't even photograph you. Does he?'

He had done, but Alice had decided that she looked undistinguished, with no trace of individuality, and ever since then she had avoided standing in front of a lens. But at least she now had an opportunity to lessen the tension by talking about Thomas.

'He takes photographs of archaeological sites. Wherever we go on holiday, he goes to see old forts, stone circles, barrow mounds. Things like that.'

'I see. Is it interesting to live with someone who is so bound up with the past?'

'It would be if he could get a decent job.'

'Ah. Problems.'

'Thomas lives on short-term contracts and low-grade work. He does some teaching, but he doesn't really like it. I don't think his degree is all that good: that's the real problem.'

Gregory had a faint smile. 'As long as he finds beauty somewhere. Even if it's just in heaps of old stone.'

Ready to move on, Alice became brisk.

'I think it's time I saw those photographs you promised, don't you?'

'Of course, we'll do that now,' Gregory replied, as if his only true purpose were to keep her happy. 'Remember to be careful of the stairs. They made them steep back when this was built.'

They descended a bare echoing stairwell whose walls had been

46

left unpainted for decades. Only a few minutes ago Gregory had led Alice past the door that he now opened.

Behind it was a room that was the same size as the upper studio. Roller blinds the colour of onion skin had been pulled down across the windows. He raised each one so that light gradually strengthened across files, cabinets, tables and computer screens. Copies of photographs, mostly black-and-white, had been placed around the room like offerings. Some were close-ups of faces that appeared familiar to Alice even though she could not put names to them, but most were of strangers. Some of these people, she realized, might already be dead. And for Gregory that might not even be important; what was important was the image they had left behind.

For a few vertiginous moments Alice imagined that she had entered a region composed of nothing but surface, spectacle and deceit. And then she gathered her thoughts and told herself that she was meant to be here. The physical world had a shadow, a twin, an undetected ghost. Somewhere alongside this very moment there was an indefinable space that was both analogous and aloof. In a way that Alice could not comprehend, she was fulfilling an arrangement that had been determined without her knowledge.

Alice believed in fate. She believed that lives crossed and became entangled in patterns that were not immediately detectable. She thought it probable that she had not been robbed merely by chance. Instead she had been humiliated and injured for a higher purpose; one that she could not yet discern, and one that the robbers would never appreciate because there was no need for them to understand. They, she and Gregory were all unconscious agents of an obscure force that lay outside the boundaries of the material world but which oversaw and guided it.

Such a belief did not seem fantastic to Alice. It was as rational as Gregory's faith in the immortality of the image, as certain as Thomas's belief in the processes of time. It was even possible that neither she nor Gregory would ever grasp the true meaning of this synchronicity. Perhaps they were never meant to, for as Alice walked around his room any hint of purpose was clouded and puzzling.

Gregory watched and wondered what was occupying her mind. 'Take a good look round,' he said. 'Feel free.'

Alice wondered if the hidden intention of each event was to guide her towards a re-evaluation of her life. Perhaps her feelings had to be intensified, or an impetus given to decisions over which she was hesitating. Most unsettling of all, it was conceivable that the robbery had happened purely so that she and Gregory Pharaoh would meet and become involved, and that her choice of the Weston postcard had unwittingly sealed that pattern. Why else should she have suddenly decided to walk down that pavement at that specific time? Since she always carried her bag on the inside to lessen the chance of theft, why had she decided, without reason, to hang it from the other shoulder? It could not have been mere coincidence that she and a strange photographer had been in the same part of the city at the same time, just as it was more than just chance that had led her into being robbed. Gregory could just have stopped her, as he had said he would have done; but if so, she would undoubtedly have ignored him and walked on. Or he might not even have noticed Alice, not spoken, and allowed her to walk past. That was why it had been necessary to have the two of them thrust together in a manner dramatic enough to make it certain they would meet again.

She looked round for the photographs he had taken of the robbery, but found none. Instead the first print that caught her attention was a portrait of an adolescent girl wearing what looked like a communion dress. The girl stared out of the limits of her life with a kind of mute integrity.

'This was taken a couple of weeks ago,' Gregory explained.

'Who is she?'

'She has visions of the Madonna. Some believe that she's been singled out and touched with holiness. It's the usual kind of set-up. It won't be long before her village will be marketed as a shrine.'

'She looks as if her mind is elsewhere, as if she doesn't even belong to this world.'

'You think so? I don't know what to believe about her. Maybe her story is a fantastic lie that she has to maintain because everything has gone too far and now there's no way out. Or maybe she really did see something. Or imagined she did.'

Looking at the pinched, closed face, Alice became certain that the girl had indeed witnessed something extraordinary, and that she would always be convinced of the integrity of her vision. It was only the rising clamour of the encroaching world that she could not deal with.

'She's not making it up,' Alice said.

'Well, schizophrenics don't, do they? They truly believe in godlike voices that only they can hear.'

'I'm sure it's not just saints and martyrs who hear voices. Ordinary people must have had visions too. They must have had them before history even started.'

'Ah, this is your boyfriend talking.'

Alice was irritated by his presumption. 'No, Mr Pharaoh, it's *me*. And what I was going to say is that their minds must have been filled with beliefs that would seem alien to us. Just like this girl's mental world couldn't be understood by you.'

'Photographers can't enter an internal world, but we *can* demonstrate its surface effects.'

Alice nodded at the surroundings. 'And all these demonstrations were arranged to impress me?'

'It took a long time to set it all up,' Gregory answered. She was not sure if he smiled as he said it.

'And *my* photographs?'

'Look at this one first.'

And he indicated a large print of a serious-faced man wearing bishop's regalia. Every line on his face was clear as a contour on a map. The lens had captured a variance in the sheen of his vestments. An ornate ring demonstrated a jeweller's art.

'I'd been photographing him just before we met. That's why I was carrying the 5D; it's designed for close detail.'

'You must specialize in taking religious subjects. But I don't know who he is.'

'Actually I'm much more interested in the worldly. As for this subject, well, the photograph tells you all you need to know – his position in the Church; his character. You can't read that kind of formal information in the shots I took of you.' Gregory indicated a desk with a screen and printer. 'I left the best copies there. Should I ever want to exhibit one, I'd pick it from them.'

Aware of his judgemental stare, Alice approached the desk with deliberation. Now that the promised images were in front of her, now that she could study them closely, even touch them, she was unsure how she would react.

At first she hardly recognized herself. The prints had been

arranged to give prominence to extreme close-ups, and each had been scrupulously balanced for tone and form.

'This could be anyone,' she said after a few seconds. 'They're like . . . pieces of me. Although it's not really *me* at all.'

'You're wrong,' Gregory said.

She lifted one of the prints to peruse it. Light from the high windows flexed along its surface.

'It's what *was* me. You've reduced me. I'm nothing but a kind of geometry.'

'You're not reduced at all. I've taken aspects of you and enhanced them.'

'Like what?'

'Like your hair. Look at the way the light flows across the frame from the upper left quadrant, and how the strands of hair pick up on that motion and break parts of it into tiny fractures. Or this one here. The fallen sunglasses suggest that something unusual has happened, or that it may still be happening. A sense of unease, of the incorrect, is magnified by the tension in the hands below the fallen body. And the next print, where—'

'That's what I mean. None of them give any idea of what I'm *like*. There's nothing of my personality in these.'

'If you want your personality to be shown, then you have to let me take your portrait in a studio session. You know I want to do that.' After a short pause, Gregory added: 'I'm being honest and I'm being straightforward.'

Alice put down the photograph and picked up another before she answered.

'But you don't even know what my personality *is*.'

'The lens will show it. It showed the bishop and it showed the girl who has the visions. You saw that it did. People will look at your face and they'll know, just as *you* knew when you looked at the face of the girl. You could see the past and the present in her face, and maybe you could see her future, too.'

Alice stared hard at the sleekly doctored fragments of herself.

Only one photograph showed her entire body. It was pitched forward with outstretched arms. It appeared to Alice that she was not falling but rising, borne aloft on invisible wings. Only one foot was still in contact with the ground, and that was lifting from her shoe as if to abandon it.

'A portrait can't show a whole personality,' she objected. 'It would be just an aspect, as incomplete as these are. And maybe just as misleading.'

'A portrait is never misleading; it's illuminating. If the photographer is good then the subjects will discover things about themselves. Things that they had never known.'

'Do you say that to all your sitters? They must think you unusually arrogant.'

Gregory raised an arm to show that she should look more carefully around the room.

'You see those faces? They didn't think I was arrogant when they saw the results. They knew I was speaking the truth. Deep inside, so do you.'

Outside the immediate world something weighty and mysterious gathered momentum. Alice could sense its motion, but neither its direction nor its mass was clear.

'I spend a lot of time thinking about decisions before I make them,' she said.

Gregory nodded.

'For instance,' she continued, 'before I made any decision, I'd want to know if your daughter would be present.' Alice waited a moment before she went on. 'I know you told me her name, but I've forgotten it.'

The deliberate echo of his own question was not lost on Gregory. He answered without emphasis.

'If you wanted Cassie to be here then she could be. But I'd ask her to leave if I felt that the chemistry worked better without her.'

'But she would stay in the office downstairs?'

'If it made you more comfortable.'

'I'm sure it would.'

'We'd have to see,' Gregory said, as if he found the discussion irksome.

Alice wondered if his relationships with women were always fleeting and without depth. Perhaps that was the way he preferred them to be.

'But if you took my portrait – if I *let* you take it – then what could I possibly find in it that I didn't already know?'

'We'd both find signs that we hadn't expected. There are things going on inside you that I don't know about. I don't think you understand them, either.'

Alice felt that Gregory would argue anything to get his own way. It was quite likely that he often did not believe what he was saying. He probably saw no contradiction in this. Stung at being patronized, she turned on him.

'Why do you expect me to respond to flattery? You told me I was special. I knew you didn't mean it. If you really thought I was all that special then you wouldn't speak to me as if I was just another face to frame in your viewfinder.'

The accusation irritated Gregory more than she had expected. He had reached the end of his patience, and it would be reasonable if he demonstrated anger.

'Do you think I speak like this to anyone?' he demanded.

'Don't you?'

'You keep asking questions – now let me put some questions to *you*. Why are you so suspicious of my motives? Why can't you accept that I have an eye for composition, and for human features and form, which is out of the ordinary? Are you simply incapable of understanding that I can look at you and see things that you'll never find in any mirror? You could stare at your reflection for days and never discover what I can show you. I know what I'm talking about – this is a job that I've done very, very successfully for more than thirty years. And I've always, *always* followed an honourable protocol, just as I would do for you.'

He bent over the desk monitor and switched it on. Taken aback by the energy of his response, Alice took a step further away. After a few moments the screen flickered into life and Gregory moved the cursor to an icon. His voice had thickened.

'Those prints are all enlarged detail, apart from one. These are the originals. All of them were taken on the spur of the moment. There was no time for proper composition. I knew I'd be able to work on them later to bring out their best qualities. But you can't or won't see the value in those versions. Instead you just want to study the raw material.'

Twelve photographs appeared on the screen, lined up like cards in a game. Capping them, at their end, was the thirteenth, a blurred image of a distant motorbike about to enter a stream of traffic.

'I'll print out a copy of each one and you can take them away,' Gregory said angrily. 'I don't want them back. We're not likely to see each other again.'

Alice saw that Gregory had lied when he told her that he had taken only five or six. But she did not protest, and instead stepped closer to the screen.

What she saw did not involve her. Instead she felt detached from the woman in the photographs, the woman who looked like her, wore her clothes and was thrown forward in the way that she had been. The sequence appeared as inauthentic as a re-enactment by impersonators.

'These don't seem like me either,' she admitted. Alice wondered if she might not even have recognized herself if she had not been told the truth.

The comment made Gregory pause. From somewhere in the studio there came the sound of a ticking clock; Alice had not noticed it before. She turned to him.

'Of course I *know* that it's me – or rather, a semblance of me. And I know this is a record of what actually happened. But it seems to be happening somewhere else and to a different person.'

'Why should you think that?' he asked quietly. 'You recognize that all of these images are truthful. This isn't your double, is it?'

'Of course not.'

'Right. Do you often have a feeling of not belonging to the world?'

'Sometimes,' Alice admitted, and would not look at him.

Gregory became as sleek as a tempter.

'Maybe you were just thinking of the girl with the visions. Maybe she's been on your mind without your realizing it. You've been infected by a sense that the real world is a kind of illusion.'

Alice shook her head. She was no longer sure what to think. Gregory went on.

'When you looked at that girl's face you must have seen that she was a contradictory mixture of the worldly and the unreal.

What I told you was true. A successful portrait opens up the personality.'

But Alice would not discuss it, and broke the spell.

'Can you put these on a full screen? Or enlarge parts of them?'

'That's how I decided on the characteristics that were best.'

'This one,' Alice said, pointing to the image of her body as it was flung towards the lens with its arms outstretched.

Within a second it filled the screen. Alice stared hard at it, searching for signs that she could not detect.

She held out one finger near to the screen and traced the shape of an oval around the head.

'Can we get closer?' she asked.

Gregory zoomed in on a close-up of the angled head. All that Alice could see was her hair, the dark glasses, a face so foreshortened it could have been that of a child being born. And no matter how hard she stared, there was nothing unusual, nothing unexplained and nothing unidentified that could be seen around her.

'And my hands?' she asked.

Again, there was nothing to the hands other than their reaching out in a reflex.

'What are you looking for?' Gregory asked.

'I'm not sure. I thought that maybe something would be made visible. It was all so sudden, so hurtful . . .'

'*Made* visible? Objects are either visible or they're not. I don't understand.'

'No. No, I imagine that you wouldn't.'

Gregory leaned purposefully on the table. It creaked slightly beneath his weight.

'When we met by the river you hinted at something that might be found in the pictures. I told you there was nothing unusual about them. Do you want me to ask you again what you're looking for?'

Alice was aware that, for Gregory, the idea of the immaterial suddenly irrupting into the visible world was absurd.

'I've heard it said that sometimes cameras catch light patterns around people. Light patterns that can't normally be detected with the naked eye.'

Still Gregory did not grasp what she meant, and he spoke as if he expected Alice to find his answer reassuring.

'Photography has been going beyond the visible spectrum since just after its invention,' he said, and then he paused. She looked down at the prints again. 'You mean auras,' he said.

Suddenly defensive, Alice folded her arms tightly around herself and continued to examine the prints.

'They don't exist,' Gregory said flatly. 'Oh, there are charlatans who doctor their photos to show faces and bodies surrounded by haloes of colour, but that's easy manipulation. Only the gullible would believe it.'

'I see,' Alice said quietly, although it seemed to her obvious that under certain intense conditions the body would throw off an energy, a vibration, a shield that perhaps only certain kinds of photography would be able to capture.

'I'm not interested in metaphysics,' Gregory said. 'Meaning resides in the here and now. Truth lies in how a body moves or facial muscles react. There is no mystery, no transcendence, no Great Beyond. Images and memories are the only things that people leave behind. There's nothing else.'

Alice remained silent.

Confidential, brotherly, apparently trustworthy, Gregory edged a little closer. He lowered his voice as if they could somehow be overheard.

'It would be a big step for you; I know that. But it's one that you should take. You have nothing to fear.'

Alice did not react, but stared hard at the woman in the photographs.

'More than anyone else I can think of,' Gregory went on, 'you deserve to be in front of a lens. When you go home to Thomas Laidlaw I want you to think about that. And I want you to know that I'll be considering the best way to pose you.'

The muscles at the back of Alice's legs had begun to tremble as though under pressure. She wondered if that shaking would be visible to Gregory if he stepped back and studied her again.

'I'll portray you in black-and-white prints,' he said. 'Humphrey Jennings said that black-and-white film lives on ideas but colour lives on sensation. That's why I'll show you in black-and-white. I think you'd approve.'

Alice was not sure whether or not she had moved her head.

'Promise me to think about it,' Gregory said, and then waited. 'Of course,' he continued, 'we'd save a lot of time, and a lot of uncertainty, if you agreed now. We would each know where the other stood.'

Alice remained silent. Her mouth was dry.

'Wouldn't we?' he asked.

Thomas lay with his feet up on the sofa and a book open in front of him. Apparently absorbed, he was surreptitiously watching Alice. All was quiet but for the sound of her shoes on the floor. She paced the confines of the flat as though forbidden to leave.

The book was a gazetteer of European archaeological sites, its text liberally illustrated with maps, plans and photographs. On the previous night Thomas had returned to the flat to discover Alice examining its images of tilted monoliths, collapsed tombs, and half-robbed mounds of stone. When he asked if she wanted to know more about the sites she had shaken her head and not looked up. But she had carried on turning the pages, apparently at random.

Thomas was puzzled. Some time ago Alice had insisted that she had lost interest in the technicalities of archaeology, but now she appeared to be discovering something unexpected in bleak images of deserted remains. He was not to know that it was not historical data that intrigued her, but composition, lighting, and atmosphere. It was as if Alice wished the sites to be stripped of all investigation, to become once again unknowable, and to exist purely as mysteries or symbols.

Thomas felt an ache of regret. In their early days together he had enjoyed telling his lover about the evidence of lost worlds that was still scattered across the European landscape. Even the names were evocative – Los Millares, Long Meg and Her Daughters, Rocha dos Enamorados, Grime's Graves. For Alice this knowledge was intriguingly arcane, and she had always been attracted to people who were experts on subjects about which she knew little. What had been especially appealing about Thomas's expertise was that within it she could always read an inference of development, of improvement, of ascent. No matter how much he insisted that such a model of progress had been discredited, to Alice it still seemed as if the world had been programmed to improve.

Now, alive with nervous energy, Alice prowled the flat while Thomas eyed her like a keeper. She checked the contents of drawers, moved ornaments fractionally, touched the corners of a framed poster to make sure that it hung straight on the wall. Then she stared out of the window at the busy street below for several minutes, all the time swaying almost imperceptibly from side to side. Thomas recognized that these were displacement activities. Alice had begun to exhibit them with increased frequency; often they led to distressing scenes.

When she left the room and went into the tiny kitchen he waited for a few moments, put down his book, and then followed her. Alice was kneeling in front of the refrigerator making a silent inventory of its contents. Her blouse with the vertical blue stripes was open one button too far and the sleeves were pushed up to her elbows.

When he told her that there was no shortage of food, her distracted expression made him think that she had not heard.

'There's something on your mind,' he said. 'Why don't you come back and sit down and we can talk about it. Or maybe we could go out for a few hours. We could go anywhere you want.'

'I'm just making sure nothing has been forgotten. Someone has to keep on top of these things. Who else is going to make sure that everything runs smoothly?'

Alice closed the fridge door, stood up and folded her arms. Her fingers tapped against her own skin with the rapidity of a Morse signaller. When she next spoke she did not look at Thomas but to one side, as if a third person stood within the room, invisible and silent. He thought it best not to break the spell.

'I may as well tell you,' she said at last.

Whenever she made a comment like that, a tide of panic rose within him.

'Tell me what?'

'What I've decided to do. You see, I found out something from Gregory Pharaoh.'

'There's something in those photographs?'

Alice was silent. She did not seem to have listened.

'You could identify the people who robbed you?' Thomas suggested.

She shook her head in dismissal. 'No, it's not that. That doesn't matter any more. Those two men were just means to an end.'

Thomas waited. He could hear traffic noise filtering up from the street.

'He told me that I have a certain . . . quality.'

'Quality,' he repeated flatly.

'He told me that I'm photogenic. I didn't expect that.'

Thomas felt a surge of relief. All that had happened was that Alice had been flattered. A photographer such as Pharaoh would be prone to exaggeration; sooner or later Alice would realize it. There was no cause for Thomas to worry.

But she acted as if the word had set a seal on her uniqueness, and when she continued she spoke like an advocate.

'It's a professional judgement made from experience. Made by an *expert*. I hadn't thought it, but that's what he says.'

Thomas considered how he should answer.

Although his feelings for Alice were what he classed as love, sometimes – too often – he was unequal to the demands that coursed through her life. But Thomas had never doubted his own emotions. He knew that it was impossible for him not to love her, as it would be impossible for him to leave. If anyone were capable of turning away brutally and forever, it was Alice.

And if that happened, he suspected that he would never be able to deal with the consequences. Thomas would always love Alice: he was certain of that. But aside from the emotions of loss and grief that would forever needle and bleed him, there would be everyday practical problems that he was not sure he would be able to solve. One of these would be where he could live. This was Alice's flat, and Thomas made no financial contribution to it. He had an older brother, Richard, whom he hardly ever met, so it was doubtful if he would be able to stay with him for more than just a couple of days. Thomas was unsettlingly aware that it was not only his heart that was vulnerable.

His response had to be tactful. If he offered too much praise, Alice would accuse him of cynical embellishment. He cleared his throat.

'I think you're very attractive.'

It was not enough. He had to say more.

'You know that's true.' Even as he spoke Thomas recognized the weakness and miscalculation of his words.

Alice appeared to be brooding on an approach, a suggestion, about which she was not yet able to speak.

'But do *you* think I look good in photographs?' she demanded. 'Has the word *photogenic* ever crossed your mind?'

'I've often asked to take your photo. Usually you refuse. The only ones we have of each other were taken on holidays.'

'Maybe that's because you don't ask in the right way.'

'What do you mean – the right way? There's only one way to ask and that's what I do. It's not my fault when you say no.'

Alice shook her head in disbelief.

'Thomas, you never make me feel that you want to photograph *me*. You just want me to be part of an arrangement. Like posing against a view to give it scale. I always feel that I'm just a kind of ornament. Or, even worse, a measure, like a surveying pole. I may as well be divided horizontally into black-and-white sections.'

'How can you say that?' he asked, the timbre of his voice shifting as he sensed control slipping from him. When Alice descended into doubt her behaviour was unpredictable and some-times intolerable.

'Once I allow myself to think it, then saying it is easy. Telling the truth isn't difficult once you've thought everything through.'

Her fingers had stopped tapping her skin, and now they dug into the flesh. He could see the force in her grip. Without relenting, Alice went on.

'In fact, telling the truth becomes a necessity. It's something to do with ethics, about being honest with yourself and those around you.' She waited a moment and then spoke again. 'And you know about being honest with yourself, don't you?'

Thomas stepped away, put his hands behind his back, and leaned against the wall. His palms were flattened against the vertical, fingers pointing down, and he pressed hard against them as if they had to be kept under control. The texture of the wall was slightly uneven and he could feel its blemishes against his skin.

It was unreasonable of Alice to suggest that he could not face the truth, because she had always avoided candour about her own past. Thomas knew that she had had several lovers before they had met, but he knew little of their names or their personalities. Retorting that she had always been silent on such matters would, he knew, only make things worse.

'Alice, I know why you're acting like this. By chance you met a man with a camera and he's been fabricating some tale or other—'

'I told you. He's a professional. His latest work is printed in next Sunday's—'

'I'll believe that when I see it.'

'You'll see it all right. I'll make sure I buy a copy.'

Thomas waited for a few moments. 'You can't believe a person like that.'

'He sees things in me that you can't. And *I* know they're there, even if I'm not sure exactly what they are. That's why I believe him.'

'He's trying it on. Can't you see that? He thinks that compliments will work because he assumes you're either vain or vulnerable.'

'Is that what you think about me?'

'You know it isn't.'

'Then why should Gregory Pharaoh? He wants to take my portrait, that's all. At first I said no, but then I thought – why not? He can make his choice from hundreds of women. *Hundreds.* Maybe that should tell you something about me.'

To Thomas, it seemed absurd that they should be arguing. The kitchen flattened and degraded their voices so that both he and Alice seemed like immature versions of themselves. Even the words they used did not sound fully formed.

'Let's go and sit down and talk this through,' he suggested again.

'No, Thomas, let's stand here. There's nothing to discuss. I'm going to sit for a portrait. That's my decision. I'm just telling you what it is.'

He nodded mutely. Her next question was put like a demand.

'Are you angry?'

'No. No, I'm not angry.'

'Jealous, then?'

Thomas denied it with a shake of his head, but he was acutely aware that jealousy was a constant measure in his life.

Everyone else seemed to have been given opportunities that Thomas had been denied. For years he had remained at the shadowy periphery of research, excavations and lectureships. Not for him the glamorous finds that so excited the media; he could only imagine what it must be like to be wooed by television producers. In acceptance of his lowly status, Thomas had even begun to consider investigating sites that, if they had been examined at all, had only been dug by wealthy Victorian amateurs who had never unearthed enough to satisfy their curiosity.

That, he thought, was burden enough, but he was also obsessively jealous of Alice. Until he had met her, his sexual life had been unimaginative. Plainly hers had not, for she had awoken responses in him whose existence he had always doubted. Now, when he lay with her in bed, or when she evaded questions about her earlier life, or simply when he watched her walk across a room, Thomas wondered if other men had made more proficient, inflamed and sensual love to Alice than he had ever been able to do. And all the time, in a drumbeat forever sounding in his imagination, he wondered if she had been closer and more comfortable with those lovers than she had ever been with him.

He had never dared admit any of these fears.

'You're jealous,' Alice said with grim triumph. 'I can tell.'

'What do you expect me to say? What do you *want* me to say? I'm doing my best to keep things calm.'

'Maybe it would be best if we weren't calm. Is that what you secretly think? You think you've got a good reason to feel agitated, don't you – and we both know why. It's because you've failed.

And because every now and then you come face to face with the truth. That's why.'

The sound of their breathing filled the room like that of animals within a cage.

'Alice,' he said wearily, 'don't let's fight each other. I don't know why you feel a need to argue. You're always the one who starts it.'

'I don't *start* it. It happens because of who we are and what we do. Do you think I enjoy being so upset? Don't you realize how often I've been reduced to tears because of what we are?'

Thomas was silent. A few nights ago, after they had made love, Alice had begun to weep. Naked, inconsolable, she had trembled helplessly within his arms and refused to explain why.

'The other week, when I had my bag stolen,' she continued, 'I told the people at work I was going to take a walk rather than eat lunch. They must have seen how near the edge I was. I started to cry before I even got out of the building. I remember keeping my head down in the lift in case anyone else got in. I knew my eyes would be so ugly and puffed up that I would have to wear dark glasses as camouflage. That's what I was doing when I was robbed. Just walking aimlessly, but fast, as if I knew where I was going. And covering my eyes in case anyone noticed how distressed I was. I thought Gregory Pharaoh hadn't spotted that. But he had. He notices everything.'

'Pharaoh.' The name tasted bitter in Thomas's mouth, so bitter that he spoke it again. 'Pharaoh the expert. I don't even believe that's his real name. Why do I feel I'm being compared to this man? You don't even know him. Not really.'

'Of course I don't.'

There was another pause in their confrontation, like an unexpected lull in battle. Alice's face had tightened, her breathing rose and fell, and the skin shone at the base of her throat. And then she went on.

'I don't really *want* to know him. I'd have told you that before, if you'd been concerned enough to ask. But it never occurred to you to ask, did it? You were too busy daydreaming to think about me; too busy fantasizing about schemes that never work out and contracts that are always short-term and plans that always fail.'

It was a familiar accusation, but one that always hit home. Even as he answered, Thomas knew that his voice was dulled, like that of a man interrogated for hours who finally confesses.

'I'm not a failure. It's just that success hasn't happened yet.'

'And until it does? Until then I work at jobs that I don't particularly like and sometimes hate. You should try lowering your standards like I have to do – it gives you real insight into how things are.'

Thomas turned away.

'Don't turn your back on me,' Alice shouted.

He was sure she had become so strident that she would be heard in the neighbouring flats. There was a self-serving streak of drama in Alice. He decided he must say this, and turned back to face her, but then he stopped.

Thomas thought that he simply did not care any more. His apparent resolve was as false as it was momentary; he knew it was impossible for him to walk out on Alice. Just as he knew that he would always be hopelessly, helplessly in love with her.

He forced himself into extending the confrontation. 'Why shouldn't I turn my back? You're not worth listening to.'

'Bastard,' she said, and clenched her hand into a fist.

'If you hit me,' Thomas said, 'I'll not respond. I've done enough of that.'

Alice seemed poised on the edge of striking him. He could see the strain in her face, the dilation of her eyes, the slight trembling of her arm.

He had to do something.

Suddenly confident, Thomas reached out and put his hand round her fist as a restraint. Alice turned her head to one side, either in acknowledgement that the instant had passed or because she could no longer bear to look at him. He was momentarily lost between rage and appeasement, but then he forced himself to calm down.

'This is crazy,' he said.

Alice did not answer, but stood still before him: a frightened yet stubborn captive.

'After all this time, we should learn not to tear each other apart,' Thomas continued. 'We should know each other's personality well enough by now.'

Her lips moved, but he could not hear what she said.

'What?'

'But you don't. That's the trouble.'

He was puzzled. 'Don't what?'

'Don't know me.'

It was the kind of complaint she made often. Thomas would have liked to consider it worthless, but he knew that it was true.

'Of course I do,' he told her, but he knew his confidence was hollow.

'It's not a failing,' Alice answered. 'Often I think I don't even know myself.'

Thomas waited for a second, and then impulsively became

more conciliatory and put his arms round Alice. Like a third invisible figure, a sense of desperation embraced them both. Alice did not move away but she was rigid and unyielding, and even when Thomas hugged her tighter she would not raise her face to look into his eyes.

Alice thought of the men who had loved her as rungs on a ladder whose top could still not be seen. When each relationship was over, she felt that she had moved higher. Anger, distress and recrimination were consequences she knew how to deal with. They were transitory and left no wounds. The next affair was always more exciting than the last.

She could never see where she was going, but she always knew that she was climbing.

5

At first Alice Fell is able to reject the lens, to nullify its inquisition, so that the earlier portraits will reveal almost nothing of her personality.

She has chosen sensible clothes – a black blouse, grey trousers with a subdued fleck, little black boots with side zips and wedge heels. Gregory has asked her to take off her watch and bracelets. A high-backed wooden chair is placed in the centre of the studio with a neutral backdrop of very pale blue. Natural light enters from windows and skylight, tall lamps with adjustable panels provide additional illumination, and circular reflectors are stationed just outside viewfinder range.

As Gregory checks the light meter he mentions that his daughter helped with the set-up. He believes that Alice will find this information reassuring, but when she was admitted to the building the two women were immediately cool with each other. Alice thought that Cassie's greeting was reserved and possibly resentful, and she wondered if a daughter's natural jealousy had worked its way into her demeanour.

Gregory explains to Alice that he will effectively be shooting digital black-and-white with the equivalent of a low ASA and a shallow depth of field. At first he has her standing with arms folded, and then he asks her to pose with one hand on the back of the chair, and then both. He puts a few impersonal questions to her that she barely answers. After a few minutes he motions her to sit.

Gregory obtains both aesthetic and intellectual satisfaction from photography. He finds pleasure not only in technical calculations and in the arrangement of lighting, but also in the actual handling of a camera, in its shape and weight, in the changing of lenses and the twist of the focus ring, in the responsiveness of the shutter release. He enjoys the way the camera body seats itself on a tripod, the coded display on its screen, the unison of flash and shutter, and he enjoys the power of having his models pose exactly how he wishes them to pose.

At first Alice does as she is told. She stands and turns and sits at the centre of the cluttered studio, her black blouse fastened primly at the cuffs and opened at the throat by only one button. She stares back into the curvature of the lens, into its deep arc of colour like spilled petrol, and all it can detect is her bland impenetrable surface. It cannot find a hidden aspect of the self. At this point she is no different from thousands of others who have sat in front of a photographer.

Gregory recognizes what is going wrong. Alice is wary about answering the questions that he usually puts to his sitters. For many years he has followed a procedure that loosens up his subjects and then triggers an emotion, no matter how fleeting. This reaction he is able to catch on the instant. His technique is one of kindly but persistent interrogation. Seduced by the unwavering attention of both photographer and camera, the subject talks openly, as if to a confessor. Gregory has listened so often to intimate admissions that they seldom surprise him. They have become part of the protocol. The act of photography opens the door on hidden rooms of emotion and belief.

Alice will have none of this. Instead of eagerness she exhibits caution. Perhaps her stubbornness contains an element of mistrust. With other models, Gregory has been confident enough to move rapidly to the most personal kind of inquiry, for it is in the disclosure of the most private experiences that the features of sitters come alive. He knows that men and women habitually present a face that attempts to disguise feelings that are of particular interest — melancholia, longing, obsession, arousal and mystery.

With Alice, it becomes obvious that she is deliberately evading familiarity. She does not even answer questions that she has answered freely in the past.

Gregory is frustrated. He realizes that he is shooting too many unusable frames and forces himself to step back and pause.

What progress has he made? In each succeeding shot there is nothing extra; there is only repetition. He connects the camera to a monitor so that he can use a larger screen to show Alice some of what has been taken. She shrugs and says nothing. He cannot tell if she is puzzled or uninterested.

Gregory stands with his hand on his chin and studies his subject. Her very silence is a challenge. He admits to himself that his fascination with Alice has to do with his uncertainty about her character. There is something about Alice Fell that eludes him, and it eludes his camera as well.

When he is able to look back on the beginning of the session, Gregory will realize that this moment of contemplation allowed him to think of a way forward. There are books on his shelves that contain hundreds of classic images, some of which he could copy. Alice's blouse would show as the deepest black on any print. It took him only a few seconds to think of Man Ray's 1930 study of Lee Miller. What he had to do now was demonstrate how that composition worked.

He showed the picture to Alice and explained that he intended to make a variation on the original. It would be a kind of homage, recognized as such amongst aficionados. Alice should keep her top button unfastened; the inverted triangle of bare skin would provide an interesting geometric shape. She should turn her head to the left and raise her left hand, fingers extended, almost to the collarbone. Light would appear to suffuse across the right-hand side of her face and a sharp line of brilliance would run from her left eyebrow, down the side of her neck, and touch her fingers as they rested against the black blouse. As he told her this, Gregory could smell her hair, the perfume she had sprayed on her skin, a lotion she had rubbed on her hands.

Alice was unconvinced, but took up the posture. 'I have no idea who that woman is,' she said.

Although he could not decide whether Alice expected him to follow up her admission, Gregory saw that he had been given an opportunity. He began to shoot at a steady pace, and as he worked he talked quickly, timing his phrases to fall between each release of the shutter. What he could not remember, he invented.

Lee Miller, he told her, was an independent woman, a great beauty who sought pleasure in several affairs, a model for Edward Steichen as well as Man Ray, a socialite and photographer who became famous for her unflinching studies of the collapse of the Third Reich. These basic facts Gregory embroidered, importing fictionalized tales of other photographers, other subjects. He even credited Miller with work that he knew for a fact was that of both Gerda Taro and George Rodger.

He did not have to look at the screen to know that Alice remained awkward rather than confident, stiff rather than glamorous. Nevertheless there was a hint of relaxation, as if hearing his stories had aroused her interest; as if, after a time, she could even become fascinated.

And now Gregory produced an even older photograph. It was from 1864 – Julia Margaret Cameron's portrait of a sixteen-year-old Ellen Terry. The model is bare-shouldered, head inclined, her eyes downcast towards the lower left corner of the frame. Natural light spills in from the right to illuminate her collarbone, neck, left cheek and the underside of her jaw. She clasps a necklace with her right hand.

As Alice studied the image, Gregory asked about its constituents. Here was a portrait of a pretty girl, but what gave it that tactile quality, that distinctive energy?

Alice waited for a second before replying.

'The necklace?'

'We'll come back to that.'

'The shoulders?'

At last Gregory believed that he was making progress.

'Right,' he agreed, 'the shoulders. You can see how their angle and their nakedness control the spatial dynamic. By posing her model like that, Margaret Cameron allows us to see into the thoughts of a young girl almost 150 years ago. Look at the expression on that face. The model recognizes her own attractiveness. She knows she has a future. Were it not for the bare shoulders, that muted eroticism would be lost.'

Alice stared at the photograph as if she were contemplating her own past.

Gregory waited for several seconds before asking the next question.

'What have you got on under that top?'

'You want me to have bare shoulders?'

'The Margaret Cameron shows how it would work.'

The response was swift enough to make him realize that she had anticipated his suggestion. For a few seconds she might even have considered it.

'It wouldn't work,' Alice said. 'I'm wearing a black bra. And I'm not taking that off.'

'You needn't do anything that you don't want. There's no pressure here. I'm not as manipulative as you suspect. But you should understand that I've photographed so many women, and a lot of them naked, that I'm used to it.'

'You're indifferent to nakedness?'

'I'm professional about it. But you and I aren't talking about nudity, are we? We're talking about bare shoulders and that's all. Pity you're not wearing a necklace. It would have had to be substantial. And with rounded forms.'

'I'm wearing a crucifix. A tiny one.'

'It wouldn't work so well. Would you object to taking it off? Are you religious?'

'No. Not conventionally.'

'Then why wear it?'

'Does there have to be a reason for everything?'

'Not at all. There's nothing wrong with people doing things just because they like it. But there's certainly a reason why I think you should take off that crucifix and be photographed in the way that Ellen Terry was photographed. You don't have any tattoos on your shoulders, do you?'

'I don't have any tattoos anywhere.'

'Thank God for that.'

'I don't have a necklace either.'

'That's easily arranged.'

'What – you have a box of props?'

'I have lots of things. I can get a necklace. I can get one now.'

'But there will be shiny black straps over my shoulders.'

Gregory nodded. He and Alice stared at each other for a moment. He was not sure what was passing between them. He did not think that Alice knew, either.

'I'll bring that necklace,' he said quietly.

Gregory descended the flights of stairs too quickly. Their hollowness echoed around his footsteps. And then the handle of the office door unaccountably slipped from his grasp with a clatter like a sprung trap, and he had to turn it on a second attempt.

Cassie looked up at him from the desk. 'Is there a fire?' she asked drily.

'I'd like to borrow that necklace. Please.'

Cassie raised her fingers to touch the lower beads. They were imitation ivory and had been strung so that the largest hung several inches beneath the base of her neck. Her fingers moved across the surfaces as if testing for smoothness.

'They're Mother's,' she reminded him.

'I haven't forgotten.'

A few seconds passed. Gregory wondered why his daughter did not speak.

'And you don't have a problem about using them?' Cassie asked at last.

'No. They improve the composition. That's the only reason I'm asking.'

She stared at him, fingers still on the beads.

'Other than that, it means nothing,' Gregory insisted.

For a moment it seemed as if Cassie would refuse.

'If you're comfortable with this,' she said at last, putting her hands to the back of her neck. Her disapproval was quietly evident.

Again Gregory tried to justify himself. 'All I'm doing is trying to take the best pictures that I can.'

'They won't even suit her. She hasn't got the right shape of face.'

Cassie unclipped the beads and held them out as if she were relinquishing a prize. As they swayed they made a noise like tentative friction.

'You've never asked to borrow them before. Never.'

Gregory hesitated. Perhaps Cassie was right. Perhaps the necklace was still so closely associated with his wife that it would be wrong to place them around the neck of Alice Fell. And yet he believed that inanimate objects had no intrinsic emotional value. Only superstitious people imagined them to be somehow imbued with the spirit of others. Objects were *things*; they had form in space and duration in time, and that was all.

He took the beads from Cassie's hand. As he did he felt a mild tingle of static electricity.

'I'll bring them straight back,' he promised.

As he climbed back up the stairs he remembered his wife unfastening the same necklace as she sat in front of her dressing-table mirrors. Taking off his clothes on the far side of the bed, Gregory had glanced across and something inside him had lurched. Ruth's pale back and raised arms, and her reflection divided in a vertical line by two of the mirrors, had combined by chance into an ideal composition.

Gregory had never photographed his wife naked; she had not wished him to. Only after Ruth died had he begun to work on extensive studies of the female form. But on that day, as she calmly and systematically took off her clothes, he had felt a need, an ache, to record the specifics of her body while he could. He had even suggested it. But Ruth had laughed and insisted she was no model; besides, she would be embarrassed.

One year later, as the disease took hold, she had not at first complained when he obsessively photographed her decline. Seemingly she had understood it was his way of coping with her approaching death. Only in its later stages had both his wife and daughter seen Gregory's professionalism as exploitative and callous. Sometimes he thought that Cassie had never really forgiven him for those last few weeks.

Gregory neared the top of the stairs. He paused at the entrance to the studio, overtaken by a sudden boyish fantasy of seeing Alice standing naked. But when he entered he found her seated on the chair and dressed just as she had been when he had left. For a moment it seemed that borrowing the necklace had been a waste of energy. Nevertheless he held it out in an unconscious repeat of Cassie's gesture.

Alice did not move. 'This isn't a prop out of a box,' she said. 'When I arrived here your daughter was wearing it. Doesn't she mind?'

'She understands.'

'It *is* your daughter's, isn't it?'

'Of course.'

Alice took the string and held it between her hands. 'I haven't said I'll do this.'

He said nothing. Quite suddenly Alice turned her back.

Gregory crossed the room to adjust one of the lights. He had the sensation of a door being opened somewhere out of sight. He paused behind the tripod and put his fingers around the focus ring. His mouth was dry.

'Are you ready?' he asked.

Methodically, as if she had reached an unpleasant decision and wanted no further delay, Alice began to take off her blouse. Watching from behind, Gregory noted the poise of the upturned wrists as she unbuttoned her cuffs, the flexing of the shoulders and extension of the arms as she slipped them out of the black sleeves. The material whispered faintly, like discarded clothing falling from a bed.

A thin gold chain glinted at the back of Alice's neck and the sheer straps of a black bra clasped her like a harness. Angled light shaded the plunge of her spine; Gregory could see the shapes of her vertebrae beneath the pale unblemished skin.

She sat with the blouse in her hands as though uncertain where to place it. Gregory walked to her side and she passed it to him without a word. The material was warm in his fingers. He knew that if he lifted it to his face he would be able to smell her body.

'I'll put the cross over there,' he said.

She lifted her arms to unhook the clasp and he saw that she had not recently shaved beneath them.

The crucifix was light, almost insubstantial. Gregory placed it on the shelf and then hung the blouse on a hanger with a metal hook that clicked with a noise like a turned key when he placed it on the hatstand. The beads slid against Alice's skin as she fastened the necklace. As soon as it was secure she turned back to the lens with her arms folded protectively across her breasts as if they were naked. He could see the edging of the bra cups beneath her hands.

'What would Thomas say if he saw me posing like this?'

'If I were him, I'd feel proud.'

'And the people I work with?'

'Are they likely to? Do you care?'

'No. But maybe I should.'

Gregory gave the tolerant, experienced smile he had perfected over the years.

'You can't keep both your hands there,' he said. 'I want one of them to be fingering the beads. Don't worry, I'm framing your head and shoulders, and nothing else.'

'I know.'

There was a moment's silence before Alice spoke again in a different register. This time she was gently interrogative, as if she were imitating Gregory's own technique.

'But do you really want just to copy an old photo? I don't want to be a copy of anything. Wouldn't it be better to do something different?'

He looked more closely at Alice. She dared him to read her face, but he was not sure that he could. In expression and stance and word, she lived by a vocabulary that Gregory could only partly understand.

'I'm trying to get what I promised I'd get,' he told her. 'Up until now, I haven't been able to. But I'm not going to give up.'

'If this is proving a lot more difficult than you expected, then I take that as a compliment.'

Gregory continued to stare. To look away would be to fail. Silence lay between them like an invisible history.

Alice's mouth moved almost imperceptibly; he was sure that for less than a second her lips parted before they closed again. A light in her eyes made him believe that she was expecting some form of challenge, perhaps even a confrontation. Maybe she was readying herself to insult or repulse him.

'Just touch the beads with the tips of your fingers,' he instructed.

Alice raised her left hand. The bra cups were trimmed with black lace and he could see the plump milky curve of her breasts above them. The necklace contrasted too severely with the skin and the black straps heightened the pictorial discord. He had made a miscalculation.

'No – the right hand.'

Alice did as she was told and let her left arm fall by her side with the fingers spread. The beads still looked bulky, too round, too much like ivory. Gregory considered them from where he stood beside the tripod. A tiny wry smile showed momentarily on Alice's face. He wondered if his doubt was apparent.

'Let's go,' he said. 'Try to look *through* the lens, rather than at it.'

She did not imitate the Margaret Cameron by turning to one side and looking down, and Gregory did not ask her to. Instead she stared directly into the lens without moving and without blinking.

The camera was neither instrument nor barrier but a conduit to whomever would study her image. At last Alice was making an imaginative link with observers whom she would never see and never know. Excitement touched her and the air in the room grew warmer. Gregory began to believe that the sitting was successful. He was on the way to getting what was needed.

After more than a dozen shots he paused with his finger resting alongside the shutter release.

'Those were just head and shoulders,' Alice said.

It was neither question nor statement. He need not have answered, but he did.

'That's what I promised,' he said.

'And were they what you wanted?'

'I think we're making progress.'

'But the beads are too heavy, aren't they? I could tell by your expression.'

'I didn't think it was obvious.'

'It was. And what you really want is obvious, too.'

Although he had no need to, Gregory busied himself at the menu screen. 'And what's that?'

'You know there's a better arrangement,' she answered.

'You're quite a mind-reader, aren't you?'

'Only when a mind is easy to read.'

'Well, if it's so easy then you'll be able to tell me.'

'If you want.'

'Go on.'

'You think the necklace will look better if I'm naked to the waist. I'd have to hold my chin higher because then the proportions will be better balanced. My neck will be elongated and the curve at the base of the necklace will complement the curves on the undersides of my breasts.'

Gregory looked swiftly at Alice and then back to the menu. It was possible that she was goading him. For a wild moment he thought of telling her that the circularity and pallor of the beads would emphasize the shape and darkness of her nipples.

'You have an eye for composition,' he said.

'I'm a quick learner.'

Gregory remained standing beside the camera as he looked

her up and down. He expected Alice to wait for his response, for she seemed confident in her control, but unexpectedly she was the one to make the next move.

'Or I could put my hands behind my head. That would give greater definition, don't you agree?'

Again Gregory waited for a moment before answering.

'Of a certain kind, yes.'

'And would you like me to do that? To see how I look?'

'Try it.'

Alice lifted her arms. Her belly hollowed. A narrow bulge of the undersides of her breasts edged from below her bra. She locked her fingers together behind her head and the fall of light shifted across her face. The sparse hair within her armpits divided naturally along the line of the junction of body and limb. She stared back at Gregory as if to prove she would always be unreachable.

'Is that better?'

'Arguably. But you've said yourself how you could look even better.'

'Ah, but I'm not going to take this bra off and let you photograph me. Even though I'm falling out of it.'

'I hadn't even planned that you would strike the pose you're in.'

Alice lowered her arms, tugged at the front of her bra until she was comfortable, and then folded her arms across her chest again.

'Sometimes things don't work out as they're planned,' she said. 'Instead they work out because of some sort of necessity.'

'The necessity I have is to portray you in a way that hasn't been done before. I haven't succeeded yet. I'm on the edge, but I haven't got there.'

'Maybe you're not as good as you think you are.'

Gregory's frustrated response was evenly paced. Keeping his eyes on Alice, he spoke as if addressing an observer hidden within the room.

'Oh, I'm good all right. The problem is not with my technique. The problem is Alice Fell.'

'I don't think that's true. If you're so eager to claim success, then any failure is down to you, too.'

But Gregory would not accept this.

'The problem is Alice Fell,' he repeated with extra emphasis, 'because she plays around with the lens. She's not nervous and she's not uncomfortable, but she doesn't like being told what to do. She doesn't accept that I know more than she does about how to get the best out of a camera. She can't decide about her part in our agreement because she likes to change her mind. She changes it a lot – that's what gives her energy. She likes to disconcert people. She's the kind of person who only feels good when she can fuck things up.'

Alice's face hardened. She was angry and perplexed. Gregory pressed the shutter release. He had taken about seven frames before she began to regain her composure.

'You tricked me into that.'

'There was no trick. All I did was say what I think.'

Her features set in disapproval. Even though the expression was staged, Gregory took another three or four shots.

'And now you look truculent,' he said.

'That's what I feel. So would you.'

'I don't think *my* ambition would be to look like a spoiled adolescent. Alice, you photograph better when you're caught out, angered, stung. If you don't believe me I'll put the images up here, on this screen.'

'Maybe I should just turn my back on you. Maybe you'd be happier if my face didn't even appear in your precious photographs.'

Gregory's confidence began to build. He raised an ironic finger in the air as if to register the value of her comment.

'Great idea. I'll concentrate on your back and nothing else. I knew you had an eye for composition.'

Alice responded angrily.

'And you'd be able to show me books with dozens of photos of women's bare backs, wouldn't you? Including Lee Miller's?'

'Hundreds. I'll lend you one. All you have to do is ask.'

'You keep telling me that you want the camera to see into the hidden parts of my personality. They won't come through on photographs that don't show my face.'

'No?'

'You know they won't.'

'It's not that straightforward. I would argue that the body is an expression of the personality. And I would say that generalities come through, but not specifics.'

'And what good is that?'

'Oh, you can find out a lot about a woman by the way she holds herself, or lifts her arms, or tilts her head. An image of her back would ignore the one part of the body that is most obviously a record of particular experience, and that's her face. It would be a study of form that makes a point about the nature of being human.'

'I don't want to represent anyone other than myself. I'm not a type, I'm an individual.'

'You're both. We all are.'

Gregory paced back and forth across the studio. The rush of confidence was an intoxicant. He felt that photographer and sitter were on the brink of an achievement, even if they would be unable to recognize that achievement until they actually reached it.

And now Gregory was certain that eventually Alice would do whatever he asked her to do. There was a direction, a mechanism, to everything.

'You should stand up,' he said.

She remained seated. Still Gregory had no doubts.

'Stand up because it'll look better that way.'

Alice stood.

'And now turn round so that you face away from me.'

She turned. Gregory stared at her like a man assessing a purchase. Alice felt both objectified and honoured; the paradox made her blush.

'I love the female body,' he said quietly.

'That's all right for you to say. You don't have to live in one.'

'It's because I don't that I can see it better than its owners can.'

He took a step forward. As he did so, his fingers rose to his mouth.

There were layers to Gregory's fascination. At times he treated women in a functional, mercenary manner, and gave no thought to anything except sexual pleasure. He understood the mechanics of gratification as easily as he understood the workings of a camera, and it was with a camera that he often recorded the objects of these briefly energetic liaisons.

But sometimes, in contrast, Gregory loved women for their natural softness, their comfort and tolerance, and he took delight in simple closeness, as though he were a trustworthy brother or father to those he befriended. And at other times his enjoyment of a woman's body was aesthetic, objective, and confirmed to him that he was like any true artist in being able to study female nudity for its sculptural beauty. Sometimes, very rarely, he had passed through this stage into a state resembling a trance and that was both spiritual and erotic. At these moments it was made clear to him that what distinguished a woman was something akin to blessedness, as though design and function were identical to the sacred and the ultimately mysterious. Sometimes he even thought that when he treated women uncaringly, he was taking revenge because they could generate such feelings of awe within him. And sometimes he felt that this revenge also had something to do with the death of his wife.

The difficulty with Alice was that she encouraged all kinds of response, and Gregory could not be certain which one he should aim to develop. As she stood before him now, facing away, he began to fantasize that, uniquely and contradictorily, she was so protean that he would be able to treat her as all things.

The necklace clasp was partly screened beneath hair that had been cut to fall along the base of Alice's neck. There were faint pigmentation marks across the shoulders where she would perhaps have had freckles as a child, and a dimple set like a small crater into the skin below the right shoulder blade. A small white label on her bra was sticking out above the fastenings. The plunge of her spine led beneath the high waistband of her grey trousers and a thin black line that was all that was exposed of her underwear.

Gregory stepped closer. 'The necklace doesn't work,' he admitted.

'Why?'

'It detracts.'

'You want me to take it off.'

'Yes.'

As she reached to the back of her neck and unfastened the clasp he watched the muscles slide beneath her skin.

'I'll take it,' Gregory said, stretching out a hand.

Alice turned a little to one side and let the necklace coil into his palm in a series of tiny clicks. The beads were warm from the touch of her flesh. He walked across the room and placed them next to the crucifix. She folded her arms across her chest.

Gregory held the light meter a few inches from her skin and noted the reading.

'You look good,' he told her.

'You want my arms like this?'

'For the moment. The label is sticking out, here. I'll just hide it.'

Alice did not complain. Gregory pushed the tag so that it was hidden, felt for the first time the warm texture of her flesh, and imagined unfastening the clips so that the tight black straps relaxed from her torso and then fell away. And then he imagined sliding his hands around her body and cupping her breasts in them so that her nipples were between his fingers. He lifted the camera from the tripod, took several more shots, and spoke again.

'And now I want them raised, with your hands at the back of your head.'

'You can see that I haven't shaved under my arms. Does that make a difference?'

'Mapplethorpe's photos of Lisa Lyon show underarm hair.'

'Why do you mention other photographers so often? Aren't you confident of your own opinion?'

'I like a little body hair on women. In the right places it's natural and it flatters. That's my opinion.'

Alice lifted her hands slowly and gracefully, like a swan about to fly.

'I never expected to pose like this,' she said.

Gregory did not answer. When she continued, he could not tell if it was wry amusement that he could detect in her voice.

'I think that maybe this is what you were after all the time. Am I right? And I think you'd *really* like to photograph me in just a pair of knickers and nothing else.'

'Of course I wouldn't. That would be a glamour shot. I don't do glamour shots.'

'And naked wouldn't be a glamour shot?'

'Not the way that I would do it. If I were to photograph you nude I'd have you stretched out with your arms above your head, maybe against a background of plush, maybe just against a rumpled sheet. Female body geometry is more pleasing than a man's. You can see it in the form of triangles. One triangle has its points at the armpits and the pubis, another starts at the eyebrows and finishes at the same place, and yet another draws imaginary lines across the nipples and down to the navel. There are more examples.'

'Do you always think in abstractions?'

'I see what's there.'

'But you're not going to see me. Because I wouldn't let you photograph me without clothes.'

'No? I still think you should consider it. For now, what I'd like—'

'Shall I guess? You'd like me to take off this bra. Am I right?'

'You needn't turn round. Unless you wanted to.'

'It will leave marks on my skin.'

'You're young. They vanish quickly. And I can adjust things so they don't show.'

Nothing happened for several seconds.

'No one can see in through those windows,' he promised, and glanced up at the skylight. Clouds had gathered over the city.

'After this you can leave,' he added.

'You think you've done enough?'

'No. But we'll call it a day.'

There was a moment's hesitation, and then Alice crooked her arms around her back. While Gregory watched she lifted the straps from her shoulders and then stood with the bra dangling from her right hand. Her left hand appeared to be held firmly across her breasts as though she still wished to protect them.

'Just drop it on the chair,' he said.

She did so.

'The waistband of your trousers is too high,' Gregory said.

'They're staying on.'

'If you just unfastened them and pushed them down a few inches, along with your underwear, I could photograph the small of your back.'

'Is that important?'

'For symmetry, yes. And suggestion.'

'Suggestion?'

'The body changes into rounded forms, and it divides. The spot at the base of the spine is a pictorial node.'

Alice loosened buttons at the front of her trousers and pushed them down about four inches with her thumbs. The swell of her buttocks protruded from above the waistband.

'You want my hands behind my head again?' she said flatly.

'No. I want them stretched out.'

She put out her arms.

'No – straight out, as if they were taking your weight. Imagine that you're being crucified. That's it. And your head down a bit – not too far; no, raise it slightly. That's perfect. Hold it like that for a few seconds.'

Gregory moved in, bringing the margins closer so that only the upper part of Alice's arms were in the frame, emphasizing her shoulders, her neck and the long fall of her spine. The shutter clicked as rapidly as an animal's warning. He knew that all the frames would be what he wanted.

'That's it,' he said, at first triumphantly and then quietly, 'that's it.'

'Happy?' she asked.

'Not happy but content. For the time being. But I feel we've only just begun.'

'And I feel that we've finished, so I'm getting dressed now.'

'Right,' Gregory said.

He turned away so that he was not watching. Even so, he was sharply aware of Alice's presence. He could smell her perfume, sense her warmth, and the small noises that she made while dressing disturbed and excited his imagination more than he was able to admit.

And now he knew for certain what he had always suspected; that he needed Alice Fell in his life, and that he wanted to know far more about her than she was willing to reveal.

A steady pulse of images flicked across the screen. Chin resting on one hand, eyes rarely blinking, Gregory was absorbed in the sequence. Whenever the slide show came to a stop he started it again. He had done this three times already, and so far he had not deleted a single shot.

Gregory had been aware of the increasing number of exposures, but now that they were parading before him it was evident that they were both too many and not enough. Too many because he had taken more shots of Alice than he had expected, and not enough because, despite the quality of those taken towards the end of the session, neither photographer nor model had advanced to the obvious next step.

Any professional, Gregory believed, would look beyond this accumulation of images and see that it concealed an unexplored level of honesty. Once that was acknowledged, then even his best compositions would be judged as frustrating configurations of hints, approximations and evasions.

Alice stared out at him. At first her character seemed as flat as the rectangle that contained her; later she appeared to be play-acting, awkward, coy. What had been teasingly promising in the studio appeared archly counterfeit on the screen.

Gregory leaned back in his chair, put his hands behind his head, scratched the back of his neck, then bent forward and put his hands back on the keyboard. The chair squeaked like a hinge that needed oil.

For more than a minute Cassie had stood beside the door, a printout held in her hands, and carefully watched how her father was absorbed in the display. Eventually she drew up a chair and sat down.

'A problem of choice?' she asked.

'You can tell which ones are the best. They're obvious. Just as it's obvious that the session can't be called an unqualified success. You can see that, can't you?'

Instead of answering, Cassie placed the printout next to the keyboard. It was a page from the website of a hotel chain, and it showed two watercolour sketches of a modernist hotel built in the 1930s. Across them Cassie had written dates, figures and question marks. Gregory had already worked for the company four times.

He glanced at the printout and then looked back at the screen. 'I'm trying to get out of brochure work.'

'But this is quality: rich guests only. The relaunch is costing a fortune. Whoever takes the photographs will make a lot of money.'

Gregory nodded, uninterested.

'Designed by Lubetkin and there's a mural by Eric Gill. They say the building is in Pevsner. So it would be an interesting shoot.'

'Right. So you could do it.'

'Dad, they want *you*, not me. They know you. And sometimes you forget that I don't work here full-time.'

'Maybe you should do. That cancer charity can't pay you much.'

'Neither do you. And I need an answer.'

'I'll think about it.'

Cassie persisted. 'If you're interested I can phone them now. The refurbishment won't be completed for a couple of months. The dates would fit in easily with your diary.'

Gregory pointed at the screen. 'From this point on there's an improvement, but the necklace didn't work as well as I imagined.'

'I told you it wasn't right.' Cassie paused for a moment before continuing. 'I'll go back and try to agree terms. Is that all right?'

'Can you see that the compositional dynamics are wrong? That wasn't obvious at the time.'

Cassie looked at the screen again. Alice sat with her shoulders bared and her fingers resting on the necklace that had belonged to Cassie's mother. She wondered if it was her imagination that lent a particular suggestiveness to the touch of those fingertips on the beads. The part-smile on Alice's mouth hinted at a triumph.

'The studies of her back are an improvement,' Gregory said, 'but we didn't get to the point I wanted to reach. I mean, technically the work is fine, but there's no true excellence. I have to be honest and admit that none of it is *unique*.'

Cassie understood that her father was expecting too much.

'You can't be unique all the time,' she told him. 'Maybe you've got all there is to get. Maybe there's nothing else that's worth retrieving.'

She sat motionless and waited for his response.

Cassie prided herself on assessing people within a minute or so of meeting them, and had seldom been wrong. She had shared brief exchanges with Alice Fell at the beginning and end of the studio session. Alice's evasions and forced pleasantries had convinced Cassie that beneath that blandly attractive exterior there was an untrustworthy and manipulative woman.

'Meaning?' Gregory asked after a few seconds.

'Meaning that maybe you're looking for something in your model that isn't really there.'

'It's there all right.'

'You can't be certain. Not really.'

'I've got a sixth sense for hidden qualities. This subject is more difficult than most. She works hard at being a challenge. In a way, you've got to respect that.'

'But if she's so resistant to being photographed—'

'I didn't say she was.'

'That's what it sounded like. *If* she's so resistant, then what's the point? Why play a game it's impossible to win?'

Alice gazed out from the screen. The lens had caught reflections in her eyes. To Cassie it was obvious that Gregory should forget the session and move on to more rewarding subjects. She opened her hand to the image as if she were casting pebbles into a still pool.

'It's not worth anyone's while for you to continue,' she said.

Gregory did not answer directly, but mused on Alice as if she were a conundrum that only he could solve.

'She protects herself all the time. Even when she's partly stripped and with her back turned she looks protected. She can't look as natural as I want, because she's not in a relaxed state. If she can use something as a shield then she will do, even if it's just a string of beads.'

He sat back and announced his conclusion.

'It would be better if I did some nude studies. There would be nothing for her personality to hide behind.'

Cassie was unsure if she should respond. What her father saw as deep insulation she saw as brittle coating. Alice Fell's mystique was thin and as easily cracked as lacquer.

'Not everyone wants to be photographed naked,' she said cautiously.

'True, they don't.'

'So Alice Fell may not.'

'Cassie, she's not like your mother.'

The remark was as unexpected and cruel as a shower of ice. For a few seconds all was silence.

'That's an insulting comparison to make,' Cassie said at last.

Gregory made a nervous motion with one hand, as if his words still hung in the air and he was able to erase them, and then he shook his head.

'It's just a difference of people,' he said. 'Women like Ruth are uncomfortable with nudity on camera. Other women aren't. Even though she doesn't know it yet, Alice would love to pose naked.'

'Dad, this sounds like a daydream.'

'She'll come round, I'm sure she will. I've lent her the Eastman book on the development of photography. She'll see the argument more clearly once she's studied the history. She'll be able to concentrate on the results that gifted photographers can get. Now, look at these.'

Alice posed naked to the waist, back to the camera, shoulder blades prominent and arms folded protectively in front of her body. Cassie studied her with a disaffected eye.

'Her strap marks are visible. There, you see? Where they cut in under the arms? They ruin the grain of the picture. You must have noticed.'

'I took all these as a kind of test.'

'I see. Does she turn round?'

'She didn't want to.'

'And yet you think she'll be easily persuaded to take off all her clothes?'

'I didn't say it would be easy. Most people don't like to admit to what they secretly want.'

'Well, I think we could agree that Alice Fell has secrets.'

'She's a different kind of model,' Gregory insisted. 'Sooner or later she'll understand that we can't remain where the session stopped. We have to go on.'

Alice had stretched out her arms horizontally. She could have been awaiting some kind of brutal punishment, the lash perhaps, or she could have been preaching to an invisible crowd. Under the studio's angled light her hair shone as it fell across the base

of her neck. The skin on the long track of her spine was illuminated like ivory.

Gregory tapped the keyboard with one finger and then turned
to Cassie.

'You don't trust her, do you?' he asked, with unexpected
directness.

'Dad, I have no reason to trust Alice Fell. I don't *know* her. It
seems that you don't either.'

'I don't have to know people. It's enough that I sense their
capabilities.'

Cassie paused only for a moment. She did not want to think
of her father as suddenly vulnerable. Perhaps, she thought, Alice
Fell had qualities that she was blind to. Or it was possible that
Gregory had reached that point at which middle-aged men
become overwhelmed by irrational dreams. The hope of a trans-
cendent passion was, she knew, powerful enough to eat at the
roots of male stolidity and destroy all caution. Whatever the
truth, Cassie had no reason to be gentle when she asked her
next question.

'Surely you realize that there's something strange in the way
you talk about this woman?'

'I talk about her in the same way that I would about anyone.'

'That's not true. You don't.'

She stared directly at Gregory, but he kept his concentration
on the screen. Even his posture was defensive.

'You think Alice Fell is different in some way that you can't
quite pin down,' Cassie went on. 'Whenever you mention her
it's as if your imagination is intense and unfocused at the same
time. And when you look at her face or her body, just like you're
doing now, your mind isn't on what I say, or what anyone else

would say. It doesn't even appear to be fixed on where we are or what your future commissions could be. Your concentration isn't professional concentration. This isn't like you. Not at all.'

He answered as though testifying. 'I'm *always* professional. If I'm intrigued then it's on a professional level. I always want to portray things about my subjects that I'm sure are there.'

'And for Alice Fell, what do you think that would be? Self-regard? Avarice?'

'Don't be so bitchy, Cassie. I don't know what her qualities are until I find them. Direction, maybe. Yes, one of them could be direction. I'm sure she's looking for a pathway in her life. I'd like to be able to get that on camera.'

'Dad, I've met women like this before. They have no sense of direction whatsoever. They're adrift, like castaways. They just cling onto any passing man in the hope that he'll take them to a friendly shore.'

Gregory reached forward and switched off the display. Light collapsed inside the screen.

'Now you're being petulant,' Cassie said. 'It proves my point.'

'You know me better than anyone else. But I'm not some foolish moonstruck kid, and you should stop talking to me as if I were.'

'It's also true that I know you better than you know yourself. You're going to tell me that you've had affairs with your models before—'

'I make no secret of that. You've even seen the photos.'

'But those girls were nothing very much to you, were they? You shared relationships that you both understood. In a way, you each got what you wanted and that equalized everything. But you're right: Alice is different. She's capricious. Maybe she hasn't decided what she wants yet, but she knows that you can offer something that other people can't. And once she's got that she'll just throw you away.'

'You can't know that. You met her for a few minutes. Hardly long enough to make a judgement, is it?'

'It's time enough. I wouldn't trust her an inch.'

'Besides, she was probably nervous and eager not to show it. So you couldn't be more wrong.'

'We'll see. How many times have you told me you rely on my opinion? Are you going to rely on it now?'

Gregory made a formless sound under his breath. He hated arguing with his daughter, and always did his best to avoid it. Even if everything else in his life were to become unstable, he knew he could always rely on Cassie. It made him feel particularly uneasy that she had taken against a woman he found so intriguing.

Impulsively he reached forward and took Cassie's hand. His felt large and clumsy in comparison to hers.

'I'll be all right,' he said. 'You needn't worry about me.'

Cassie did not move her other hand.

Unspoken between father and daughter was the knowledge that throughout her life Cassie had avoided being either transported or harrowed by sexual fascination. Her involvement with men had never been wholehearted; even the break-up of her last relationship had caused her only minimal distress. Cassie had closed the door on affairs of the heart and did not wish to open it again. Often she wondered if the time spent on her brief dalliance with romance would have been better spent elsewhere; it had, however, helped her understand why her father treated women in the way that he did.

Gregory could never recover from Ruth's death, but it was

impossible for him to spend the rest of his life pursued by fantasies of a return to their shared happiness. His world had changed too much. Instead he took refuge in affairs that lasted for weeks, or sometimes only days. Cassie was content that her father should seduce women or be seduced by them, but if he were ever to fall in love she would believe that her mother had been un-forgivably betrayed.

Eventually she extended her other hand so that Gregory's was encased in both of hers.

'Dad, you're too old to be infatuated.'

'I'm not too old for anything. And I can never be infatuated. I'm far too wise.'

'Look, nowadays you and I share the same belief. Love, or whatever you want to call it, simply isn't worth the trouble it causes.'

'Cassie, I've been here before. It's old territory.'

'I don't think so. In all your dealings with women there was never any sense that you could lose control. You knew that and your girlfriends knew it. You were in charge, Dad. That's your personality. That's what works best. You shouldn't let that part of you be eaten away.'

'There's nothing wrong with being excited by someone new.'

'But there's something wrong in reaching out for a thing that isn't there. We both felt abandoned when Mother died. We both fastened everything in, even the best of emotions. But it would scare me if you decided that it was time to find her successor. We only ever have one chance with the life of the heart. You and I, we've had our time. Both of us have.'

'There's always another chance, Cassie. Even for you.'

'No, there isn't. That's just a kind of spectre. Sometimes people are left with empty spaces that get filled up by dreams – the kind of dreams that are so disorienting that it makes them fall into the arms of fantasists. I don't want that to happen to you.'

She and Gregory looked at each other in silence.

And for a brief hallucinatory moment it seemed to Gregory that he should take his daughter's advice and forget Alice. He should write off the studio session as something that had not quite worked, despite all his efforts. He should move on. After all, he had other assignments waiting to be fulfilled. Within the next few days there were portraits of an actor and then a foot- baller, just to begin with. And there were always other women.

And then it seemed that it would be cowardice if he turned away. With each day that passed he grew older and his energy levels declined. Perhaps he was condemned to brief unsatisfac- tory liaisons such as the one with Carla, but perhaps Alice was his last opportunity to enter a relationship exciting enough to effect a change in his life. Cassie had talked of foolishness, but the real foolishness would be if he remained safe and secure.

'Don't worry,' he told Cassie, as he smiled broadly and falsely, 'I'm not going to fall into any trap. I'm an expert at avoiding them.'

'And Alice?'

'You're right. In the end, she was just another model.'

But even as he spoke Gregory realized that he was treating Alice as an incarnation of the complexities and allure that he found in all women. In refusing to admit that he secretly wanted Alice, he had not admitted to himself the strength of his need for her.

If only he could photograph her without compromise. If only he could produce an image so charged and so powerful as to be overwhelming. All he had to do, Gregory thought wryly, was find the location, the confidence and the pose. And most of all, and most difficult of all, he had to find the decisive moment.

She spoke his name and he did not answer, but Alice was convinced that he had heard.

Thomas sat at the table on the other side of the room, his head down and his hand held so that a pen jutted upwards from between his fingers. In front of him were two open textbooks and an A4 writing pad whose pages he was covering in notes. Another three books were stacked to one side. A CD of the 'Goldberg Variations' was playing, but he did not appear to be listening. It was one of Alice's favourite recordings, and had been given to her by a former lover. Her knowledge of classical music had come only from him, and now she could appreciate how the interleaving and mathematical progression of the work appealed to her innate sense of patterning.

Thomas was too shallow, Alice thought. He was a clever man but she was a complex woman, not easily understood, and far beyond his comprehension. Most people found her to be a challenge; why should she ever have believed that Thomas Laidlaw would be any different?

It pleased Alice to be thought of as unfathomable. To her colleagues at work she was personable and attractive, although far from beautiful. They had noted how she avoided involvement; superficial friendships were all that she needed. Sometimes Alice joined them on infrequent celebratory nights out, but remained sober and in control when drink and proximity made others loose-tongued. On the hangover mornings many of those were subdued, but Alice Fell was always calmly assured. She never had anything to regret.

Little was known about her. She made no secret of the fact that she lived with a man called Thomas, apparently an archaeology expert – some believed that he was a professor – but no one had ever seen him. Everyone assumed that her past must hold other men, but Alice never mentioned them. Occasionally she held intriguing telephone conversations with callers from outside the office, but afterwards she expertly brushed away questions from anyone intent on finding out more.

In contrast, she was unabashed about questioning others, particularly if they possessed specialist knowledge. Whenever overseas buyers or agents visited the building she sought conversation, not about their businesses but about their countries, customs, languages, lives. Varieties of religious faith so fascinated Alice that more than once she had asked visitors about their personal beliefs. Often this had disconcerted them, and on one occasion she had been forbidden by management to ask such questions.

Because she guarded her own privacy Alice was considered mysterious and enticing. Several members of staff, both male and female, thought of her as intriguing but unwinnable. Not only was she delighted by this, she encouraged it.

Alice also knew of the rumour that she had once had a passionate affair with a director, a married man no longer with the company, and that it had ended dramatically. But she had had no such affair. True, she had been charmed by the man, but she clearly knew that if she had allowed that attraction to develop then her life would have become too restricted. Besides, beneath the sheen of his experience there had been a bruise of desperation. Her potential lover was so needful of an escape that he was bound to have become irrationally possessive. Involvement would have hindered any progress she wished to make. Because sometime, maybe soon, Alice was sure to find a lover who was not only better than anyone she had ever had, but who would be more exciting, more inventive and completely in tune with whatever it was that she needed. So far, none had been able to come close to that promise.

Despite the brevity of her relationships, despite the frustrations of the jobs she had taken, Alice remained confident that a rewarding future lay just beyond her reach. The right lover would help her to seize that future, and once it was in her grasp its momentum would drag her free.

A man was always a part of her ambition. Alice loved men — passionately, wholeheartedly, but temporarily. Over several months, perhaps longer, she would devote her life to one particular partner. Without exception, towards the end of that period she would stare clear-eyed into the heart of their love and find that it had become empty. She would be distressed and tearful, but unmoving in her determination. It was always Alice who found the courage necessary to put an end to the relationship; always Alice who delivered the final blow.

Her betrayed men were often distraught. Up until the last days they imagined that she was content. But because it was so evident to Alice that a break-up was unavoidable, she was puzzled by the lovers who clung so despairingly to the past — could they not see that there was nothing of any value left?

At the end of these intense romances she believed that she had learned all that was worth knowing about each man, but every one of them felt that they had not known Alice at all. She recognized this and took pleasure from it. Alice had a need to be unlike other people. Ever since her adolescence she had been convinced that she was destined for excitement, progress and revelation; it was just a matter of events being allowed to fall around her in a particular pattern.

So it had become obvious to her that her time with Thomas was reaching its natural end. It was also obvious that, like most men, Thomas would choose to ignore the evidence, or perhaps be unable to comprehend it.

She spoke his name again, more sharply this time so that it carried over the Bach, and he looked up.

Alice picked up the remote control and lowered the volume by several levels. Thomas did not react. She waited for a few seconds before putting her question.

'Thomas, why don't you do something that you *really* want?'

His expression was at first startled and then suspicious. She gazed back at him with innocent eyes and he moved one hand across the textbook as if he were throwing dice.

'I have to know all of this. In case I'm asked.'

Thomas was teaching mature students, many of them retired, who had enrolled on his short local history course because they needed to occupy their time. Alice knew that such a group was unlikely to ask the kind of precise technical question for which undergraduates might anticipate a detailed answer. They would expect to be taught in broad sweeps, with points of vivid colour to maintain interest, and their concentration would always remain on the local. Afterwards they would forget most of what they were supposed to have learned. There was no need for specialized expertise.

Thomas had second thoughts and attempted a direct answer to her question.

'Besides, in a way, this *is* what I really want. Part of it, anyhow.'

Alice carefully placed the remote control alongside a book she had been studying. The book was the George Eastman House history of photography that Gregory had lent her. She had noticed Thomas glance at it and then turn away.

'I don't think you want to be teaching pensioners and the unemployed. You want something a lot bigger and a lot more important. You see yourself as a professor, giving lectures, writing books, heading up excavations. Being an occasional tutor for continuing education is a long way from that ambition.'

Thomas looked back down. His voice bore the weight of hurt. 'We've had this argument before. Please just let me get on with my notes. If you want to needle me I'll go somewhere else to work.'

'And where would you go, Thomas?'

'A café, a library, a friend's. I don't know.'

'You don't really have friends. Or a family.'

'I have a brother.'

'You never see him. And you hardly even speak.'

His answer was so aggrieved that it surprised her.

'Richard is still a brother. I should be able to rely on him if I needed to. You don't have a brother or a sister or anyone. Unless you count your photography man as a friend. Which he isn't.'

Alice sat forward. The light inside the room brightened momentarily and then returned to what it had been.

Thomas pretended to be once again absorbed in his textbooks, although for him the words were being drained of meaning. Most of what Alice had said was a kind of challenge. Even her evasions were a form of confrontation.

There was a sudden deafening crack, as if a huge flat surface had splintered just outside the window. Air pressed against their eardrums. Startled, they both looked up and heard the noise of something distant, massive and rolling, which faded within seconds.

Later Alice was to persuade herself that this had been the moment when a fireball struck a church some miles away.

'That was close,' Thomas said, almost under his breath. He had begun to sweat a little and he passed his fingers across his brow.

After a while Alice spoke again.

'You're right about the arguments. We shouldn't get into another. We have too many.'

There was no humour in Thomas's smile. Alice went on.

'I'm not trying to taunt you, I'm trying to help. All I'm saying is that you should give yourself time and space to do what you've always wanted.'

'I see. And what would that be?'

'Thomas, *I* don't know. What *do* you want?'

Fearing a trap, he did not answer.

'It has to be something to do with archaeology,' she suggested, 'something that's easily arranged and isn't just a daydream. Something *realizable*. You've told me before there are places in Britain that every archaeologist knows about but that you've never visited. Hadrian's Wall?'

'*Everybody*'s been there.'

'Skara Brae? Callanish?'

'They're not easy to get to.'

'Well, go somewhere that *is* easy to get to. When we first met you told me that there are dozens of places in the north that only a few people know about. I remember some of the names. The Langdale axe factory. Samson's Bratfull.'

Thomas corrected her pronunciation. When threatened, he

often took refuge in pedantry. '*Samp*son's,' he said. 'There's a *p* in the name.'

'*Samp*son's,' she repeated with too much emphasis. 'Whatever. Go there. Give yourself a treat.'

'Sampson's Bratfull is just a featureless heap of stones on a remote moor. There's not much of it left. It's not even worth seeing.'

'I didn't think you'd seen it.'

'I haven't.'

Alice sighed. 'Thomas, those were just names I could remember. I'm not an expert. How should I know what's worth visiting and what isn't? You shouldn't be so defeatist. You spend time looking at plans and photographs of places like those. We both know they fascinate you, so why not go and see what they're really like? Pick the good ones and just visit those.'

Thomas jotted down some words, stared at the page as if he could no longer read his own writing, and then looked at Alice.

'Will you come with me?'

She had anticipated the question.

'Thomas, this is for *you*, and not for both of us. Treat it as work, or research, or recreation – maybe all three. You don't want me trailing with you across moors to see heaps of stone that are miles away from anywhere. That wouldn't involve me in the way that it would involve you. Why don't you just go travelling for a few days, on your own and at your own pace, following your own route, and enjoy it?'

'And then come back here?'

Alice did not answer. Thomas felt his heart contract. He looked back down at his notes.

'Maybe I'll do that,' he said.

'Maybe?'

'Sometime.'

Alice watched him for a few seconds, but he did not raise his head.

Thomas was his own worst enemy, she thought. What he saw as integrity, others saw as pettiness. Sometimes, and increasingly often, he was as moody and unresponsive as a child.

They sat in silence for several minutes. After a while, the urgent blare of a police siren drifted up from the street.

Thomas, too, was aware that there was something immature within him. For years he had been desperate to replicate the closeness and exclusivity of a lost childhood friendship. Others knew that it would be stifling and restrictive to come too close to Thomas, and kept their distance. Already infected by a sense of righteousness, Thomas felt noble just as much as he felt jealous or spurned. There was a certain perverse pleasure in the sense of being crushed. His brother Richard's lifelong indifference had merely strengthened his misplaced sense of honour.

Only at university had he learned how to mix freely and even to be a winning conversationalist. A brief affair with a fellow student had left him fantasizing that the most appropriate reaction to its end would be his suicide, but he was astute enough to know that this was just an imaginative way of coming to terms with loss. And besides, he lacked the courage to kill himself. Nevertheless, the failure of the affair, and what the woman had said as she left him for the last time, seemed to confirm to Thomas that he was a man who would remain on the margins. From that he drew further justifications of himself.

He was sharply alert to this aspect of his character. For most of the time he controlled it, but sometimes he indulged it. He saw it either as a crippling imposition from his youth, or as a gigantic psychic wound that he romantically compared to those suffered by doomed heroes from myth.

When Thomas had first met Alice he was not sure why she had responded so positively. Partly, perhaps, she had an intuitive understanding that he lacked experience and that this could easily be remedied. And, partly, it could have been that he had been schooled in subjects so arcane that they could never form part of everyday discussions.

Thomas had dreamed that Alice had never before known anyone quite so learned and quite so compromised. In those moments he was possessed by an optimism that was almost euphoric. He was able to think of himself as unique, as a man so distinctive that only a woman equally distinctive could recognize his qualities and love him for them.

He could not continue to believe this. More and more, Thomas felt that he had misjudged Alice. She had always hidden her past from him, but from the way in which she made love he knew that it must have been erotically adventurous. Compared to her inventiveness, his own sexual techniques were merely dutiful. For Thomas could scarcely have imagined a woman so uninhibited in her actions, so direct in her language and demands, so thrilling in her relish of unembarrassed physicality. Every intoxicating action seemed to confirm their indispensability to each other.

But now Alice was retreating into herself. She was no longer interested in Thomas's displays of knowledge. His eloquent descriptions of the past had begun to bore her. He spoke less and less frequently about henges, burins, the Neolithic, the Catuvellauni. If he visited museums to look at flint axes or bone needles or antler harpoons then Alice no longer came with him. He had begun to expect that one day she would openly state that Thomas was not special after all. He wondered if she wanted be rid of him so irrevocably that in the future his name would not even pass her lips. He brooded that she had become fascinated by Gregory Pharaoh because he was a man with a different expertise who would perhaps offer her a different future. No longer would Alice tolerate what she judged to be Thomas's inertia, but which in his eyes was nothing but an unbroken run of bad luck.

And yet, if this were to end, Thomas had nowhere to go and nothing to fall back on. Whatever Alice might think of him now, he loved her. Maybe his passion bore a greater emotional similarity to the intense friendship of his youth than it did to a mature relationship; it was uncomfortable to contemplate that. But he also knew that he loved Alice with a kind of tender ferocity that no one else could have nor ever would.

Now she sat opposite him in silence, and even though he did not lift his head Thomas was aware that she was studying him, reading his posture, thinking forward.

In a deliciously slow torment of self-pity, he wondered what she would decide and when he would be told.

6

More than sixteen hours had passed since the lightning strike, but the air inside the church was still vinegary with the smells of flood and smoke. By the time the first of the fire brigades arrived the conflagration had already spread to the support beams, and within minutes an entire section of roof had collapsed and fallen into the nave. Crews fought most of the night to extinguish the blaze. Gregory had watched the television footage of water jets arcing onto a dark roof that gaped apart to expose a glow as fierce as an entrance to hell.

Now the building was cordoned off behind police incident tape and classed as unsafe. The floor was awash and littered with struts, panels and stonework. Fragments of coloured glass lay scattered across the marble as if from the wrecked kaleidoscopes of giants. Lead panels on the roof had melted, flowed and solidified again in bizarrely shaped and motionless cascades and pools. Some of the wooden beams had burned in irregular textured sections so that they resembled incinerated totem poles. From where it had accumulated in hidden reservoirs, water still trickled down the walls and across memorial tablets to subalterns who had perished in India and firstborn buried on the veldt. Every few minutes a fall of ash smudged the weak sunlight that leaked through the ragged gaps where a stained-glass window had been.

Gregory stood beside the rector in an aisle resembling a muddy track. Holding up a tiny camera further down the church was a man who had arrived only a few minutes earlier. The imprints of his boots were fading in thin grey ooze. He was the only one who was wearing an industrial hard hat. Its shell gleamed white in the subdued light. He even had his name printed on it: Adrian Wells.

Wells had handed a business card each to Gregory and the rector, and explained at length that he was here on the instructions of the church authorities to carry out a preliminary investigation; afterwards, he and a specialist team would carry out a detailed assessment. Gregory had slipped the card into a pocket of his camera bag. He seldom threw contacts away; Cassie now had a file with hundreds, perhaps thousands, of names.

The rector, small, bald and with glasses, held the card in his hands as if about to lay it down in a game. He shook his head as though compelled by shock to repeat the motion every few minutes.

'I don't know,' he said, 'I don't know.'

Around them the ransacked space trickled and murmured with clicks, drips and creaks. Traffic noise drifted in through the opened roof and broken windows. A carpet, its pattern no longer discernible, squelched like upland peat whenever anyone walked across it.

'It's like the Blitz,' Gregory said, his voice echoing down the cavernous space. He knew that he would not be the only one to make this comparison.

Wells was in his late twenties, bumptious and eager to impress the others with his research.

'Parish records show that an incendiary landed here in early 1941 but did little harm. Yesterday must have been very like incendiary damage. We have several contemporary photographs in my office.'

'I know them,' Gregory answered, slightly aloof. 'They're famous.'

'Sure, but photographs can't convey the heat and the noise and the smell. That's what one misses.'

'No? It seems to me that those sense reactions are all implied. You can't get more vivid illustrations of destruction than those old wartime pictures. I'd like my work to have the same effect.'

Wells smiled sceptically and walked further along the nave. Gregory looked at the rector and raised his eyebrows.

'He's young,' the rector murmured by way of explanation. Then, keeping his voice low, he added, 'Some will say this is more than destruction.'

'*More* than?'

The rector had placed one hand on the back of the nearest pew. When he lifted it away the skin was coated in particles of ash the colour and texture of wet cement. He began to clean his fingers on a handkerchief drawn from his pocket.

'Many of our worshippers will think in terms of desecration, Mr Pharaoh. They will find it hard to credit that this is only an accident.'

'But it was a lightning bolt,' Gregory said. 'It was just bad luck that it hit here.'

'A fireball, most say. Sent for a reason.'

'A fireball, then. With no reason behind it other than the laws of physics. Even your parishioners are bound to understand that the world is an accumulation of chance events.'

The rector smiled wanly. Gregory looked up to the ceiling.

'Will all this be rebuilt to be identical?'

'If Mr Wells approves such a plan. I have no idea how much a restoration will cost, but I'm sure there will be an appeal.'

From where he stood further down the church Wells could still hear them if they spoke at normal volume.

'At the moment,' he called back, 'I'm not even sure how much more of the roof and ceiling will have to come down to make it safe. Scaffolding is an urgent necessity.' He pointed towards the undamaged windows. 'Those need to be covered for their protection.'

Gregory glanced across at a stained-glass shepherd Christ, his crook in one hand, immaculate white lamb in the other.

'Victorian?' he asked the rector, but Wells replied.

'Later than the fabric. Standard iconography and somewhat mawkish for my tastes. Sensibilities have changed, thankfully.'

Gregory raised his camera between his hands and held it like a trophy. 'I need to do my job. Unlike you, I don't have much time.'

Wells looked at him and suddenly said, 'Pharaoh: of course. I can place you now. You took a portrait of one of our bishops. Very recently.'

Keen not to be left out of the exchange, the rector spoke up. 'I believe Mr Pharaoh also took some photographs of a little girl who has visions of the Virgin Mary.'

Gregory looked askance at him. The rector shrugged, a little embarrassed. 'When the newspaper phoned for permission I asked who you were,' he explained.

'The girl being one of our faith's many fantasists, no doubt,' Wells said. 'Tell me, do you make a speciality of religious subjects?'

'You're not the only person to ask me that,' Gregory answered as he moved into position and checked out the sight lines. 'The answer is no, I don't. In a couple of weeks I'm due to photograph an ossuary, but after that I want to move away from any subject that could be labelled religious. I'm like an actor who doesn't want to be typecast.'

'I believe I know of that ossuary. There's a dispute over what to do with the bones.'

'A journalist is doing a piece that will need illustration. I'm told that the parish only reluctantly agreed to let me work in the crypt. Do you have any influence?'

'None at all, Mr Pharaoh. I'm an architect, not an archaeologist.'

Gregory walked back along the sodden carpet and framed both rector and architect in a wide shot. Wells deliberately turned to one side so that he would be seen in profile.

'Rector,' Gregory said, 'just stand as you are. No, don't move; right in front of me is fine. I can get you nicely in focus and also pull in much of the background with a wide-angle.'

The rector demurred. 'I'm really not sure that I should. This isn't about me.'

'No, but you've been interviewed by reporters and it's important that the public sees your face. They'll be able to read things into it.'

The rector's hands fluttered across his scalp as if checking on hair that had vanished long ago. Gregory made the exposure but, knowing he was being taken, the rector unintentionally stiffened his facial muscles.

Wells moved closer. The rector was still uncertain.

'Our bishop should be standing here, not me.'

'The bishop isn't available,' Wells explained to Gregory. 'Yet another conference agonizing over social problems, I'm afraid; attendance compulsory for scholars.'

'I'm pleased he's not here. To have him in the picture would be something of a cliché.' Gregory nodded at the rector. 'You're much better.' And then, after a pause, he looked at Wells and said, 'But you would make this an interesting piece of photo-journalism.'

'Really?'

'Don't be so coy, Mr Wells. You know I'm right.'

'Well, I have no objection. What do you want me to do?'

'We should wait for a minute or so. The light is strengthening, I think. When it slants in through the hole I'll take you looking up at the roof.'

The three men walked further down the church and came to a heap of debris resembling a pyre that had collapsed inwards as it burned. Glass fragments lay across the floor like bright discarded tiles. Both Gregory and Wells took photographs, but Gregory did not have to check to know that his would be unsatisfactory. There was no form to be found within the wreckage, only ruin.

As Gregory neared the altar there was the sound of a shutter clicking. 'I heard that,' he said, without turning round. Incinerated spars were strewn on the floor like the remnants of a sacrifice.

'I had the altar and the painting framed,' Wells explained. 'Thank you for giving a scale.'

Beyond the altar, set within a gilded frame, was a large canvas of a Christ with sad eyes and one raised hand. In the centre of the palm, like a small target, was a circular spot where the cruci-fixion nail had been driven. Behind and above him the painted clouds parted. A coating of stippled grey covered the surface of the painting so that it was impossible to make out its true colours.

'We are proud of this,' the rector said quietly. 'Many of our worshippers find solace in that face.'

'Pre-Raphaelite,' Wells said briskly. 'Unfortunately not the Brotherhood, just a minor follower. You can tell by the inferior brushwork. Nevertheless it's certainly worthy of preservation.'

'It looks filthy rather than damaged,' Gregory said. 'You'll be able to get it cleaned and restored, won't you? Like the church as a whole, I suppose.'

'If you come back in a year,' the rector said, 'all this will be cleared up and restoration almost complete. I'm certain Mr Wells will help us with that.'

'Only a year?'

'Perhaps a little more. It takes a long time to rebuild order from chaos.'

'I'm not in a position to give estimates,' Wells said. 'This was a freak accident and I know from experience that freak accidents cause damage that isn't always obvious.'

He received no reply other than a shake of the head. Gregory began to wonder if the rector might not be able to believe what was so obviously true.

'You do see that it was an accident, don't you?' he asked.

The rector nodded. 'Of course. Chance operates beyond the will of God. Although some – a very few – believe that the fireball was a divine warning.'

'God sends a lightning strike as a punishment?'

'They see it as a purifying force.'

'Against what – ungodliness, blasphemy, sexual licence?'

'You can see why they should think such a thing.'

'It's difficult to argue against the irrational.'

The rector spread his hands. There was still a smudge of soot on his fingers.

'Some of us live in a world of signs and portents,' he said. 'That girl who has visions – who is to know if what she sees is a hallucination or a true revelation?'

A hazy shadow moved across the floor and all three men looked up as they heard a flapping of wings. A bird descended through the hole in the roof, settled on the summit of an exposed pillar, and looked down into the nave.

'If this is a sign,' Gregory said drily, 'then that should be a dove.'

'Sad to say, it's a pigeon. There are hundreds, thousands of them round here. Last month one got in somehow. It took us weeks to get it out. Its droppings were everywhere.'

Gregory smiled. 'At the moment, rector, a pigeon is the least of your problems. I'm sorry it wasn't a dove.'

'Even then it would have been chance and not design. Look around you – see what has to be done here. The church has more to worry about than false signs.'

At that moment there was a sharp crack from somewhere in the roof, followed by a rattling sound like a handful of gravel falling against a board.

'That certainly wasn't a divine sign,' Wells said drily. 'It was a physical one telling me that the sequence of destruction isn't finished yet. And that the two of you should be in hard hats, too.'

Gregory rubbed his hands together to signal that he was ready to take his photographs.

'I think it would be good if you could look up towards the source of that noise,' he told Wells. 'I need just a handful of shots. And if you could stand over here – a bit closer; yes, there.'

'I'd be in profile again.'

'Yes, and in shadow. Believe me, it will be an evocative image. Not quite St Paul's in the Blitz, but near enough.'

Wells posed with the efficiency of a model, taking his stance and tilting his head exactly as Gregory asked him to do. In silhouette the brim of his hard hat was a thin diagonal sliver of blackness against the verticals of the church. A check on the Canon screen demonstrated that the images were effectively dramatic. Even Wells nodded in agreement when he was shown them a little later.

Gregory shouldered his camera bag. 'I'll take my leave and let you get on with things,' he said.

As he looked round for one last time he realized that he did not like the church. It was too dark, too formal and too cold. The architecture was both lofty and restrictive, the memorial tablets all spoke of a demanding but complacent imperialism, and the dark hardwood pews were uncomfortable places to sit.

If God had existed and ever spoke in his ear, Gregory thought, he would want it to happen not in a place like this but outdoors, on a road or on high ground, with space around him and a wide clear sky above.

'When they built this,' he remarked, 'rank and social order and penitence must have meant a lot more than they do now.'

'A different world, Mr Pharaoh,' Wells said airily. 'Everyone will want this building restored so that it still conforms to that world. Perhaps if the destruction had been greater – and many would say it was sacrilegious for me to propose this – then we could have built a modern church on this site: one that was welcoming, inclusive, with closer connections to the everyday world. Are you shocked?'

'You're suggesting that destruction can bring benefits.'

'The past doesn't hold all the advantages. We have to rebuild – but perhaps we have missed a chance to build something better. You say that the world is full of chance events. It's also full of chances that are missed. And you, Mr Pharaoh, strike me as a man who misses very few chances.'

Gregory laughed. 'I try not to. I don't always succeed.'

He shook hands and prepared to walk away, but the rector had a question for him.

'Tell me: I was told only about your spiritual work, and yet you say you will do no more of that. But what else do you specialize in?'

'I've worked across a wide range of subjects, rector. I think you could say that I've taken almost everything.'

'I see. And your next project? Apart from those bones?'

Gregory laughed. 'Flesh, rector; I shall be working on studies of the flesh.'

After a few weeks, Alice was able to look back and see clearly that the crisis of one particular day had gained direction and force far away from Thomas; instead its origin lay amongst the half-truths and recriminations of business life. As the working day progressed it became increasingly obvious that to remain working in that office would be corrosive.

Alice realized that matters would only get worse shortly after she arrived at her desk. A particular transaction had been dogged by weeks of misunderstandings, errors and delay, and now it appeared probable that the entire contract would collapse. She was held to be partly responsible, but to Alice it was evident that a vindictive management had merely selected her as a scapegoat. To that management, however, her opinion seemed uninformed, and her questioning demeanour little short of insolent. When she was reprimanded in front of her colleagues, all of them sat with averted eyes. Not one voice was raised in her defence. After all,

Alice Fell had always been aloof, had never tried to be popular; why should she expect support now?

Aggrieved at her treatment, Alice was certain that her life would become intolerable if she did not take action. Her imagination had been shaping the decision for weeks. She would, of course, walk away at a time of her own choosing, and when her departure would cause the greatest possible disruption. The more she thought about it, the better it seemed that she should work a few more days, perhaps secretly degrade or hide several important files, and then walk out.

When she arrived back at her flat Alice was in no mood for compromise. Even the way she closed the door was notable for its controlled aggression. When Thomas asked how she was, she saw only the falseness of his concern.

She waited for several seconds before replying that she was fine. The words displayed her resentment like a badge. When Thomas nodded and told her that was good, it was clear to Alice that his pleasure was counterfeit.

Thomas was attempting to ingratiate himself by preparing a meal. It was a simple pasta dish, but he fussed over it as if it required particular expertise. He realized that Alice could turn on him at any moment.

She walked across the floor, pacing out the width of her property like a letting agent. Thomas glanced at her and smiled, but then looked away. There was a fluttering around the muscles of his heart.

'I was hoping you wouldn't be here when I got back,' she said.

The flutter became a hard fist in the centre of his chest. It stopped him breathing freely. Not knowing how to respond, he began to check the temperature controls on the cooker as though they were complex devices.

'I said,' Alice repeated, 'that I was hoping you wouldn't be here.'

'I'm not teaching today,' he answered weakly.

She walked across the floor again. For the moment Thomas dared not turn. Her glare would be enough to unman him. A part of him knew he should say nothing, but another part lacked the resolve to remain silent. He spoke as if they were continuing a discussion Alice had begun days ago.

'I've been thinking about journeying north to visit those locations but I haven't been able to plan it out yet.'

The speech collapsed around him like a deflated balloon.

Alice paused and folded her arms. She knew what the truth was. Thomas would never get to see his overlooked and un-impressive sites. The Neolithic axe factory on the side of a mountain, the stone circle that was too far off the beaten track, the high barren moor with its near-formless mound of stones – these were all destinations he would never reach. These bleak locations, unvisited and ignored by his peers, were emblematic of Thomas's modest, unadventurous life. He was a clever man but so flawed that all his potential had been wasted. It was too late now for any form of recovery. Thomas Laidlaw was beyond redemption.

And what terrified Alice most of all was the suspicion, the threat, that in many ways she and Thomas could have similar futures.

'I wasn't talking about your travels,' she announced. 'I was talking about you moving out.'

The expected blow always falls the hardest. Thomas drew his elbows in at his sides and raised his shoulders as if a current had passed through his body.

Alice moved a step closer, but stayed far enough away to be

out of reach were he suddenly to whirl round. She went on.

'I was hoping you'd be gone. Because we both know there's no future for us.'

It felt as if she were inserting a knife, but at the same time she knew that such a moment of truth was justified. She continued. 'I thought you would have read all the signs – they've been clear enough. I thought that maybe we could avoid a scene like this. But if you'd understood you'd have offered to go before now. What is it that makes you want to stay? Nothing that you can do will take things back to what they were. I'm sorry, you're sorry, we're both sorry. Why do we say that? Our apologies make no difference.'

She paused, took a breath, and said what had to be said.

'Thomas, I want you to leave. I want you to leave straight away. I want you to go and not come back. I don't want you to phone, I don't want you to write, I just want you to go.'

He turned and looked at her, his face stricken into a kind of paralysis.

'We have to talk about this,' he said.

'No, we don't have to talk about it. Words will change nothing.'

'We can't just give up on things.'

Exasperated, Alice shook her head. 'I've told you, there's no point in discussing it. It's settled. Whatever you say I'll not change my mind. Look inside yourself and you can see that I'm right. If this didn't happen now then it would happen tomorrow or next week or next month. It's better for us both if we just end it today, now, this minute.'

Desperation laced his speech. 'Whatever happened today has got you in such a mood that you see everything as black. But it isn't. We have a future together.'

Thomas held out his arms to embrace Alice, but she moved away.

'Hold me and it will be all right,' he pleaded. 'I promise you everything will be all right.'

And he stepped forward, his gait as ungainly as any monster's, his arms stretched out as if in parody. Alice raised a hand. It stopped him like a charm. He stood there looking at her with shocked eyes.

'This is it,' she said firmly. 'End of the road. We both knew it was coming. It's here. Understand? It's here *now*.'

And he looked so helpless, so unequal to everyday life, that for a moment, but only for a moment, Alice pitied Thomas and hated herself for making him suffer.

The mood passed as suddenly as it had arrived. There was no alternative. He was a dead weight, he was manacle and shackle, and she needed to be free. What happened to Thomas now was his own concern; Alice was not his keeper.

A part of her life closed behind her and a new part began to open up. She could sense its energy and its heat. And although Thomas had been a small element in the past, he featured not at all in the future.

Alice had the lock changed the day after she had finally succeeded in banishing Thomas. Only then did she feel secure and confident that she was moving on.

Getting rid of him was prolonged and distressing, and she could not fully understand why he had to cling so desperately to the past. Men were like that, she thought – fundamentally they were needy and unambitious. Their braggadocio was nothing but a threadbare camouflage for insecurity. Usually they wanted a wife to come home to, although not necessarily to be faithful to. At deep levels that they were unwilling to admit, men were always anxious for affirmation. They constantly hunted for compliments but if given one were never sure how to deal with it.

Before he was shamed into leaving, Thomas exhibited a range of emotions that were unpleasant and annoying. He walked around, he stayed still, he sat down and immediately stood up, and he moved from room to room as if he expected Alice to follow, crumple, and then tell him she did not mean what she had said. Alice was always determined, but Thomas tacked back and forth across the sea of his emotions as if he did not know which course was best. In turn he was jealous, bumptious, angry and craven. When he left, he was like an innocent man found guilty of a terrible crime.

Soon after she had closed the door on him, Alice began to cry.

At the end of each of her relationships she always wept spasmodically for two or three days. After that she was calm, she was happy, and the rest of her life seemed as though it would be worth living. And although she wept because she could not avoid inflicting pain, Alice was never overwhelmed by guilt.

Her lovers, on the other hand, were never able to forgive. Even though each affair had turned stale, they all acted surprised, wounded and betrayed. She believed that this could only be because of an irrational masculine pride. As a young woman Alice had expected men to be tougher, even unfeeling. She had not known that their emotional bruises never faded. Men who had craved affection were unable to recognize its decay and hopeless at recovering from its collapse.

As soon as the lock was changed Alice began to clean the flat, move the ornaments and rearrange the furniture. This was important even if the differences she made were only minimal. On several occasions she had to stop, sit down and weep. But after a few minutes she was able to stand up and carry on as if nothing had happened.

She energetically polished the worktops and the table, and then washed the cutlery and every plate and cup and glass. She found the last two bottles of wine that Thomas had bought and poured them down the sink. There was something comforting and final about the way in which the wine swirled red against the white surface before disappearing down the waste pipe in a series of expiring gulps. Every book, every CD and DVD was checked; if there were any suggestion that they might belong to Thomas, they were placed in a cardboard box with a lid that was closed and which she would later tape shut. Three wallets of old photographs, very few of them featuring Alice, were also slipped into the box. In the bathroom a bar of soap, two unused razor blades, and an almost-empty can of shaving gel had been left behind like relics. These were collected and put into a black refuse bag. Joining them was a supermarket ready-meal that Thomas had asked her to buy and that she no longer wished to eat. Also dropped like a contaminant into the bag was an unused packet of condoms from the table on the side of the bed where he had usually slept. Alice tied the bag with a double knot before dropping it down the rubbish chute.

When all this was completed she looked round the flat and decided that soon she would repaint part of it, hang new curtains and buy a new duvet and perhaps a new standing lamp. Then she sat at the dining table and spread out the appointments section of a daily newspaper, glancing as quickly as she could through the jobs that were on offer. She would walk out of her present employment in a day or so, claiming irreconcilable differences as if she were a board member. There was enough money in her bank accounts to allow her if necessary to live without worry for several weeks. After that she would have to start earning again.

When she had considered the advertisements and found nothing Alice checked her phone and found that Gregory had rung from his mobile. She had not responded to an earlier call, and she was not fooled by the apparent casualness of his message – something about asking if she wanted to help on a project that he did not describe. For a few minutes she considered ringing him back, but then decided to let him wait. Every trivial reason not to return such a call now began to seem increasingly important.

And yet she could not stop thinking about Gregory. He was a strange person, certainly someone worth cultivating, and, as with all men, he used professionalism as a mask for his uncertainty. For him a camera was both shelter and probe. He was content to objectify Alice and yet eager to please her. There was little doubt that he wanted to have sex with her, but nevertheless he seemed conflicted about his reasons.

As for Alice herself, she had grown used to the idea that she could enjoy sleeping with him – the trouble was, she was not sure if it would be worth it. Had she not by now had her fill of love affairs, of their profligate squandering of emotion? Gregory Pharaoh must have had many women, and he could never be as much trouble as Thomas had been. But something happened to men when they fell in love; it was as if they were no longer capable of reason. Would it not be wiser to keep Gregory at arm's length, to use him when he could be useful and not to enter with him into the broken maze of an affair? Besides, Alice thought, it was possible that she had already been given the best that he could offer. What could he do now but take even more photographs? Was this the help he was requesting?

She knew that all of these questions had a rational, considered answer. She had already had enough lovers; there was nothing to suggest that an affair with Gregory would be different from any of the others. But Alice also knew that she was a woman who had never been able to resist the intoxicating temptation of an unwise action.

7

The underground vault lay behind an oak door that was bolted, padlocked, and always remained unopened except for authorized visits. These were always arranged to take place when the church was quiet. At exactly the specified time a churchwarden arrived with a heavy key strung on a rope as thick as a lanyard. He opened the padlock and slid the long bolt right back so that it made a noise like a stone hitting raw earth. The churchwarden would adjust his glasses, grip a handle, and pull hard so that the door slowly moved, its iron hinges creaking like hawsers. The door had sunk under its own weight and could not be opened fully. Its lower corner ground so harshly across a flagstone that over the years a pale arc had been scored into the surface.

Just inside the door was a switch that operated an electric light fixed to the wall in a metal cage. The cable for the light was bracketed to the wall at head height, and led down a stone staircase that turned to the right. The steps were narrow and gloomy and there was no handrail, making any visitors descend gingerly with arms outstretched and fingers trailing along the cold stone.

This is what Gregory did until he grew used to the descent. Alice was less confident and continued to touch the walls for security.

At first the size of the vault was difficult to gauge. The ceiling bulb was dim and a yellowish deposit coated its underside, further weakening its glow. Traceries of decaying cobweb were strung around the fitting. At the end of the room a tiny barred window looked out onto the churchyard. Grass grew unchecked on its outside and the inside had been colonized by pads of moss. Most of the panes were level with the ground so that apart from a thin strip of pale daylight the window admitted only a murky green.

When she first saw the bones piled on the wooden racks Alice could not think what she should say. Instead she remained silent and unmoving in the gloom at the bottom of the stair, tightening her arms around herself because of the cold. As Gregory walked along a narrow aisle, checking the perspectives, his breath turned to cloud and his voice was metallic and unreal.

'There are hundreds – can you see? Look at the numbers. This one is 248. Another one over there is 316.'

The crypt was stacked with human bones – not every bone, only the skulls and the long bones from the limbs. These, Gregory had been told, were the bones that were considered essential for resurrection. At some moment in the past the ribs, pelvises, vertebrae and digits had been lost, disposed of, perhaps thrown into the nearby river and washed away. Now all that was left of the dead was piled on the tiers and rows of grubby wooden benches, each one slatted like a barracks bed. As though arranged by a weaver or builder of stone walls, the long bones had been placed in configurations that steadied them against each other so that they did not slip or roll away. On top of these secure layers the skulls had been set down in rows, some with their jawbones, some without. Every relic was shaded in colour from pale yellow to dark brown, like nicotine stains, and every skull had a number inked on its forehead. Each number was fading into the bone, and none was in sequence, as though at some point the entire collection had been taken apart and then reassembled at random.

Alice found the ossuary macabre and uncomfortable. She could see no value in keeping these part-skeletons where they lay. Far better, she believed, to act on the recommendation of the church authorities and have them buried with due ceremony in a mass grave in the churchyard; after all, they might originally have been exhumed from there. But a local debate about the future of the crypt had turned into a national argument between clergy, parishioners, historians and forensic archaeologists. Some claimed the remains were those of plague victims, others that they had been massacred in the English Civil Wars; no one truly knew. Gregory had already photographed spokespeople on opposing sides of the dispute; now he had to complete his work by taking studies of the relics.

Before he drove to the church to unload the car he had parked at a café overlooking the village green. Preoccupied throughout the journey, Alice had constantly checked the screen of her mobile phone in case she had somehow missed a call. Fortunately Thomas had not rung; unfortunately, neither had any prospective employer.

Gregory did not realize the extent of her concerns, although he was aware that Alice had had arguments both with her employer and with Thomas. As they relaxed in the sunshine, however, Alice began to express doubts as to what she was doing there, and why she had agreed in the first place. Was it really true, she asked, that Cassie was working for her charity that day? And had Gregory told his daughter that, for this day only, Alice was to be his assistant?

Smoothly reassuring, Gregory told her that there was no actual reason why Cassie *should* know, or why she should ever be told. Alice read more into his words than had actually been spoken.

Then, as if once again striving to prove the longevity of his profession and its continual reinvention of themes, Gregory produced a copy of Nadar's 1861 image of the Paris catacombs. Those bones had been separated by type and stacked like wood in a timber yard, he explained; Nadar's problem had not been in the framing but in the degree of illumination and length of exposure necessary for the wet-collodion plates. Framing would, however, be a problem for Gregory. No matter how wide the angle of the lens, space restriction within the crypt would limit him severely.

Now as she stood in the gloom at the foot of the steps Alice could see that he was right – there were difficulties of height, angle, light, perspective. She understood why, along with all the metal stands and extension leads, Gregory had brought along an aluminium stepladder. At the same time his reasons for requesting that Alice assist him seemed even more perverse.

'Why did you ask me here?' she asked, and was surprised at how eerie her own voice sounded within the confines of the vault.

'You volunteered.'

'I didn't know it would be like this. Did you want to scare me?'

'No. I thought this would be—' Gregory paused a moment before he went on, '*instructive.*'

'I certainly wouldn't have come here on my own.'

'But would you have come with your boyfriend? Wouldn't he be interested in these relics?'

'Maybe. His real interest is in prehistory.'

'You didn't ask him his opinion?'

'No.'

Gregory read the pause.

'You didn't tell him you were coming, did you?'

'I didn't need to. Whatever Thomas thinks, it doesn't matter much. It never has done.'

Gregory did not speak, but examined her face for any movement. She knew it would be best to admit the truth.

'Thomas isn't with me any more. He'll not be coming back.'

They each felt their hearts beat a little more heavily.

'Do you want him to?'

'No,' Alice said flatly.

'Well, then,' Gregory said, 'it seems that being my assistant for the day is the only way that you could have got to see such an extraordinary spectacle.'

Relieved not to be asked any further personal questions, Alice took him up on his remark.

'Being extraordinary isn't a convincing reason to come here. I feel that we're intruding. You'll tell me that's not a rational response, but I still feel it.'

Gregory nodded towards the racks.

'These people stopped having opinions a long time ago. We can intrude all we like. They're not going to bother when we rig up the equipment, and the sooner we start doing that, the better. My optimum position will be higher than the uppermost skulls, so I'll need that ladder. We'll move the lights around. I don't want the full-on, empty-eyesocket look, because that would be a cliché. Let's start moving, shall we?'

They both had to make several awkward descents to the vault before he declared himself satisfied with the amount of equipment below ground. To Alice it felt strange even to be in motion in the crypt, as though she and Gregory had broken a seal on darkness and silence, and each time she came back underground she was filled with unease. The breath from their lungs smoked in the light beams, and each new positioning of the ladder or movement of the stands could not be made without harsh unforgiving scrapes and clatters that seemed to verge on sacrilege. When Alice looked into the shafts from the lamps she could see thousands of dust motes drift and lazily rotate, and she wondered if she were breathing in fragments of the dead.

And she imagined that somewhere there would be another dimension in which she and Gregory were being observed and their clumsiness fretted over. Perhaps they were already being judged for their noise, their boorishness and their lack of respect.

At one point the churchwarden appeared, seemingly taking shape out of the gloom at the foot of the stair to watch them, the light reflecting in his round glasses so that the lenses were like silver coins placed on the eyes of the dead. After standing quietly for several minutes he turned and went back up the steps as silently as he had arrived. Gregory winked and smiled at Alice to indicate that he had found the churchwarden's presence oddly amusing. She smiled back without thinking, and immediately felt that she had been tricked into becoming complicit.

With the new lighting, the skulls began to acquire shape and depth. Alice thought that if she stared at them long enough then she would be able to distinguish different characteristics, be it the shape of the cranium, the number of teeth, or the diameter of the sockets. But all the time she could not help but think that this was a demeaning and inhuman way for any life to have ended. Whoever had lived within and around these skeletal remains deserved more dignity than a number inked in the centre of the forehead.

Gregory moved the ladder noisily and climbed it, only to descend and move it again.

'Look at this,' he suddenly said, and brushed his middle and index finger across the top of a skull. Moisture glistened on his fingertips. 'Condensation,' he explained, 'our breath is condensing on the bone.'

Alice shuddered. She had no intention of touching these objects.

And yet, as the camera shutter repeatedly clicked like a measure of each passing sliver of time, she began to feel not only discomfited but also strangely exhilarated. She was pleased she had come here. This reliquary was also a library of the dead, an assembly of untitled books whose pages had all been ripped out and scattered. It was both a memorial and a prophecy. Death was an inescapable solvent that stripped away personality, history and identity. These people, whoever they were, whichever sex they had been, had left nothing behind but their bones. Their lives had vanished without an entry in a ledger, or a name on a gravestone, and, most cruelly of all, without an image.

She found herself thinking of the book that Gregory had lent her, of the studies of Ellen Terry and Lee Miller, of women long dead but whose character and force were still visible on the page. There were bodies, thousand upon thousand of them, whose flesh had turned to dust but whose glamour still shone despite the silt of accumulating decades.

The ossuary dead were beyond any form of recovery. This uniformity of bones had once possessed *difference*. Those nearby skulls had been home to a range of features: handsome to ugly, young to old. The colour of their eyes and hair, texture of skin, expressions, even the way they walked, would have made them identifiable as individuals from a hundred yards away. The same fears and passions and hopes had swept through them as swept through everyone. Those heads could have lain together, side by side. Their arms could have held each other, their legs could have been intertwined. And yet, in the end, everything that had distinguished them had been stripped away. Whatever had defined them had been eliminated. These were frameworks and nothing more.

Quite suddenly Alice felt neither distance nor revulsion but a strange kind of kinship. And then the feeling vanished as quickly as it had arrived, and was in its turn replaced by one of unexpected euphoria.

Alice exulted that she was palpably, effortlessly, thrillingly *alive*. Blood coursed through the chambers of her heart. Sense impressions poured into her memory. Every movement she made was a gift that was her due, a triumph of the evolutionary drive and yet also somehow miraculous. The tips of her fingers tingled, as did her toes. There was pressure at the small of her back, a slight tugging around her nipples, an increase in the heat around her vulva. She was a compendium of sensation, emotion and thought. For a dizzying moment it seemed unbelievable that her body with all its energies and memories could ever be reduced to an unfeeling pile of bone. The dead were another country. Especially if she were naked, Alice could have walked between these racks as an example of life at its fullest, of the senses at their most receptive, of the body at its most exemplary.

Heat from the lights made the air grow warmer. Gregory hung above the ranks of skulls like a puppeteer. A lone spider with spindly legs ran across a cranium the colour of excrement and then vanished into the latticework of bones. It seemed to Alice that she had been given a licence, and that this had been Gregory's secret purpose in bringing her to this chill hidden chamber.

'All right,' she said.

He looked across at her, his eyes drowned with reflected light.

'I'll do it,' she told him. 'I'll pose for you. I'll do what you want.'

Alice remembered daguerreotypes of women whose physicality was still vividly present a century and a half after they had posed. If you looked at them carefully you could study their hairstyles, fingernails, navels, their distribution of fat, their posture as they sat on a chair, the way they lay across a bed. None of them had been given names; everyone was anonymous.

'I don't want my name to be known,' she said forcefully. '*Ever*,' she added.

'I can arrange that.'

'And I don't want the session to be held in that studio of yours.'

'All right.'

'*Or* have my photos stored on a memory card with photos of someone else. I'm my own person. I'm not just some model you could hire.'

Gregory was still in position, suspended above the dead, his tongue protruding slightly from his lips. The numbers on the skulls were like an account. Alice went on.

'You said I deserved to be photographed at a special place. You agree?'

'I'll find somewhere unusual. Just for you.'

'There are other conditions.'

Gregory stepped further down the ladder, but halted on the lowest rung. 'Don't make too many,' he said.

'I want copies of every photograph. I don't want a selection and I don't want to be shown what you think is good and not shown what you think is bad. I want the complete file. You may be the man behind the shutter, but the photographs will be of *me*. I have a right to them all. I have a right to see how I look.'

As Gregory stepped onto the stone floor of the crypt, the ladder scraped along it with a metallic squeal.

'You have no legal claim on my work,' he told her. 'I've said before that they are my copyright and that's how they'll stay.'

'I don't want control over what you take. I only want an agreement as to where you could show them. Or *if* you show them. I don't want to find myself in some magazine that everyone can read.'

'I understand. And where would you like to find yourself?'

'A print hung on the wall of an exhibition would be different.'

'It would.'

Alice stepped back and almost knocked into the wooden upright of the nearest rack. The empty sockets stared outward.

'I'll arrange it,' Gregory said quietly.

Excited, uncertain, she nodded and was suddenly breathless.

'Right,' she said.

In a hundred years' time, Alice thought, people would be able to study her body as she was able to study the daguerreotypes. In however partial or incomplete a way, a part of her would be made permanent. She would have achieved a kind of success. Her image would live forever in the present.

★

If Gregory had been completely financially independent and free to photograph whatever subject he wished, the bone crypt would still have been among his choices. The unsettling atmosphere of the underground chamber appealed to him. From it he obtained images that were lit and balanced with an exactitude that few of his competitors could have matched. When he examined them he could see that several were good enough to be classed among his very best work. He visualized them as gelatin silver prints hung in his planned exhibition, the hard curves of the skulls providing a memento mori to the organic softness of his portraits and nude studies. The ossuary's bleakness would counterpoint the detailed clothing, finely textured faces and candidly shot flesh displayed on the adjacent walls.

But as he daydreamed about this triumph, Gregory was also imagining Alice naked and enticing in front of his lens.

At her desk on the other side of the room Cassie finished her conversation, put down the phone, and fingered a necklace fashioned from metallic loops. She had not worn her mother's necklace since Gregory had borrowed it to hang round Alice's neck.

'The picture editor says they'll go ahead as planned. First week of next month.'

'That's good.'

Gregory asked no further question. More and more he was coming to rely on his daughter. Last week she had taken his place on one of the less important assignments, and next week she was due to cover another. As usual Cassie had protested, albeit briefly, but Gregory had insisted. After all, he reasoned, his name was also the name of the company, so the sessions need not involve him personally; his daughter was just as much part of the Gregory Pharaoh business as he was. Afterwards and as usual he had checked

Cassie's work and found it imitative. It was, therefore, perfectly acceptable.

'We still have to discuss these,' Cassie said.

Gregory moved his fingers across the keyboard in apparent idleness, but then opened a file of the photographs of Alice that he had taken weeks ago in the studio. He was determined to study them again. Sculpted by light, motionless, Alice gazed out at him like a provocation. For more than a minute he did not speak.

Cassie watched him. Often she could not decide whether Gregory had begun to daydream, or whether his extended silences were expressions of a growing melancholia.

'Dad,' she asked, 'are you listening?'

'Of course I'm listening. Why wouldn't I be?'

Cassie picked up a thin file of papers and stood up. As soon as Gregory's screen was in view she noticed what he was studying. Gregory considered exiting the picture file but did not. After all, he had nothing to hide.

A chair with castors stood in the corner of the office. When Cassie moved it so that she could sit next to him it rumbled across the uneven floorboards like distant thunder.

'There are six potential commissions here,' she told Gregory. 'Four are probable, but two of those are due soon. I need you to comment.'

'Are they in this country?'

'Yes. Why?'

He shrugged defensively. 'At the moment I don't feel like travelling overseas.'

'It's never bothered you before. You always said you liked to get away.'

Gregory did not answer. Cassie looked askance at the screen.

A spectral Alice Fell stood with her arms raised like a dancer in an unexplained rite. High contrast made her skin flare white, as if lit by burning phosphorus, while her eyes and lips were darkened like kohl. A well of shadow behind her collarbone was as sharp as a crescent. To Cassie she looked like a woman who would stop at nothing to get what she wanted.

'Can't you stop looking at these?' she asked.

'It's important to be self-critical. You know that as well as I do.'

Cassie decided not to answer. The images moved onward.

After a few seconds she spoke again. 'You took this sequence from eye level or below. The viewpoint favours her.'

'I hope you're not trying to say that I glamorized my subject. These are conventional dynamics and you know it.'

Immediately Gregory felt that perhaps he had responded too harshly, but that it would be inadvisable to retract what he had said.

Cassie ignored him and placed her hand on top of the folder as though it contained documents for a court case. 'This is your business, not mine. I'm just an employee. Part-time, at that.'

Gregory saw the chance to recover a balance. 'I've been thinking about what I said. Maybe the business needs you more than either of us has ever fully recognized.'

'Maybe, but you're still the one who has to decide what you want to accept and what you don't.'

'But you must have been considering the options,' Gregory said.

Cassie did not answer, but opened the file and indicated the uppermost printout. It concerned a musician, in the country for only a week, with distinctive features and the air of a man used to posing for his portrait.

'You could do it,' Gregory suggested. 'It would be good for you.'

'Dad, he's *important*,' she said.

But Cassie also thought that if her father were so lacking in energy then it would indeed be rewarding if she were to take some of the more interesting commissions. Maybe she had let her life become stale; maybe she should be thinking forward to the time when her father would retire.

'And the hotel?' Gregory asked.

'What?'

'The hotel that's having thousands poured into its renovation. When am I supposed to be covering that?'

'I wasn't talking about the hotel.'

'No, but I am. Do we know the dates?'

She waited for a moment before replying. 'I'd have to check the calendar, but it's not for weeks. They'll still be working on the last phase of the refurbishment.'

'Have we an estimate?'

'If you like I could phone and ask for an update. But we need to sort out this musician first.'

'I'd like to take a look at the rooms beforehand. Just to get a sense of the perspectives. Can you tell them I want to do that?'

Cassie looked closely at him. Her father had never been so unduly concerned about a shoot. Very quickly she began to wonder if his request had something to do with Alice Fell. She indicated the screen.

'Do you mind turning this off while we talk?'

'It's all right as it is.'

'No, it isn't. Neither of us will be able to concentrate.'

Gregory pressed a few keys and the file collapsed into its icon.

Seeing that he would go no further, Cassie reached out in front of him and switched off the monitor.

'You're determined,' he told her.

'One of us has to be.'

'I'm going to say yes to the musician.'

'Good. That's the right thing to do. There are these others, too. You have to think them through. Or both of us have to do that.'

Gregory nodded. He was aware of his own behaviour patterns and was faintly embarrassed at seemingly being unable to alter them. When he saw how Cassie was reading his mood he shrugged and then tightened his mouth in a fatalistic smile.

'All right,' he agreed. 'But I'll need to know about the hotel.'

'Do you want to use an unfinished hotel as a location?'

'It's an idea. It could work.'

Cassie took a chance. 'And you want Alice Fell to be in that room.'

Because he considered lying, Gregory waited before responding. And then he spoke.

'Why not?'

Cassie looked down at the papers on the desk and smoothed the uppermost document with her fingers even though it was already flat.

'We really must come to an agreement on these,' she insisted.

'Cassie, I know what you think about Alice.'

'Really.'

'You don't mince your words. You see things in her that I don't see. But all she is to me is a professional challenge. I'm annoyed with myself because I haven't been able to do her justice yet.'

'Photographically,' Cassie said.

'I wouldn't be speaking in any other way, would I?'

His daughter said nothing. She just kept looking down at the file. Gregory felt impelled to speak again.

'Cassie, I haven't slept with Alice.'

She did not think that he had. But she kept silent.

'I'm telling you the truth.'

'Dad, you might not have slept with her, but it's obvious that you want to. And that's getting in the way of your professional objectivity. You're a photographer, not some kind of suitor.'

Gregory had not known that his desires were so easily read.

'What is she after, really?' Cassie asked. 'You must have your suspicions.'

'I don't think she's after anything.'

'She must be. I can see the calculation in her eyes.'

'I don't think so. Maybe she seems aloof, but actually she's unusually responsive to the world around her. I enjoy her company and I enjoy photographing her. And that's it. That's all. I've told you not to worry.'

'But I do.'

Gregory said nothing.

'Dad, let me make a suggestion. It's very forward of me.'

'I'm not sure I want to hear this.'

'Of course you do.'

'Cassie,' he said warningly, but she would not be stopped.

'Why don't you just sleep with the woman? Seduce her. Take the initiative. It's easy for you. Put yourself back in control. In all probability you'll wake up the next morning and everything will seem ordinary and everyday. You'll not be bothered any more. You'll see Alice Fell for what she is.'

Gregory put both hands up to his face, spread his fingers across the top of his eyebrows, and pushed his thumbs into his face just below the cheekbones.

'But I don't know if I *should* sleep with her.'

'But you want to. I know that and she knows that.'

'*Most* of the time I want to. But there's a part of me that says that I'd be doing wrong.'

Cassie leaned back. The chair creaked a little, like a rope under strain.

'You make it sound even worse than I thought,' she said.

8

Off-white sheets were spread across the floor and draped across the furniture. Each sheet needed to be washed, and many were marked by dried paint that had accidentally been dripped on them. Most of the spots and smears were of muted pastel colours, although sometimes a cluster of vivid primaries stood out from the surface. A fractured wave of bright blue, as if from a carelessly dropped brush, ran along a fold of cloth near the far wall, while the sheet thrown across a nearby couch was starred with a constellation of red that was the colour of arterial blood. Any sound within the room was both hushed and hollow, and Gregory's tread was muffled as he walked to the window and stood against a glare of afternoon sunlight. Outside he could see the hotel gardens. A sprinkler threw out water in brilliant whirling fans, but no one moved through the landscaped greenery.

He turned back and pushed the shirtsleeves up over his forearms. His favourite Canon had been placed like a sentinel on a tripod in the middle of the room. Beyond it Alice stood in a white towelling robe fastened by a loosely knotted cord. She had undressed and fixed her lipstick and hair in a bathroom that had already been converted into something gleaming and pristine. As she did so, Gregory had found himself wondering if she would take a shower afterwards, and how she would look naked with water coursing across her skin. He spoke gently to encourage her.

'Whenever you're ready.'

'You have to give me some time.'

'Of course. But the sooner you take off that robe the sooner you'll feel comfortable, and the sooner we can start.'

Alice did not move. The milky varnish on her nails was the colour of the internal curves of seashells. Raising his hands for emphasis, Gregory used a line of argument he had often used on others.

'You have to be confident in yourself. Sessions like this always make my models feel liberated and alive. They have their pride validated. And they tell me that the feeling never leaves them.'

He paused, as if deciding whether he should risk the next sentence.

'You must have known men who delighted in seeing you walk naked across a room.'

Alice did not answer, but continued to look at him as if she were wondering what would happen next.

'Remember the sense of power that must have given you,' Gregory told her. 'Imagine the camera is one of those men. Because the camera is just as fascinated, just as transfixed.'

And Alice remembered a time when she strode across a floor with such naked confident grace that her lover merely sat motionless in rapt attention, and then told her she was the most sensual creature he had ever seen. She remembered her own feelings clearly, but could not remember which of her lovers was the one who had been so entranced.

'I'm ready to get started,' Gregory said.

'Give me a few more seconds. Maybe I'll surprise you.'

Alice reflected that Gregory did not know, just as` Thomas would never know, of the lovers she had enjoyed, or of the abandonment that had often transported her. And yet that sensual paradise had never lasted. Instead it had always become jaded, unoriginal, emptied.

It was almost certain that if she were to take Gregory to bed then their relationship would follow the same downward curve and terminate in a wasteland of boredom and distrust. And then she would become distressed and angered if he did not also recognize that the affair was exhausted.

Without ever having a clear sense of destiny, Alice had always aimed to discover something different in life. She believed herself equipped for deep insight, and at the start of every love affair she longed for a sense of meaning to strike her with a force so illuminating that her life could suddenly be seen to have shape and purpose.

One of her lovers had been a lecturer in drama, steeped in literary history, from whom she had learned that all of life could be viewed as fictive, as conforming to known archetypes. Every relationship she had had, and every one that she would have, could be deconstructed into a set of games: into strategies, advances, feints and negotiated settlements. More than once he had told her that ancient drama often allowed conclusions to be wrought by divine intervention, and that a god would appear from the edge of the stage and arrange the fate of every character. Alice could not believe in the divine, but it seemed plausible to her that similar energies must be at work in the present-day material world – if not, then perhaps her own life was just a sequence of variations on lives already lived by others. These energies were always just at the edge of detection, as they were at the edge of reason, but a nearby revelation could sometimes be partly sensed, like a change of pressure in the air. Alice strove to be convinced that a system of equity would somehow ensure that eventually she would be awarded a form of enlightenment that she could not as yet imagine.

For a while it had seemed that sensual ecstasy was part of a transformative power. Now it was beginning to appear possible that Alice had been wrong. All of her lovers had given her pleasure, diversion and new perspectives, but not one of them had enriched her understanding beyond limits from which it would have been impossible to return. Even though that kind of transformation could often seem to be just beyond her reach, perhaps it was actually illusory. Even in its most modest forms it would never be found within an embrace. Like a mirage, true enlightenment lay both elsewhere and nowhere.

And yet here in this pale, hushed room, with her bare feet testing the weave of the sheets, the air infected by smells of paint, the sun warm by the opened windows, Alice wanted to intrigue and excite the man who was about to take her photograph. Gregory Pharaoh was her object and her victim, and she wanted him overtaken by fascination and lust. She needed to see this abstracted, overconfident man made awkward by desire, to hear his voice dry like a husk within his throat. She wanted him to stumble, and she wanted him to glow.

'I'll stand over here,' she said, walking to the window so that her back was to the lens.

'I decide the shots,' he told her.

'Then maybe you should decide on this one.'

On a low hill in the distance cloud was building. Alice unfastened the robe and let it fall open as she looked across the gardens. The sun was hot on the exposed vertical strip of her skin, and her breasts tingled slightly. She stood at the window as aloof and as unabashed as a Surrealist muse. If anyone had been walking in the grounds they could have looked up and seen her, but no one did. At her back there was silence. The shutter did not click. Power surged within her like a tide.

'Do you want me to turn so that you can see me?' she asked.

'Yes,' Gregory said.

A corona of sunlight flaring about her, the sides of the white robe framing the length of her body like shutters, Alice turned to face Gregory. She remembered what he had said about the geometry of the female form. And she knew that for the length of that bright afternoon, in this quiet cocoon of a hotel room, she was being captured, fixed, immortalized.

Gregory had his camera lined up, but he did not take the shot. Alice waited. She wanted him so consumed with excitement that his limbs would be drained of their strength. If at that moment he had fallen on his knees in front of her then she would have stopped forward to stand with her pubis only inches from his face.

'Do you think this pose is good?' she asked, challenging him with her gaze.

'No. It's too much like a glamour shot. It's not what I want.'

'Then what *do* you want?'

'Honesty,' he said.

Gregory could not help but remember how once, years ago, he and his wife had been staying at an expensive continental hotel in a room facing into the sun. Ruth had stood at the bathroom door, fresh from a shower, a white towelling robe open down the front of her body, the room behind her bathed in light. They had been married for years, had made love hundreds of times, and yet Gregory had found himself so overcome with tender passion that at that moment he wanted to be nowhere else. His wife's body, her companionship, her very nature were so comforting that the rest of the world, and all other women, were made insubstantial.

He cleared his throat. 'I think if we begin with you standing over there, behind that couch.'

'Why there?'

'Because its shape and the folds in the cloth and the spots of paint will act as counterpoints. Just accept that I know instinctively what will work. I can't explain myself all the time.'

Alice waited for a moment before walking to the couch. 'Should I take this off?'

'That's the idea. When you have, put your fingers on the back of the couch, as if you were resting them on piano keys, and look straight into the lens.'

'This back is too low.' She gestured downward with one hand. 'My body hair will be in shot.'

'I know.'

Alice waited for a moment, imagining how she would look, and then eased the robe from her shoulders and threw it to one side. As soon as she had done so she wondered if she should have trimmed her pubic hair. Actresses and models did that, and yet all of her lovers had been excited by it and begged her to keep it as it was; often her drama lecturer had teased it with a brush prior to making love.

Afterwards the lecturer would lie beside her, sated and dreamy, and rather than ask Alice about her own feelings, he would talk about his work, about stagecraft, acting techniques and pretence. He knew all about pretence; he was married to an actress who was often away on tour or on location, and whom he had no intention of leaving. Alice was happy with that; she had not wanted anything permanent. Later she came to recognize his monologues as tutorials, and as examples of his self-centredness, but to begin with she had been fascinated by what he said. The personality, it seemed, was not fixed at all, but was malleable and more subject to change than Alice had suspected. Perhaps her own self, too, could undergo a transformation.

'Is that all right?' she asked Gregory.

'I'll tell you when it's not,' he answered, running off several shots. With each one Alice appeared to relax further and then to grow more confident.

'If you would stand to one side,' he requested.

She came out from behind the couch. There was nothing between her body and the lens. Her pubic hair was a shock of russet against the pale skin. Gregory was on the edge of arousal, and at the same time he felt guilty. He cleared his throat.

'Put your right hand on the couch back again. That's it. Use it to keep your balance if necessary. Now, put your other hand behind you so that it rests at the base of your spine. Good. And your right foot behind your left, and lift your body a little from the floor. Like a dancer. Great — that's great.'

'It would be easier if I was wearing heels.'

'But I wouldn't get the natural weight distribution that I want. And besides, I'm not Helmut Newton.'

Gregory had a twinge of guilt that shaded into a feeling of protection. He was not certain that Alice knew exactly what she was doing in this wide, unhelpful world. He suspected that although she had had several lovers, she had become too involved, too dependent. He thought that each one must have broken her heart in ways that she would never speak about. Only Ruth had ever broken Gregory's. She had not intended to. She would never have anticipated the way that he had been unable to recover from her death.

'Standing like this is uncomfortable,' Alice said.

'OK, that will be fine. Take it easy and relax.'

As she did he noticed two things. Firstly that, rather than stand with her legs too closely together, she kept them very slightly apart. And then Gregory also noticed that there was a crooked blue line raised on the skin at the inside of one thigh, just above the knee. Alice saw him register the vein.

'I never said I was perfect.'

'There's no such thing as perfection. And who would want that?'

'I thought of having an operation. They say it's easy. It'll show on the photographs, won't it? People will say "Look, that woman has a varicose vein."'

'If you cared about that, then you wouldn't have volunteered.' And then, after a pause, Gregory chanced a further question. '*Has* anyone ever said that to you?'

'Any men, you mean? I don't know. I can't remember.'

She knew he recognized that she was lying.

Besotted by intimacy, Alice had once shared a bathroom with a man who had insisted on knowing all of her body, and expected her to know all of his. When she had shaved his chin she had been so inexpert that excess foam from the razor had covered her fingers and dribbled on her naked belly. When her partner bent to wipe it away with a towel he noticed the vein for the first time, and traced it with his finger as if it had been something distinctive and precious.

He was a physicist, and during the time that they lived together he had taken her to parties where he and his university colleagues had bandied undefined words like 'hadron' and 'quark' and phrases such as 'quantum vacuum' and 'the Copenhagen interpretation'. These concepts were so impenetrably specialized that Alice felt they might as well have been mathematical formulae. Sometimes, indeed, they were, but sometimes they opened into seemingly irrational theories, usually and paradoxically called solutions, such as that of an endlessly proliferating multiplicity of universes.

She had found it curiously exciting that there was a body of knowledge to which she had no access, for no matter how often the basics were explained, she found that they slipped too easily from her understanding. It was enough that a man of such intellect, and capable of thought that was so unreachably abstract, should find her appealing. But later she found her physicist to be self-centred and the workings of his mind unreachable.

She looked across the room at Gregory, wondering when he would cease to record her body and instead move his fingers across it in wonderment. Perhaps in some alternative universe he was already doing that.

'What should I do now?' she asked.

'There's a chair over there. I'd like you to sit on it.'

'It looks uncomfortable.'

'I won't keep you there.'

Alice sat down. The coarse sheet was cold against her flesh. Alert to appearing unaware, she was careful to hold her knees together and angle them away from the camera. Gregory took the Canon from the tripod and knelt down so that he was on a level with her torso. For the next few minutes he directed Alice into the postures that he wanted; all of them were discreet.

In the alternative worlds that her physicist had talked of, perhaps another Alice, a different Alice, was leaning back on an un-covered chair, feline and available, her arms thrown back and her legs wide apart. More than once she had asked her lover if there were indeed such alternative worlds, for when she tried to think of them they receded to infinity like the images in parallel mirrors. And if they existed, was it possible that one could irrupt into another, and could this be an explanation for all the things that happened in our present world that were mysterious, unbeliev-able, impossible?

Her physicist had laughed. These things were theoretical abstracts, and unknowable; earthly perceptions would judge them less real than fantasies. But still Alice felt that at some time in the future there could be a revolution in thought, a breakthrough. Somehow it would be proved that the everyday sensory world was more irrational than had previously been suspected, and that the only way it could be made explicable would be by reference to forces that lay outside the simply observable.

Gregory retreated behind the tripod, lowered its height and spread his legs to look in the viewfinder. For a moment he appeared to be a creature drawn from both flesh and metal, and then he stood straight, placed his knuckles against his chin, and stared hard at Alice.

'Could you stand up again?'

She obeyed. He studied her. She could not tell what was going through his mind.

'I want to take side views. Profiles.'

'I'll look too big round the midriff.'

'Of course you won't. And don't breathe in too hard – it will be obvious if you do.'

Alice shuffled round to stand sideways on to the lens.

Unexpectedly she felt more vulnerable than she had done for the frontal shots, and her confidence began to fail. Perhaps her nose would look too large and bony, her breasts too small and not swelling out from her ribcage with an appealing round fleshiness, her nipples too prominent, her buttocks too large, her belly not flat, her pubic hair too bushy. She could never resemble a model in the prime of youth, or look anything like the other women who must have posed nude for Gregory. Instead his work would portray her as a woman in her early thirties with all the signs of her age. It would be obvious that she was pretending to be someone she was not.

Quite suddenly Alice wanted to screen herself from throat to ankle. Even the white bathrobe would have revealed too much, and instead she wanted to swaddle her body in a shapeless blanket.

Gregory sensed the change of mood and tried to soothe her.

'It's all right,' he told her, 'you look fine.'

Alice looked askance at him and he saw a thin film of concern shine across her eyes. She folded her arms protectively across her breasts and then she raised one hand and left it poised in mid-air above her belly. It was as though she wanted to screen her pubis but dared not for fear of appearing irrationally frightened.

Gregory crossed the room. The wrinkled sheets on the floor made his footfalls resemble the soft padding of an animal. Defiantly Alice raised her head higher, but she could feel her heart beat faster.

'It's all right,' he repeated quietly.

Each aware of the other's nearness, they stared across the narrow gap and did not blink.

To Alice it seemed that they were like magnets, unable to approach any closer because a similarity of aim kept them apart, and that if one of them said the right words then the polarities would be suddenly reversed and they would fall into each other's arms.

Gregory cleared his throat. 'You're going to look good,' he said, attempting to be gentle but finding that the words had roughened on his tongue.

Alice still guarded herself with her arms. 'I don't like looking at myself in profile,' she confessed, flattening her raised hand. 'There doesn't seem to be much of me in a pose like this. I'll just be a kind of cameo.'

'Your personality will be clear in these shots. I can guarantee that. I told you I'd find things that you weren't able to find.'

Unconvinced, she said nothing.

Gregory moved fractionally closer and stopped. He seemed to hang there, almost swaying, prevented from coming any nearer. Alice wondered what his attitude would be if he were the subject and she the photographer. Would he complain about too strong a light on his thinning hair, or a penis that would appear too small or too wrinkled, or a sagging belly that would prove how little exercise he took?

'I'm going to move in and take you from your hips upwards, and I'm going to use the space above your head. So I want you to stretch out your arm – nearest the camera, that's right, push it up high because it will look like ivory against those walls. And as you do, incline your head.'

Alice hesitated.

'Soon, please,' he told her. 'Immediately would be even better.'

She stretched up her arm as though grasping for something just out of reach.

'Right, so if you could just lower your head – not too much; a little more; that's right. Perfect.'

The camera click was loud in the hushed room.

'You still haven't shaved your armpits.'

'You disapprove?'

'No. I photograph real women; I have no interest in centre-folds.'

'That sounds like faint praise.'

'I photograph *natural* women, if you want to put it another way. Ones without silicone implants, or tattoos, or wax jobs on their—'

He suddenly stopped, as if uncertain what he could say. Alice realized that she could assert control by being brutally frank. And at times she liked to shock.

'Cunts?'

Gregory nodded as if he had been about to say something else, and then smiled quietly to himself. 'If that's the word you want to use.'

And suddenly she remembered Thomas.

What would he think of her now, Alice wondered, as she stood before a lens with her arm raised like a victor and her head lowered as if in a stylized bow, her nakedness unprotected, the textures and contours of her body so freely displayed?

'I want to photograph your back,' Gregory said.

Without even asking, she turned. Sunlight flared against the windows.

'I don't want your hands by your sides, I want them above your head – this time both arms, and stretched up like an exercise. Imagine you're diving upwards into space. If you can raise your heels from the floor, that will help the posture. I'm only going to take your upper part, probably from the back of your thighs upwards. Maybe I'll crop your hands and the higher part of your arms, I'm not sure.'

Alice stretched as far as she could. She felt that she belonged to the air that flowed across and surrounded every move. Her entire body tingled unequally, as if beneath her skin the web of nerve endings tightened and relaxed in skeins and nodes of intense warmth. Somehow it would have seemed not unnatural for her feet to lift from the floor for a moment, just as they had left the pavement when she had been robbed, except that this time she really would be suspended in mid-air, held aloft by forces no one knew.

The camera noise was like a counter, advancing into the future.

Alice believed that Gregory was the most experienced man she was ever likely to meet. He was used to the female body; he had explored its characteristics and demands for years and years. She was not certain what a love affair with him would be like – she could be his adventure, his relaxation, or his solace. Whatever was to pass between them, she knew that when it was all over he would accept its end. Gregory's profession, and his true passion, was to record the surfaces of life. He would never be in danger of becoming emotionally, sexually or domestically dependent on her. Probably he would not even share the level of intensity that Alice hoped to reach. When that was depleted, she would weep as she had wept for her other lovers, but it was likely that Gregory would not do even that. He would walk away with a contented finality. And afterwards, when both he and Alice were older, and Alice less attractive than she was at this moment, his photographs of her nakedness would still be as startling and as thrilling as they were on the day they were taken. Her limbs and face, her breasts and belly and hair, had been captured for posterity. Alice Fell would have made her mark on eternity.

'One more pose,' Gregory said.

'Just one?'

'For the time being, and then we can relax for a while. I'd like you to recline on that couch.'

Alice walked back across the room until she reached the long shrouded form at its far side. Gregory followed her. She knew he was watching the way that she moved. They each stepped over a patch of crusted red paint as though it had been still wet.

'Should I lie down?'

'Yes.'

Once again the sheet felt rough against her skin. The weight of her breasts shifted to one side.

'I don't look good like this.'

'Of course you do. But that's not what I want.'

He came closer and put his fingers on the couch's covered arm. She could hear a faint noise as he moved them to the exact position that he wanted her to take.

'You should be face down, but with your hands here, where my hands are. And your head raised. And your legs stretched out behind you. You needn't keep your legs closed. If you have them more than slightly apart that will be good – but don't worry, this won't be an Araki.'

'Who?'

'I mean it won't be explicit. I want to focus on your back – on all of your back. It's a continuation of the set we just took. But the spatial dynamic will be very different.'

'All right,' Alice said, and got into position.

For a few seconds she was on all fours on the couch and both she and Gregory thought of the sexual act. He imagined his hands spread across the top of her hips. She imagined the same, and a rhythmic thrust that would make her breasts sway and that she would brace by taking its weight on her hands.

'Is this right?' she asked.

'Shuffle a bit further forward. Are you comfortable?'

'That doesn't matter. How do I look?'

'Almost right.'

'Is this a copy of another photo? That Araki person?'

'I'm not thinking of any other photographer. I'm just thinking of you.'

Gregory had never intended to portray Alice as uninhibitedly sexual. Instead he had wanted to show her as cool, alert, her sensuality available only to someone she would choose. There was something not quite right about the pose at the moment.

'Wait a few seconds.'

He stood above Alice and studied the way in which the light fell across the curves of her shoulders, the long ridge of her backbone, the pale raised buttocks above which he could just see the faintest tracery of down. Below them her legs were parted at an angle, the raised blue vein just visible, the muscle swelling high at the back of her calves.

Alice could feel his fascination. It radiated from him in waves.

'Gregory,' she said languidly, her eyes fixed on the white sheet just in front of her face. It was so close that it was difficult to keep in focus.

'What?'

'This excites you, doesn't it?'

He did not answer. She asked another question.

'You want to make love to me, don't you?'

Gregory did not know which truth he should admit. Momentarily he looked across the room. Sunlight had advanced a little further across the crumpled sheets. He imagined himself standing above Alice so that his hands traced every curve, every joint, every cleft, but dragging like a weight against the luxuriant vision came the suspicion that she could demand more commitment, more permanence than he would be able to give. And yet a hidden part of Gregory wanted an affair that was complicated, lengthy and cathartic – something that would take a torch to his memories and burn out all the longing from his memories of Ruth.

'You think so?' he asked.

'Don't deny it. I can see right through your camouflage.'

A sudden touch of vertigo made Gregory stand with his feet slightly apart.

'Whatever I feel or don't feel doesn't matter,' he lied. 'We're here to take the best photographs that we possibly can.'

Alice made a murmuring noise that sounded like a dismissal. 'You can't expect me to believe that you haven't been in this situation before. There must have been times, maybe lots of times, when you finished your sessions by fucking your model.'

'Maybe yes, maybe no. But as far as my present model is concerned, I'd be pleased if she would lift her head so that she could look at the far side of the room.'

'Ah, we're being unbendingly professional, are we?'

As soon as Alice lifted her head Gregory framed her face and back and buttocks. Light touched her like a benediction. Her profile stood out sharp and confident against the unfocused background.

'You must have carried condoms with you, just in case it happened,' she continued. 'Maybe you've brought some today. I wouldn't know.'

'My sexual life is none of your business.'

Between Gregory's hands the camera felt like a casing for something that was alive.

'You asked me to take this position,' Alice said as if she were just awakening from sleep. 'You must have known it was awkward to get into. When I was on all fours and with my backside raised, I couldn't help but imagine things, and those things made me tingle a little. When you saw me like that, didn't you think the same? Don't you think it now?'

Gregory's mouth was dry and even though his legs did not move they still seemed to be shaking as if an electric current was being pumped through them. He walked back to the tripod and fixed the camera on its apex. He wanted to put his hand down the front of his trousers and move his penis into a less restricted position.

Alice maintained her posture but turned to look at him.

'But that would be no way to start, would it?' she asked.

'I don't know what you mean.'

'I mean that the first time people make love, they should do it face to face, shouldn't they? That's the way I've always done it.'

Gregory imagined walking across to the couch, dropping onto his haunches in front of Alice, and kissing her wetly on the mouth. Immediately he knew this would be ungainly and ineffective because she had taken the recumbent position he had requested. Perhaps he could kiss her shoulder instead. Or he could kiss the skin at the base of her spine. He could extend his tongue and place its tip just at the beginning of the cleft of her buttocks. None of her other lovers, he was sure, would have made first moves such as these.

Alice sat up on the couch, knees tightly together, and placed her hands across her breasts to hide them. Gregory wondered if, impulsively, she had suddenly changed her mind. Or perhaps she was taunting him. There was an expression on her face that he could not quite read.

'We're hardly equal here, are we?' she asked.

'I thought we were,' he said, not understanding.

She clicked her tongue in mock reproof. 'How can we be? You're fully clothed and I'm not. I'm *vulnerable*.'

Was this an invitation to undress? Dizzyingly, Gregory saw himself in double focus. Firstly as Ruth must have seen him all those years ago – young, confident, energetic; and then as he might seem to Alice – ageing, somewhat overweight, his body no longer firm, and his erection perhaps unreliable now that he had once again remembered his wife.

And Gregory suddenly imagined the reproving figure of Cassie observing him, silent and with her arms folded, her mother's beads around her neck, distaste on her face.

'So,' Alice said, 'I think it would be better if I was wearing that bathrobe – don't you? It would make us more equal.'

Gregory tried to get all thoughts of his daughter out of his head.

'What's more,' Alice continued, 'I don't think I should be the one to pick it up.'

Without a word, he walked to where the robe lay on the sheets. When he came back he held it just out of Alice's reach. Tantalized but disappointed, she did not move.

'This isn't the time for *games*,' she said.

Gregory leaned further forward to allow Alice to take the robe from him. As soon as she had done so she wrapped it quickly round herself, and then stood up so that it draped the lower part of her body. Her nakedness was once more completely hidden.

'There,' she said, 'that evens things up.'

They stood facing each other across a ruche of crumpled white sheet flecked with blue like a broken wave.

'Well, Mr Pharaoh, what now?'

Whatever happened, Gregory wanted to be absolved of responsibility.

'You seem to be driving this,' he said.

They stared at each other as if they were both waiting for the other to break and confess whatever was the truth.

'I'm used to taking the initiative,' Alice said.

'I see.'

Time gathered in the room, layer pressing down upon layer.

'I don't like the obvious,' Alice told him. 'I like to be different. Sometimes, I like to shock.'

He nodded and said nothing.

She crossed the space between them in three wide strides, paused in front of Gregory with their eyes still locked, and then slid her hands under his shirt and around his midriff. He felt an inner breathtaking jolt but did not know if it would transmit to Alice's hands.

'I like to do this,' she said, pushing his shirt high up his ribcage so that he was sure she could feel the shallowness in his lungs. Then she bent and touched his left nipple with the tip of her tongue. The sensation was teasingly charged, but even as Gregory was enjoying it he wanted to step back, without knowing why.

Alice gently fastened her lips, and then her teeth, around his nipple. He wanted to break away from her at the same time as he wanted to pin her to the ground and ravish her. She sucked and slowly tilted her head from side to side. Gregory's mind grew fuzzy, as if full of cloud, and at the edge of his hearing there was an insistent, repetitive, annoying noise that made him think of a circular saw whirling as it cut through wood, withdrew and then sliced through wood again.

She stopped and leaned away.

'I have to answer it,' she said.

Only at that moment did Gregory realize that he was listening to the ringing of a mobile phone. Muffled and insistent, it echoed from within the bathroom.

'You don't have to,' he said, reaching out to place his hands on Alice's shoulders as if this would prevent her. Beneath the towelling the contours of her body were like an invitation. She broke away from him.

'Of course I have to. I left the number on the landline answer-phone. I'm just doing what you would do. And for the same reason.'

'Whatever the job is, it can wait,' Gregory said, but she took no notice.

For a few seconds he thought that Alice would not reach the phone in time and would be forced to ring back later, but then he heard her speak from the bathroom. At first he tried to ignore what was being said, and instead pretended to busy himself by dismantling the tripod and placing the camera back in its case, as if everything were happening as planned.

But as the conversation went on Gregory edged closer and closer to the open bathroom door.

Alice had not recognized the incoming number, but told herself that there was no reason why she should. She had approached almost twenty companies and organizations, and it could have been any one of them that was ringing. But the caller's voice, when it came, was neither neutral nor formal. Instead it was hesitant.

'I'm looking for Alice Fell.'

'Yes,' she said, 'that's me.'

'I'm sorry to ring you like this. We've never spoken.'

Alice waited. She did not know the voice even though there was an unclear suggestion of familiarity about it.

'I'm Richard.'

Still thinking of how she and Gregory would resume in a few minutes, she said nothing.

'Richard Laidlaw,' the man said.

For the briefest of moments she made no connection with the surname, but then she immediately knew there was something wrong.

'What is it?' she asked.

As he stood at the door Gregory began to realize that every-thing was changing. Alice's voice and the way she held her body were indicators that could not be ignored. An instinct for self-protection made him pretend that this was of little consequence. What did it matter that he would not be having sex with her that afternoon? It was bound to happen soon.

The thought immediately vanished into a regretful melancholy. Gregory knew his own mind now. He truly needed to make love to Alice. He wanted her presence to be imprinted on his body and his memory. Emotions rose within him that he had not wished for, and wanted to suppress, but he was helpless before them.

Much later Alice came to believe that the call had been made at that particular moment because it was part of a hidden design. Richard could have rung ten minutes later. Or she need not have answered. And that would have altered everything. If she and Gregory had actually made love before the call, then Alice would have had to look on their intimacy as something she should have been wise enough to refuse.

But they had not made love, and when she looked at the photographs taken that day she was able to view them as indicative of a certain kind of cleansing ritual. Although unaware that she was exactly where she needed to be, Alice had been unconsciously preparing for Gregory's future.

9

Almost two hundred images are stored in the small Kodak that Thomas kept in a side pocket of his rucksack. The first dozen are studies of the interior of a city flat, including a view from a window and one of the inside of the front door. The living room and bedroom have each been photographed from several angles. There are no means of identifying the flat, and few would recognize that it belongs to Alice. A succeeding image could be either a deliberate abstract or a mistake, but is actually a photograph of a river taken by zoom at dusk. The yellowish smears on the formless grey are lights reflected in the moving water.

The remaining pictures are of remote archaeological sites. To a non-specialist the most recognizable location, and certainly the most dramatic, is the stone circle at Castlerigg, although this features in only three shots. Perhaps Thomas felt that the site was too well known. Covered in much greater detail are the circle at Swinside and the megaliths of Long Meg and Her Daughters. Other photographs show what remains of tumuli, cultivation terraces, settlements and hill forts. The untrained eye, however, will see only low mounds of earth, grass and broken stone, like evidence that has become so degraded that it is no longer decipherable.

Other than when a brief moment of sunlight passed across these barren places, the colours are muted and the landscapes drab. Some shots have been taken during rain, with muddy puddles collected in every depression. Only twice does Thomas himself appear, posed self-consciously against a mound to give it scale. These pictures were taken early in his journey, at the Leven's Park Ring Cairn and the Bronze Age farmstead at Sealford. After that, he appears to have abandoned the idea of standing in front of the lens.

For more than a week he had been visiting forlorn, out-of-the-way sites known only to a few. The Ordnance Survey map had become dog-eared, the compass face was smeared, and the laces of his scuffed boots were stiffened and discoloured by mud. Thomas had no transport of his own, but relied on infrequent bus services and, twice, offers from strangers in cars who had taken pity on him. At night he stayed at B & Bs in villages or farmhouses and in the morning ate full English breakfasts whenever he could. For the rest of the day he survived on either bought sandwiches or Indian restaurant takeaways that he ate at bus stops with a plastic fork. Much of the time he was searching wet fellsides or moors for modest archaeological remains that were so difficult to spot that many walkers would have marched straight past. He habitually lingered at these locations for longer than was necessary.

Always sensitive about bodily functions, Thomas had developed a protocol for urinating in the open air, making use of tree plantations or drystone walls as screens. Once, in an act that had subsequently seemed to him the most absurd of follies, he had stood at the centre of a collapsed and deserted earthwork and masturbated with a kind of clinical frenzy, as if he were somehow taking an obscure form of revenge. Only afterwards did he feel ashamed, and hurry on as quickly as he could to his next destination.

Whenever he visited a site he circled or boxed its location in ink on his map and graded its interest with his own symbols. He did this so systematically that the map's red contour lines were now patterned with what looked like runic markings. By doing it Thomas could pretend, at least for some of the time, that his journey had a serious academic purpose.

On the day of his journey to Stockdale Moor he began by photographing a Celtic cross in a village churchyard. The weathered sandstone held both Norse and Christian symbols; a crucifixion was fading back into the stone. The cross was a thousand years old: by Thomas's standards relatively recent, but he had been required to teach several historical periods and the cross was important, so it seemed sensible to visit it before he began his climb to the settlements. It would join his other photographs of Norman castles, Georgian houses and sites from the Industrial Revolution. At this moment, and for most of his walk, Thomas believed he was certain to return to something like the life he had once led.

He stood among the mottled gravestones and checked his map. The thin blue squiggle of the Bleng rose below Caw Fell and Gowder Crag and flowed along the southern edge of the moor. Sampson's Bratfull was indicated in Gothic lettering, while symbols for cairns were pocked across the gradients and plateaux. All around were moors, farms and fells with names belonging to a grimly functional past during which matters of the intellect or of the heart must have been indulgences – Stone Pike, Raven Crag, Hawkbarrow, Scargreen.

Thomas folded his map and walked to the end of the village. At a signpost he struck off the main Wasdale road and set off into this bleak heartland along a narrow road that was marked as private. After a few last bungalows and a farm he could see nothing ahead but hedges, trees, fields and the sides of a shallow valley. A large bird wheeled in the sky for a long time before it was lost to sight behind the edge of the forest. Once again he found himself thinking of Alice. He could not help it. She was with him always.

Last night he had stayed at a B & B used by long-distance walkers. On a shelf there had been a scruffy collection of local guidebooks. As he leafed through one in a desultory fashion the name of Alice Fell had leapt out at him like an alarm: Wordsworth had written a poem of that name. The discovery seemed not so much of a coincidence as a goad.

For some distance the road resembled a lane and passed between wooden posts strung with wire and grassy banks topped by hawthorn. After five minutes he had to step off the metalled surface and stand close to a wooden gate when a muddy Land Rover drove towards him. Thomas moved back onto the road as soon as it had passed. He could hear the sound of water from beyond the trees on his right, and in the field to his left a few incurious sheep with ragged coats methodically cropped the grass. There seemed to be no one else around. When he reached the first conifers he looked to their uppermost branches and saw their tips sway in a breeze he could not feel at ground level. Above them the sky was cold and grey. He began to think about Alice again.

Often Thomas revisited his lost love affair like a detective searching for motivation, but this time he tortured himself by wondering what Alice was doing at this particular moment. Safe and warm in the flat that he had once called home, he imagined, and perhaps with Gregory Pharaoh, a man who was far too old for her, a man whose promises must have been exciting, confusing and misleading. Perhaps even now she was naked and straddling him. Thomas tried to imagine the scene because he knew it would cause him pain, but each time the details were about to resolve themselves they slipped out of focus. The most hurtful thought of all was that Alice could be whispering in Pharaoh's ear the endearments and invitations that she had once whispered to Thomas, and which he had always wanted to be for him and him alone.

He came to an unsurfaced area that was used as a car park. A man and a woman wearing cagoules had just opened the boot of their car and were drying two dogs with towels. The woman smiled and said that it looked as if it were going to pour down. Thomas thought of just walking on, but paused to ask if they knew the best way to Sampson's Bratfull. Neither had heard of it, but when he explained its location, the man recommended that he take the track to the left just after the lower roadbridge across the Bleng. That way was more sheltered. The river had burst its banks and taken a new course a couple of years ago, but there was an alternative path through the wood. Thomas could, if he wished, return by the upper bridge, along the road from Scalderskew Farm. That way was longer, not as sheltered and not as interesting. The two dogs jumped into the car boot, circled round each other several times, and then settled down.

For more than a week Thomas had chosen not to hold conversations, and now he found that he wanted to spend time talking to these people. He asked about the dogs. One was a Lakeland terrier, the other a cross that was often taken for a Lancashire Heeler. The man and woman took as much delight in them as if they had been children, and for several minutes they described the dogs' characters and exploits.

Thomas was slightly bored, but as he walked away he was also envious. Maybe the man and woman had as pleasant a life as could be led – a home far away from a city, a couple of dogs to walk, the natural world all around. They had appeared so happy with each other's company. There was a sense of family that was somehow extended and completed by their pets. Thomas did not have any close family connections. There was Richard, whose name he kept as an emergency contact, but they had not met for several years. Instead, they had merely kept each other informed of their latest addresses and contact numbers. Others, when they had broken up with the person they loved, would have sought refuge with a brother or sister. Not Thomas. He had not felt able to do that, and had not wanted to. Others might even have been able to ask a brother or sister if they could borrow money; Thomas could not do that either, even though his account was now dangerously low.

A light shower fell as he crossed the smooth metal bars of a cattle grid. The year's new growth shone a vivid green on the conifers. Behind their trunks the pale boulders in the river had been tinted brown with peat. Ivy grew thick enough to choke a ditch on the left.

The road turned to cross the lower bridge and then divided. The way to the right led upwards and soon vanished behind a wooded bank. Beside it a sign for Scalderskew Farm was hammered into the ground. As the dog owners had advised, Thomas turned to the left and took a broad track of packed earth that skirted the river on its southern edge. A flurry of small unidentifiable birds whirred between saplings that had sprouted from a bank of mossy earth.

A little further on he came to the spot where the Bleng had burst its banks and now flowed across the track. At some time in the past, asphalt had been laid, perhaps because that stretch had always been muddy; now the flood had lifted it in cracked plates so that the water coursed across the shattered path in a series of shallow rapids. Thomas considered the alternative path through the wood but decided to ignore it. He waited for a moment with the toes of his boots at the edge of the stream, and then he walked slowly forward. Water flowed around the soles of his boots, its noise rising to cover him in its intersecting patterns.

He thought of the time when he had shared a shower with Alice. The cubicle had filled with mist, and condensation formed on the glass so they could no longer see out. The noise of the falling spray changed as they turned their shoulders and flanks to the jet, and they both laughed when water ran from the end of his penis as if from a tap.

Thomas took another step forward and misjudged the depth of the rapids. Cold water surged above the top of his boot and poured inside. Instantly his foot became icily cold. There was nothing for it but to walk quickly ahead. He forded the rogue stream and stood on its far side with his boots squelching beneath him.

Maybe Alice and Pharaoh were sharing a shower now, he thought. Maybe she was laughing in the way she had always laughed with Thomas. Was laughter something that she would share with all her lovers? Would every man in that hazy un-focused line have been told the same things, taken to the same places, made love to in the same unforgettable ways?

Thomas had brooded many times on the mysteries of Alice's past. All he could do was speculate, as all that he possessed were the flimsiest of clues. As he walked on up the valley, the trees crowding more thickly around him, he once again began to be tortured by imagined comparison. In Alice's judgement, how had he compared with other men? In how many ways had he failed? And what was he, how *unsatisfactory* was he, when compared with Gregory Pharaoh?

The valley sides grew steeper, the riverbed more littered with boulders, the trees darker. In a patch of brambles that looped and curled across a thicket of sedge he found an entangled sheep. The ram's eyes were as shiny as new-blown glass, and it struggled to free itself in an eerie silence. All that could be heard was the squishing sound of its feet as it trampled the marsh without moving any further forward. Thomas watched it for a while. He knew there was no way in which it could be freed other than with clippers, heavy-duty gloves and enough power to lift it by the horns and haunches. Eventually he turned away. Behind him the trapped ram struggled helplessly.

The track skirted to the right of a disused ford, climbed higher, and began to fade amongst undergrowth and moss. Sodden fir cones, dark as owl pellets, were scattered across the ground. Thomas slowed and then halted until he detected an unclear path that forked to the left. A coating of fallen needles gave beneath his weight as he passed between the trunks of high dark trees.

When Alice had demanded that he leave, Thomas had refused. Only when she had threatened to have him served with a solicitor's letter did he begin to accept that she was as determined as she was cruel. Even then he had not left the area, but booked into a nearby cheap hotel and hung around for days waiting for her to ring. The bill ate into his account; he had always been dependent on Alice for money.

Because Thomas loved Alice with an intensity he had not thought possible, he could not understand the change in her feelings even when she been signalling them for several weeks. Much later, when he began his northern journey, he still hoped that somehow she would change her mind. At any moment he was ready to return; all she had to do was ask.

He carried that thought in his mind like a tune that he knew would never be sung. In a dark corner of his heart Thomas knew that he would spend the rest of his life thinking about Alice, but that she would scarcely think of him at all. And even if she did, he would be an object of derision.

He clambered across roots and down a bank that was slippery with mud to reach a narrow wooden footbridge with wet planks. Halfway across he leaned on the rail to look down on a furious deafening cascade as the Bleng was forced between massive boulders and spilled in torrents across them. For several minutes Thomas watched the river bear everything away. After a while the constant roar triggered his thirst. Along with the food he had bought in a village he carried a bottle for water, but when he took it from his rucksack he discovered that he had forgotten to fill it. He replaced the empty bottle and walked on.

The path swung across a floodplain covered in low scrub, then took a hairpin to the right and began to climb steeply through a conifer plantation. On either side lopped branches were strewn like brushwood between the standing trunks.

As the path angled right and then left across the gradient it grew even steeper. Ascending its eroded surface made him breathe strenuously. Noise from the river rose up the valley sides. Drizzle began to fall, a little heavier than before. Thomas paused to collect his breath, turn up his collar and place a peaked cap on his head. The sound of machinery drifted from some far distant spot in the plantation. He could not recognize the noise, but after about a minute decided that a team must be chainsawing wood on the other side of the valley.

Eventually, after an ascent that he guessed must have been about four hundred feet, he arrived once more on the unmetalled road that led to Scalderskew Farm. The high haematite content of the surface gravel made it a muddy red, and sheep droppings littered the surface like tiny black olives.

Thomas joined the road and walked to the left. The farm lay some distance away, in a hollow between the high moors, the heights behind it already dissolved in mist. He knew where he was going. The weather would not stop him now.

He crossed another cattle grid whose bars gleamed cold in the rain. A dozen sheep moved out of his way. A few paces further, on the far side of a stream, he struck off the road. In front of him the treeless moor rose, inhospitable and cold. Its turf and reeds were slippery beneath his feet and the rain pattered in flurries on his rucksack.

Quite suddenly Thomas was irrationally happy. A solitary expedition in such bleak conditions was proof of his individuality and determination. If ever anyone talked of his life, they would have cause to praise his unfashionable qualities – his quiet, unflashy knowledge, his modesty, the way in which he had championed the past. Surely he was due such recognition. The land sucked at his boots as he walked. Visibility shrank around him.

And then, just as suddenly and even more powerfully, he was

overtaken by a sensation that was the polar opposite of the one he had just experienced.

There was no point in tramping this moor in search of an unimportant mound of stones. No one had ever thought it worthy of serious excavation. The appeal of Sampson's Bratfull lay in its quirky, rather grandiose name, and that was all. Thomas brooded about what could have been his real motivation for coming here. Perhaps it had nothing to do with archaeology. Perhaps it was because the very ordinariness of the mound, its position at the unexplored edge of things, corresponded to his own lack of achievement, his own life. Despite its name, Sampson's Bratfull was insignificant. Who had ever visited it deliberately? A glance at the map would tell you all you needed to know. No one would even notice if this accumulation of stones somehow ceased to exist.

At the very moment that he was thinking this, he found what he was searching for.

The mist that had retreated before his progress now closed behind him. Thomas stood on the sodden ground in front of a long barrow of countless grey stones pocked with lichen. A viscous sheen of water lay across the rocks as if they had been coated in colourless oil. Rain trickled down his face and the breath rattled in his throat.

The tumulus seemed to be part of the moor itself; whether rising from it or sinking back into it Thomas was unable to decide. He walked along one of the longer sides and then stopped, looking directly at the bank of rock. The circle of mist enclosed the spot as if it were an arena. All was quiet but for the sound of his own movements.

He began to unsling his rucksack so that he could get his camera, and then he stopped and shucked it back on his shoulders again. What did photography matter? What was the point of all those pictures that were steadily filling the Kodak's memory? Photographers, Thomas thought, were people who accumulated images like others accumulated objects. There must be a kind of desperation in their lives, a drive to record everything that passed in front of them, an obsession with permanence. They were mired in the present. All that they did was record surfaces. Anything deeper was beyond their interests or their capabilities. They *watched*; that was all.

And this was why Gregory Pharaoh would never understand heartbreak. A photographer could never know despair. In that way, Gregory was a perfect match for Alice. They both moved like insects across the surface of life. Neither had been injured by it.

It seemed to Thomas the bitterest of ironies that the world belonged to people who had never been scarred. He had been a fool to get involved, and an even bigger fool to allow himself to be wounded so deeply. Alice was not even sorry for him; instead she was scornful. Perhaps even now she was discussing him with Gregory Pharaoh and they were laughing.

Thomas picked a stone from the mound, weighed it in his hand, put it down again, and picked up another. They made tiny indentations in his palm. Thousands of years ago people had collected these stones and carried them to this spot to mark something, no one was certain exactly what – a burial, probably; several burials, perhaps. Maybe a few feet below the surface there were still bones to be found. Maybe the bodies had been burned on a pyre before being interred. And perhaps the site had been sacred, placed on the heights so that the dead would be closer to the gods.

Thomas pictured himself being memorialized by such a mound. It would be much more dramatic than a gravestone or a bronze plaque on a crematorium wall. If he died here, now, this instant, then maybe his true worth would begin to be recognized. People he hardly knew would claim that he had been their friend. Alice would be struck to the heart with guilt, made dumb by her part in his death, and ashamed that she should even think of taking Gregory Pharaoh into her bed.

He grimaced and put the stone back on the mound. A squall drove in from the west, the rain hitting his face and the back of his hands as sharply as hailstones. The turf beneath his feet seemed to be a damp crust of earth suspended on mud. The temperature gradients slid around him.

That was enough. Thomas walked away from Sampson's Bratfull intending never to return.

The road was filling with opaque red puddles. Thomas walked through them with the rain driving against his back. His cap became so soaked that it tightened around his head. He wondered about returning the way he had come rather than taking the long road back, but he knew that he must be close to the upper bridge. Perhaps he could find shelter there.

On his right the plantation edge was lined with conifers that had taken the full force of winter storms. Several had fallen so that the wheels of their root systems were set on edge like gigantic toppled candlesticks, and some had been snapped apart at about two-thirds of their height. A number had been sawn down so that the stubs of trunks resembled giant studs that had been punched into the earth. One tree had been struck by lightning and was nothing but a headless trunk, its upper section split as if by a gigantic cleaver. A thick streak of charred wood ran like a trail of dried black oil from its top to the ground.

The road dipped before him and then the upper bridge came into view. Thomas saw it first through a drifting curtain of rain. Wide enough to take a lorry stacked with timber, it spanned the valley in a broad functional slab. So that the forestry vehicles would not be unnecessarily restricted, there were no railings along its sides. After crossing it, the road ascended across the moor in a curve of murky red. The next tree boundary ran in a barrier along the skyline.

Thomas hoped that once he reached the bridge he would be able to creep beneath its shelter and remain there until the squall had passed. There would be something satisfyingly boyish in that; it would make all this into a kind of adventure. Eagerly he increased his pace down the slope, but then he stumbled on a loose stone. For a few seconds he lost his equilibrium and was forced to take awkward, jolting steps to regain balance. As soon as he had done this he stretched out his arms and made a few fake movements with them, as if wishing to convince an imaginary observer that he was rehearsing a theatrical act. Even as he did so he recognized this as absurd.

Only a thin concrete lip ran along the length of each side of the bridge. It would be easy to fall from it into the torrent below. The Bleng rushed and foamed, spray lifting from its surface and rising as if forced upward by the pressure of noise. A fallen tree, stripped of all greenery, thrust its branches from the water like the arms of the dead.

Within seconds Thomas realized that it would be impossible to take shelter. The bank angled steeply down to the river, but below the bridge the rake was precipitous. He took off his rucksack and placed it on a stone at the point where the concrete slabs abutted the road. Then he opened it and took out the empty water bottle. He needed a drink.

Thomas stood at the edge of the drop and stared down. There was something hypnotic about the rush of the peat-stained water, the severity of its flickering gleam, the energy of its collapse into blinding white foam. He could not help but imagine being carried away within it.

If someone were to see him now, Thomas thought, poised with his boots on the edge of the downward slope and the water bottle in one hand; if some person were capable of looking into his mind, what would they see? What would they whisper in his ear? Would his whole life have been as absurd as the little dance he had done when he tripped? If he were honest with himself, if Thomas were as observant and as rational as the very best archaeologist, what conclusion would he draw?

There was only one.

He was a man who had failed and who would continue to fail. Defeat had locked around him like a trap. He had no worthwhile prospects. His savings had disappeared. He had never succeeded in getting employment to match his talents. The only woman he had truly loved had rejected him. For all of his life, in his family, his relationships, in the jobs he had taken, Thomas had been an obstacle for others to get round. He had always been *in the way*. And for Alice Fell, too, he had eventually become the person who had prevented her from moving on to another love and a different kind of life.

The slope down to the Bleng was slick with mud and shale. In order not to lose his balance Thomas had to stuff the bottle into a wide pocket on his jacket and descend the bank facing inwards. He did not want to slide and then toboggan into the flood without stopping. On the way down he kicked the toes of his boots into the incline and grasped clumps of turf or the occasional sapling until he could reach the water's edge.

Once there he could scarcely think because the noise was so deafening. He squatted and rinsed his hands clean. The water stung his fingers and numbed them. He took the bottle from his jacket and propped it above a flat stone that lay flush with the angle of the slope. He watched it for a few seconds to make sure it would not slip. Perhaps he would fill it in a minute or so, he was not sure.

Thomas moved gingerly along the foot of the bank, angling his boots against the gradient so that he did not lose his balance. It was still raining heavily. When he looked back at the top of the slope he saw the underside of the bridge as a dark bar against the greyness of the sky, and his rucksack beside it as a bright spot of colour.

He came to a level strand of broken stone, scarcely more than a few inches wide. From the shapes made in the flowing water he guessed that it extended beneath the surface for the length of a cautious step before being carved away by the main channel. If Thomas walked onto that level then the water would pour over the top of his boots as it had done at the start of the path. Another step forward and he would flounder. The current would seize him in an inescapable grasp. Once that happened, he would be taken beyond choice. The water would do with him what it would.

He placed one foot in the river. The water that poured into his boot was icier than he had expected. He brought his other foot in line and stood motionless in the shallows with his hands by his sides. The current tugged lightly at his limbs like a tease. Just ahead of him it was deep and immeasurable, coursing unstoppably across rocks in turbid dips and whorls and dizzying patterns of foam and spume. The soles of his feet, his toes and his ankles became clamped within a cold so intense that they lost sensation. He began to be scared.

Like an intruder hurrying from a room, Thomas stepped back onto land. But as soon as he felt it under his feet he was gripped by panic that he could lose his balance and fall by accident into the river. He did not stop to pick up the bottle, but scrambled as fast as he could up the slope. Several times he slithered backwards and hurt his hands as he grabbed at whatever was in reach. Dislodged shale slid after him down the rake.

Once at the top he stood several paces back from the edge. He was breathing convulsively and his legs were trembling. He really was a failure, Thomas thought bitterly. This was proof. He had even failed to take his own life.

He spread out his hands. The palms and fingers were stained a tribal red. One fingernail was torn and a few tiny stones were sticking to his skin from the climb. Thomas brushed them away. The rain fell all around. As the drops landed on his skin the red became watery and dissolved in widening spots.

The rucksack with the camera and his map and food and clothes and diary still lay at the side of the road. The bottle still stood where he had left it beside the Bleng. Rain dripped steadily from the branches of the nearest tree. Mist rose in the valley. Thomas put his hand to his head and discovered that he was still wearing the cap. He took it off and carefully placed it on top of the rucksack. Even the smallest movement now seemed significant.

Without fully knowing what he was doing he strode to the centre of the bridge and paused with his toes against the concrete lip as if at the starting line of a race. His feet were warmer now but the rest of his body was cold.

The river seethed and thrashed beneath him as if it were alive. Spray rose upward in disintegrating clouds. He felt that he was obeying a law that he could not fully understand and yet could not escape. It removed responsibility for his actions. He no longer had to think.

Thomas stepped into the air and toppled forward.

For a moment it seemed to him that he paused in his fall, as if the spray were bearing him aloft, and then the river rose to meet him. From somewhere came the realization that his mind should be racing, but all he could frame was a simple phrase that blotted out everything else. What a fucking stupid thing to do, he thought.

The first thing that he hit was not water, but stone.

10

Alice sat next to Gregory in one of the rear pews. She looked down the length of the chill echoing room, over the backs of the heads of the other mourners, towards the coffin on its plinth. Soon it would be out of sight, lost to everyone's gaze as it slid along rollers into the heart of the crematorium. She could not imagine what Thomas would look like inside that polished box with its brass handles. It was so impersonal, so everyday, that it seemed almost unbelievable that it should contain a body she had often made love to.

Gregory counted more than twenty people scattered around the chapel either singly or in tiny groups. He had only agreed to come because Alice had insisted that there would be no one there apart from herself and Richard Laidlaw. But it occurred to Gregory that everyone in the sparse congregation must have known Thomas to some degree, whereas he did not. And not only had he never met Thomas; he was actually rather pleased that he was dead and out of the way.

'I can wait outside,' he murmured in Alice's ear. 'I don't belong here.'

'You can't leave now,' she whispered urgently, and then took his hand and squeezed it in manner he found pleasurable. 'Please stay,' she added, 'not for Thomas, but for me.'

As Gregory waited for Alice to release her grip he slipped into an erotic fantasy on how else she could hold him. Meanwhile she gazed fixedly towards the man sitting on his own at the front of the chapel. Eventually she let go, and as she did she spoke quietly.

'That must be his brother.'

Then she turned her head and whispered so close to Gregory's ear that the words seemed to be carried within a hot wind.

'Be careful what you say to him.'

'I don't intend saying anything,' Gregory answered.

He thought uneasily that even though Thomas was dead it was still possible that he could disrupt everything. Gregory's ambition would have been satisfied by now if his body had not been discovered. Or if Thomas had not carried a diary in his rucksack then he would not have been identified for a long time, and this funeral would not have been held for weeks or months. It could even have been so far ahead that Alice would not have found it necessary to attend.

But the police had easily tracked down Richard Laidlaw. The last communication he had received from Thomas had been a note quoting Alice's name and address. At the time he had not even been curious. He had never considered that he might have cause to ring the number.

When he had phoned Alice about his brother's death Richard had shown no indication that had been told about their separation, and she had not had the heart to admit the truth. In subsequent conversations Alice wondered if Richard actually knew what had happened, but if so then he never showed any awareness of it. Evidently the Laidlaw brothers no longer discussed such matters.

She had often thought of confessing, as she felt that Thomas's brother had a moral right to know. But when she had discussed it with Gregory he had shrugged his shoulders and asked what purpose it would serve, so she had confessed nothing.

Now as she sat in the crematorium chapel Alice wondered if Richard would draw the obvious conclusion when he saw her with a male companion.

'If he asks,' she said to Gregory in a low voice, 'make sure he knows we're just friends.'

'If that's what you want.'

'Of course it is.'

And for the immediate future that was true, Alice thought. She had decided that if she and Gregory were to become lovers it would not be until well after the funeral. Somehow or other that would be more honourable.

The service was muted, its religious aspect made equivocal by the indifference of the congregation. Although the Laidlaw brothers had been baptized as Anglicans, no one knew what Thomas's beliefs had been when he died. When Richard had phoned to ask, Alice had replied that he had only ever talked about primitive ritual and memorial. Together they had agreed that an interest in polytheism was not a useful pointer for a modern committal, and Richard had therefore arranged a conventional C. of E. service.

An uninterested vicar announced that the deceased had been on the brink of academic recognition when he had lost his life in a terrible accident. As he spoke, Gregory studied the vicar's bland emotionless features and sensed that few of those present, if any, felt a great sense of loss.

Two hymns were sung to organ music whose notes were drawn out for too long. Alice attempted to sing but seemed out of breath. When Gregory looked aside he saw to his surprise that she was crying. Unsure what to do, he stared straight ahead. The vicar's amplified voice lifted above the murmuring congregation like a threadbare sail.

To Alice it was disturbingly appropriate that Thomas should have died in such a mundane and pointless accident. It was the summation of a life never fully realized. Briefly she considered the possibility that if she had not ordered Thomas to leave, and if he had not travelled north, then he could finally have had better fortune in a few weeks or months. Just what this good luck might have been remained undefined in her imagination. But a sense of guilt nagged at Alice; she had been the prime mover of this tragedy. Whether Thomas was to prosper or remain a failure, he certainly would not have trekked to Stockdale Moor if she had not ended their relationship.

Even as she thought this, she gained a little ease from believing that there must be a hidden purpose behind his death. It had not been just a simple matter of terrain and weather. Losses so tragic were never without consequence.

Gregory grew more uncomfortable as the service progressed. Any funeral reminded him of his wife's death, but cremations redefined the memory so sharply that he had difficulty adjusting to the present. At the time he had been cushioned from grief by his own systematic recording of Ruth's disease. This self-imposed task, this willingness to have his profession place its stamp on those last few weeks, had enabled him to cope in ways that friends found admirable. None knew, although some must have suspected, that he was photographing every stage in his wife's slow decline.

Now, years later, as he observed the funeral of a man he had never met, Gregory had no need of the detachment a camera could bring. All he knew of Thomas was what he had been told. He did not even know what he had looked like.

Gregory should have been indifferent, and yet the progress of this Christian ritual, its reassurances and what he considered its absurd but touching promises of resurrection, were poignant and moving in ways that he did not wish to admit. So that when the curtains at last came together, cutting off everyone's view of the coffin, he was eager to leave the scene as quickly as he could.

Outside the chapel most of the mourners dispersed quickly, as though unwilling to be asked the extent of their friendship with the deceased. Alice was almost the last to shake Richard's hand. At first she could see little of Thomas in his brother, but after a few seconds she was able to detect a likeness in the shape of his face, the way that he stood, and his voice.

'I'm glad to meet you at last,' Richard said. 'And I'm sorry that Tommy never told me anything about you. Especially since you're the one who must be feeling his loss more keenly than anyone.'

Gregory, standing back, noticed Alice blink. He wondered if she had stifled an impulse to turn to him for reassurance.

Richard continued to say the kind of things commonly said at funerals – that it had been a great shock, that his brother had died tragically young. After this he seemed lost for words.

'Yes,' Alice said weakly, 'an accident like that was the last thing that anyone could have expected.'

For a moment Richard looked as if he were about to contradict her, but then he looked directly at Gregory.

'And is this your friend?'

Gregory already knew how he would answer.

'Cousin,' he lied, shaking Richard's hand. 'I never met your brother, but Alice talked about him a lot. I came along to give her some support.'

'There weren't many people here,' Alice said to Richard.

'No. After the police found Tommy's diary I phoned every address. I didn't know if it would be a friend or an acquaintance or what it would be. A few of the numbers were out of date. Some of the people who answered couldn't even remember him. And some were colleagues who'd worked on contracts so had known him only a short while. That's why I was really pleased that you could come. Tommy must have meant more to you than he did to anyone else.'

Gregory could not resist agreeing. 'That's right,' he said. 'She was always talking about him – weren't you, Alice?'

'I never stopped,' Alice said.

'I've organized a buffet at a hotel near here,' Richard told them. 'Well, it's a pub, really. I don't think many people will be coming. Two have said they'd definitely be there but they sounded as if they go to funerals just to get a free meal. Look, will you and your cousin—'

'Gregory,' Gregory said.

'Will you come along? You can tell me more about how Tommy spent the last few months.'

Alice hesitated. It seemed desperately sad that there were so few people to reminisce about Thomas, but she knew that the closer she got to Richard, the more dangerous it would be. She had avoided telling him the truth, and now was not the right time to confess it. She had caused enough pain in her life. Perhaps it would be best if she left him believing that Thomas had died in a happy relationship.

Gregory rescued her. 'I'm afraid we have to get back,' he said smoothly. 'Demands of work and all that. Sorry, but I'm sure you understand.'

'Sorry,' Alice said in a hollow echo.

Richard nodded and then appeared to be considering what to do next.

'There are a couple of his things you should have,' he said. 'I left them in the car. They're nothing much, but, well . . .'

Alice swiftly waved a hand in refusal. She did not want her home to be invaded by mementoes of Thomas. She had already packed up everything that she associated with him.

'No, please,' she said, 'they should go to his family. Honestly. I have some of his things at the flat – clothes, books, CDs. You should have them.'

'But you and Tommy lived together,' Richard insisted. 'You know we hardly ever met. You were closer to him than I ever was. There's no family left apart from me. *You* keep his things. What you don't want, give to charity.'

'Are you sure?' Alice asked after a pause.

'Positive.'

She nodded. 'All right. But I don't want whatever was in his rucksack. Or any money.'

Richard was surprised. 'But Thomas *had* no money – didn't you know? His account was almost empty.'

'No, I didn't know that.' Alice looked down. 'All he had to do was ask,' she added.

She did not know if she had spoken the truth. Probably she would have resented continuing to support him.

Richard led them towards a car parked alongside a featureless wall of red brick. Suddenly Alice felt nauseous. Sweeping through her was the vivid realization that on the other side of that wall Thomas's coffin was in place and ready for burning. The furnace door would be closed and a control turned. Within seconds gas jets would incinerate the wood and play upon his body like blow-torches. His skin would peel away like bark from a tree and his fatty tissue would bubble and ignite. Before it disintegrated his skeleton would glow dark as an X-ray against the incandescence. Smoke from his burning would flow from the chimney; she and Gregory and Richard would be breathing it in as they left the site. Soon all that would remain of the man she had once loved would be a scattering of bones being shovelled into a pulverizing mill.

She put out one hand to steady herself against the wall, but it was too far away and her fingers scratched thin air. The asphalt tilted on the parking lot.

Gregory reached out and steadied Alice before she fell. Inside her head there was a sense of lightness, of lifting from the ground. Scared of falling further, she leaned against him as if he were indeed a trusted cousin.

Concerned, Richard asked if she was all right.

'I'll be fine,' she said weakly.

'I understand. You'll take a long time to get over this.'

'Ages,' Gregory said drily.

'Don't worry about me,' Alice insisted.

Richard waited a moment and then spoke in a rush.

'You can be honest with me. Before all this happened, Thomas and you were getting on well together, weren't you? I mean, there weren't any problems?'

Once again Alice wondered if, somehow or other, he had discovered the facts but had concealed his knowledge. Maybe the truth was evident in her face.

'You must have a reason for asking that,' she said.

'Do you mind the question?'

'Of course she doesn't,' Gregory said.

'We were all right,' Alice answered, and then waited a moment. 'Yes, we were all right,' she said again, as if repetition were a guarantee of honesty.

Richard was satisfied. 'I thought you must be. I was pleased that Tommy had, you know, settled down at last. I never could. It's good to know he was happy before he died.'

'Is there something we don't know?' Gregory asked.

Richard pressed the key to unlock the car boot.

'When he was younger – when he was *a lot* younger – he had black moods. Severely black moods. It was easy to undermine his confidence. I wasn't the only one who knew how to do that because a lot of us were guilty of it. It took Tommy weeks to get out of those moods – sometimes longer. When he was in them, he used to say things he shouldn't have said. To make everyone else feel guilty, I suppose.'

Gregory expressed what was not being spoken.

'You mean he threatened suicide?'

'Often.'

Alice shuddered. 'He can't have done that. He didn't leave a note.'

'That's right,' Richard said, 'he didn't.'

'You told me that the police said there was food in his rucksack.

That he must have slipped and fallen and hit his head while trying to fill a bottle with water.'

'That's what it looked like.'

'The empty bottle was still there beside the river.'

'Yes.'

'Richard, there were still places that Thomas wanted to see. He was desperate to see them. It was an *accident*. There's no reason to think anything else.'

'I'm sure you're right,' Richard said quietly, in a way that both Alice and Gregory took to mean that he was not completely convinced. He opened the car boot fully.

'I thought you'd like his camera and his map,' he explained. 'I've scrolled through his photos. There are a few inside a flat – the one he shared with you, I suppose – but with no one there. Not a soul. I don't know why he would do that.'

Gregory improvised. 'Maybe you were planning to redecorate,' he said to Alice.

'That was the idea,' she agreed, and Richard went on.

'After those there are dozens and dozens of photographs of the places that he visited. I have no idea where they are. They all look the same to me.'

Once more, Alice hesitated.

'Thanks,' Gregory said, picking up the map and glancing at it. 'He's marked this,' he added.

'Yes, he made notes all over it. His wristwatch, would you like? His address book? He had two archaeology books in his ruck-sack – do you want those?'

'Richard,' Alice insisted, 'I have lots of things to remember your brother by. I really don't need anything else.'

'Apart from the Kodak and the map,' Gregory said quickly,

holding out his hand for the camera. 'I'll take care of it,' he said as soon as it was passed over.

'There was another thing,' Richard added cautiously. Alice noticed him tense a little, as though anticipating a dismissive reaction.

They waited. Richard looked up at the crematorium roof and then back at them. She wondered if he was looking for smoke.

'There's a memorial garden here,' he said.

They waited until Richard continued.

'I was going to have the ashes buried there. The undertaker said he would see to it. And they'll put a plaque on the wall. It'll be durable plastic because people steal the brass ones.'

Alice glanced at Gregory, but he did not look back at her.

'But maybe,' Richard went on, then stopped, then started again. 'Maybe Tommy would have wanted his ashes scattered in a different place. Maybe he said something to you about it.'

'No, he didn't. Why should he?'

Richard shrugged.

'He must have believed that his death was years away,' Alice said.

'I suppose so. Yes.'

Not knowing how to answer him further, Alice turned to Gregory. 'What did you do with your wife's ashes?'

'I buried them where we had been happiest,' he said.

'I thought, perhaps,' Richard said tentatively, 'one of those ancient sites that so fascinated him – you know, circles, mounds, things like that, the ones in his photos . . .' His voice tailed off. 'But maybe not,' he added defensively.

Once the suggestion had been made, it seemed to Alice that this was the best ethical solution. It would be fitting if all that remained of Thomas were interred in a place that had informed his ambition. It was the least he deserved.

'You're right,' she agreed. 'Why don't you do that?'

'But I don't know anything about archaeology. We were very different people, and what interested Tommy never interested me. If you shared his life, you must have shared his interests — at least to some extent. So I thought that maybe you would have the best idea.' And before Alice could answer he went on, rushing out his suggestion so that the words collided with each other. 'And I thought that you would like to do it — bury his ashes at one of his favourite places, I mean. Or scatter them there. Whatever's best.'

'I don't know if I want to do that.'

'It seems right to me,' Richard insisted. 'I don't have to be there. In fact it's probably better that I'm not. I don't even need to know where the site is. Because I think it's something that should be done by the person closest to him. And that's you. It could be your secret. I wouldn't mind.'

Even his own brother wasn't concerned, Alice thought. Thomas had been more alone than she had ever fully realized. He had always needed someone; even his remains still needed someone.

'What do you think?' she asked Gregory.

'Maybe it would just be best if they were scattered in the memorial garden. Look, let's be frank, Thomas is dead. He's not going to know or care where his ashes are.'

'But you felt a duty to your wife to leave her at the right place,' Alice said. 'Maybe this is about duty.'

Gregory said nothing. His suspicion was confirmed: Thomas was a problem even in death.

The three of them stood together and said nothing until Richard looked at his watch.

'I have to go,' he said. 'Maybe you can think about it and let me know. If you can decide within the next hour or so that would help.'

Alice came to a decision.

'You're right,' she said. 'Thomas shouldn't be left here. He should be somewhere else. Somewhere that he would want to be.' She turned back to Gregory. 'We should do what you did – take him to where he would have been happy.'

Richard's relief and eagerness were apparent.

'And you'll do that?' he asked, far too quickly.

'Of course.'

'And once we've got the ashes to you, I can forget them?'

'Yes,' Alice said. 'Yes, you can forget them. I'll make sure they go to the right place.'

Richard leaned forward. For a moment she thought he was about to kiss her, but instead of that he grasped her hand in both of his.

'I was never a true friend to my brother,' he said, 'but I always wished him well. You were good for Tommy. I'm so happy that he met you. You knew what was right for him. You still do.'

She nodded. The muscles in her neck felt stiff. Richard went on.

'It's sad that you didn't have a lot more time together. You must have really loved each other.'

There was no point now in telling Richard the truth. She lied to keep him content.

'Yes,' she said, 'we did.'

Minute after minute the procession of bleak, lifeless photographs slid across Gregory's screen. At the beginning of each section he halted their progress and consulted Thomas's OS map. After this he searched the internet for images that would confirm Alice's provisional identification of the locations; she needed to be certain that each stage of Thomas's final journey had been correctly tracked. Perhaps, Gregory thought, a file of digital images and a map covered in handwritten jottings were to be her dead lover's only memorial.

During this period there were three incoming calls to the office. On each occasion Cassie pointedly greeted the caller by name so that her father would know who was ringing. None was unimportant, but Gregory shook his head in dismissal and continued his research. Cassie had to promise each time that he would call back as soon as he could. Gregory had not noticed, but she was wearing her mother's necklace for the first time since he had borrowed it to photograph Alice.

There was little pattern in Thomas's map. It appeared that although his route had been initially systematic it had soon degenerated into unpredictability. Rather than pursue an itinerary based on rational topography, he had instead been prone to impulse. Sometimes he had travelled to sites that were miles away from each other and returned later to ones he had overlooked. In the final days he appeared to have crossed his own tracks several times. Alice had speculated that this might have been the result of transport difficulties, and cited infrequent bus services and poor availability of accommodation. Although Gregory had not disputed this he believed that the doomed journey's haphazard nature was the product of a disordered mind that could no longer comprehend its best course of action.

The very last photographs were of a wheel-head cross that was so tall and spindly that Thomas had evidently had difficulty fitting it all into the frame. He had also taken several close-ups of patterns and images carved into its sandstone surfaces. Although much of the detail had weathered, Gregory could identify a tree in full leaf, a snake and several human figures, one with its arms outstretched. Only when he checked further did he discover that these were representations of the sacred ash tree that supports the world, the serpent that surrounds it, and a depiction of a cruci-fied man. The cross was an amalgam of pagan and Christian mythology, with the crucifixion sharing the same column as the battle between the Norse gods.

Gregory telephoned Alice from his mobile. She told him that she understood why the cross would have intrigued Thomas; one of his interests had been the cultural impact of belief systems. New beliefs, he had claimed, entered a community first as threat, then as distortion and finally as transformation. Alice suspected that he had seen that process illustrated in the carvings.

Gregory knew that what concerned Alice most of all was that the photographic record stopped in that churchyard. The cross was its terminal point. There were no images of Thomas's planned destination.

'I know where the cross is,' Gregory told her. 'The date on the photos and the notations on the map correspond.'

'He was on his way to Sampson's Bratfull,' Alice said.

'That's what it looks like.'

'But he never got there. If he had done, he'd have photog-raphed it.'

'That sounds right.'

Alice did not answer. Some extraneous noise, perhaps an echo, rustled in his ear.

Until quite recently Gregory would have been bemused by

the name of Sampson's Bratfull, and would have assumed that it was fictitious until he was shown it on a map. And if he had then researched the mound further he would have judged it to be un-interesting and of marginal archaeological interest. Now, as the place towards which Alice's last lover had been heading when he drowned, the location assumed an importance that he could scarcely measure.

Evidence on the Bratfull was scant. Internet photographs showed a concentration of stones set on a drab, marshy, desolate moor. According to posted comment, the modest scale of the mound had disappointed passing walkers. If it had been a tumulus, Gregory thought, it must originally have been much higher; perhaps builders of stone walls or believers in pagan religions had cannibalized it over the decades. There was agreement that the name originated in a folk tale in which a giant let stones fall from his overloaded apron as he strode across the high moor. The sixteenth-century spelling of Sampson, and the Old English and Gaelic name for cloak, *brat*, testified to the antiquity of the myth. Some sources, however, claimed that it was not an earthly giant who was carrying the stones, but the devil.

'It's a rather unprepossessing site,' he told her.

'That's not the point,' Alice said.

'I mean that it's possible he got there and just didn't think it was worth photographing. Those stones wouldn't have caught my attention. There are collapsed sheepfolds all across the moor. The place is just littered with stones.'

'But Thomas recorded everything else, didn't he? So why *wouldn't* he have taken photos of Sampson's Bratfull? No, he can't have reached it. I'm sure of that. Did you study the map?'

The landline rang. Cassie picked it up and looked across to Gregory with raised eyebrows.

'Is that someone calling you?' Alice asked. 'I don't want to get in the way of business.'

Gregory shifted his hold on the mobile. 'They can wait,' he told her. 'There are a couple of bridges on the map, Bleng bridge and an upper one across the same river. His water bottle was found next to the upper one. He could have been on his way to the Bratfull, or coming back.'

Cassie raised her voice so that it carried across the room.

'Yes,' she told her caller, 'that's Gregory Pharaoh you can hear speaking on the other line. But he shouldn't be too long. Unless I can help?'

'Is that your daughter?' Alice asked.

'Yes. Go on.'

'The police told Richard that the river was in spate. It would have been easy to miss your footing. Thomas never reached Sampson's Bratfull. He never got to where he wanted to be.'

Cassie was making a note on her pad. 'I don't know,' she told her caller, 'he may be away on those dates.'

Alice spoke again.

'It's the right place for Thomas,' she said. 'I *know* it's the right place.'

'It's a long way,' Gregory said. He was already thinking about what could happen.

'Will you arrange things? Please?'

It was not in his interest to refuse. Once Thomas's ashes had been scattered then a door would be closed on the past. And Gregory imagined a comfortable, discreet hotel in a quiet part of the country, far enough away from the collapsing tumulus for Alice to be able to forget it easily, with crisp sheets and old furniture and soft bedside lights that filled the room with warm shadows.

And he thought of her body, a body that he had studied and recorded, and the presence that had tantalized him, and that Alice Fell would be his and his alone for as long as he wanted her.

'Yes,' he said, 'I'll fix everything.'

He ended the call at the same time as Cassie was ending hers.

'As soon as possible,' she said as she hung up.

Gregory returned his attention to the screen. After a while Cassie spoke again. As if in reproof, she had rested her fingers on the curve of her mother's necklace.

'You have to give me some answers.'

'Is there anything urgent?'

'It depends if you're going away next week. Are you?'

'Cassie, I know you disapprove.'

'It doesn't matter if I do.'

'And you think I'm too old to be behaving like this.'

'I can't see why you have to drop important work and drive half across England just to scatter the ashes of someone you never even met.'

Gregory ignored the comment. 'We shouldn't refuse a lucrative contract even if it has to be completed next week. You could do it. I'm happy with that. You're very capable.'

'I know I am. But I'm covering for you more and more.'

'One of these days I'll stop doing this job. But the business will continue.'

'Photographers are like actors – they die in harness. Dad, you haven't even asked what the project is.'

'Do I need to know? Is it something that I really should be shooting?'

Cassie considered for a few seconds before answering. 'I don't suppose it is, no.'

'Well then, you do it. With my blessing.'

'And the exhibition? You have to start finalizing the selection soon. You can't put that off. It's essential.'

'You could help me with that, too. Oh, and I need to sort out a hotel. For next week.'

Cassie was silent. Gregory studied the carvings on the wheel-head cross as he waited for her to volunteer. The crucified man lay within the sandstone, his Norse features as blank as those of a chessboard king.

'I'll arrange your hotel,' Cassie said at last. 'I'll find one that you'll like. Just tell me your preferred location.'

'Thanks.' Gregory paused for a moment and then apologized. 'I'm being unreasonable. I should make my own booking. You must feel you're colluding with something you don't want to happen.'

'That's one way of putting it. Another way is to say that I'm helping you get through your little bit of madness as quickly as possible, because once you've come out the other side then things will get back to normal. And I like things to be normal. A double room?'

'Let's leave it as two singles.'

'How cautious of you,' Cassie said drily.

'I mean it. You know, before you met Alice I was certain that you would like each other.'

'How could we, when we understand each other so well?'

'You don't really.'

'Dad, let's say that you think you can discover parts of her character by staring at her body through your lens, but that I can see other parts just by looking straight into her eyes. Why don't I just book you a double room? Won't that be simpler? Get it over with?'

'If you dislike her so much, then why are you so keen that we sleep together?'

'You know why. You're not very interested in women as individuals. You like them as types, as examples of some aspects of femininity that you're fascinated by and yet don't know all that much about. So losing them doesn't affect you very deeply.'

'That's not true,' Gregory insisted, and yet he thought that his daughter could be right. After Ruth's death, had he retreated from the particular to the generalized, from depth to surface, from commitment to indifference, from wise man to fool?

'Dad, Alice Fell is a schemer. She's not enigmatic and she's not challenging. Once you've slept together, she'll lose her allure – it'll fall away like a broken shell. You'll wake up and see that her ambitions are selfish and ordinary. The sooner that happens, the better.'

Gregory tapped a finger against the edge of his keyboard. 'Let's keep it as two singles.' After a few seconds he went on, 'I have to consider what happened to Thomas. Nothing will change until after his ashes are scattered.'

Cassie crooked her finger through the necklace.

'If you think about how he died,' she said, 'then it must be even more obvious why I don't trust her.'

Cassie returned Gregory's steady gaze as she continued.

'That man must have been very naïve. He was probably convinced that she was the love of his life. Even worse, he must have persuaded himself that she felt the same. It's obvious when you look at it. Thomas killed himself because of how Alice treated him.'

'That isn't what anyone else thinks.'

'Dad, you *must* know that's what happened. I don't need to hear any more detail to know that's true.'

'People don't kill themselves for love.'

'You don't think so?'

'I know it.'

Gregory believed that he had lost more than Thomas would ever have had, and yet he could never have thrown himself into a river. If he had done that he would have betrayed Ruth as well as Cassie.

'You've always had reasons to live, Dad. Maybe Thomas Laidlaw couldn't find any.'

Gregory shrugged and his eyes strayed to the screen again. He had no wish to extend the conversation any further.

'Maybe,' he said. 'In the end all that matters is that he's dead.'

He had already lost interest in Cassie's opinion, because it arose from observation and not experience. No one would ever know what had really happened to Thomas, and yet his daughter wanted to blame Alice for his death. Gregory decided that this was because she wanted to protect him; she was worried that he would take a path that would be similarly irrational.

Cassie was settled and at ease in a predictable life; Gregory accepted that. But he saw no need to be so wary in the closing stages of his own life; instead all that he saw was the necessity of satisfying a longing that refused to let him rest.

11

The road became narrow as it threaded its way between bushes, fences and trees. Gregory drove slowly, half expecting to meet an oncoming vehicle that would make him reverse to the last passing-place, but the way ahead remained deserted. Alice sat in silence, sometimes turning her head to look out of the windows. She had last spoken when he had taken shots of the cross in the churchyard. As soon as he had lowered the camera she had asked him to leave it locked in the car boot from then on. Alice did not think it right that he should make a visual record of the place where Thomas had died; and besides, she would never wish to be reminded of it. Gregory had reluctantly agreed, for without a camera he always felt strangely unmanned.

He stopped the car on an area of gravel, puddles and compacted earth marked by tyre tracks. Dead leaves were plastered on the drying mud like faded messages.

'It seems that from now on we walk,' he said.

Once the car doors were open Alice looked around and then glanced up at the sky. Little of it could be seen between the high trees. The river could be clearly heard as it coursed behind a raised bank colonized by saplings and scrub.

'Will it rain, do you think?' she asked.

'This doesn't feel like a place that avoids bad weather,' Gregory said. He handed Alice her waterproof jacket and then put on his own.

'There's something in the air. Don't you feel it?'

'I'd check the lacing on your boots,' he suggested by way of an answer, and bent to check his own.

Alice had last worn outdoor clothing when she had visited archaeological remains with Thomas, and for almost a year it had remained unused and half-forgotten in a cupboard. She had not wanted to wear it now, but Gregory had insisted. She felt cumbersome, unattractive, and with boots that were far too heavy.

He lifted his rucksack from the back seat, hoisted it on his back, and adjusted the straps over his shoulders. Spare sweaters had been packed beside the urn, but it still felt unwieldy and oddly shaped against his back.

'Should I carry the pack?' Alice asked.

'I don't mind.'

'I thought that maybe you wanted me to do that. After all, you didn't know Thomas.'

'I don't want you to do anything. What's important is what *you* want. When we get there you can be the one who empties it. – if you think you should.'

'I don't even know if I should do that. The truth is that I'm only here because no one else would bring Thomas to where he should be. But after the argument we had when we split up . . .'

She stopped and then started again.

'I had to tell him things that were very hurtful. There was no choice.'

Gregory nodded briskly. Alice had made similar remarks several times, and there was little point in entering another discussion now. He wanted the ashes carried to where they would be scattered, and once the job was done he wanted to return to the hotel as quickly as possible. The disposal of what little was left of Thomas Laidlaw would close off that part of the past. Afterwards, her duty discharged, freed from guilt and memory, Alice would wish to delay no longer. Gregory's single room was big enough for the purpose, or he could go to hers.

His imagination had already excited itself with possibilities. Secretly he had rehearsed how to make their first bout of lovemaking uninhibited and exhausting. He hoped that running through Alice's mind there would be a similarly adventurous heat: imperative, overwhelming, but as yet unexpressed.

They walked side by side down a short stretch of metalled road alongside huge trees whose shadows had starved the earth around their roots. In a field on their left a white horse stood motionless as it watched them pass.

Gregory had studied the map closely. 'The lower crossing should be here,' he said, and after a few more yards Bleng bridge came into view. They walked over it without pause and immediately came to a fork in the road. A board pointed to the right with the name of Scalderskew Farm painted on it. They stood looking at it for a moment.

'Thomas must have taken the forestry road,' Alice said, reiterating their understanding as if she expected a challenge. 'If he'd gone to the left he'd have reached Sampson's Bratfull before he got to the upper bridge. Is that right?'

'According to the map, yes.'

'And he can't have done that because there are no photographs of the Bratfull. I've thought about this and even if he'd been disappointed I'm certain he would have taken some. You agree?'

'If you think so.'

'So if we go to the right then we follow in his footsteps.'

'All right,' Gregory said, adjusting his pack again. 'The quicker we move the sooner we'll get back.'

At first the road climbed so steeply that they had to lean forward to obtain a better purchase on the surface. Gregory dropped back a little and studied Alice from behind. He liked seeing the movement of her limbs as she pressed onward, because he could not help but think of her naked body angled in such a way. And then he luxuriated once more in the memory of how, undressed, she had paced across a room that was hushed by dustsheets, had willingly laid her body open to his lens, had spoken with a goading frankness that had keyed up his sexual expectations. By now he had studied those photographs many times, stared at tableaux that both challenged his gaze and questioned it, become absorbed in her eyes and nipples, skin and hair, the shaping of ivory and shadow.

He could tell that Alice felt a satisfying pleasure in her own movements. Even the thick clothing that she wore could not fully mask her feline pride. When they returned to the hotel she could throw that clothing to one side. Would he be able to strip her with the slow, easy confidence of his many past seductions? Would she encourage him to linger over each part of her flesh as he laid it bare?

Already he imagined the texture of the nape of her neck, the curve of her hip beneath his hand, the taste of her lips, the sway of her breasts, the feral heat of her vulva. As lovers, could they be as thorough and exploratory as it was possible to be? Would she relish his timing, his touch, his attention to detail?

They laboured upwards in silence. Neither spoke. The only sounds were of their footfalls on the gritty road, their breathing and the distant muffled noise of water.

After a few minutes they came to a point where they could stand on the road's grassy edge and look down. Trees with fanned-out roots clung to a precipitous and gloomy slope. Through the dark trunks, a few hundred feet below, the riverside path could be distinguished. Water glittered across its surface like a glaze.

'It looks as if the river has burst its banks,' Alice said.

'I see it.'

'Maybe that's why he was forced to take this road.'

'Maybe.'

'If he'd gone that way, down there, he'd have been able to fill his water bottle easily.'

'Alice, you can't spend your life thinking of things that never happened.'

'You think not? I think it makes sense to always wonder why.'

Ever since they had begun the journey Alice had been brooding once more on the workings of what others called chance. If Thomas had been able to take the lower path then he would have reached his destination and returned by the same route. He need never have seen, or crossed, or paused by the upper bridge. He need never have scrambled down what had been reported to her as a steep, dangerous slope. He would not have slipped and fallen into the torrent. He would still be alive.

And yet she did not wish to believe that Thomas's death was an unforeseen consequence of chance decisions and events; she had to believe that it concealed a hidden purpose. People did not die without reason; individuals were never pointlessly destroyed. There was a kind of celestial mechanism that gave meaning to everything, even if that truth often remained hidden. Whether or not Thomas had committed suicide – and Alice was certain he had not – his death must be part of a design whose pattern she could not yet read. And perhaps, she thought, it was not intended that she should ever read it. Maybe the signs were designed to be understood by someone else. It was even possible, but unlikely, that it was Gregory who was the most important person on this pilgrimage.

They were considerably higher now, and the landscape opened out so that raw moorland could be seen in the gaps beyond the regimented plantations of spruce. The choked roadside ditches ran with thin streams.

'The air's so heavy,' Alice protested. 'This jacket feels cumbersome.'

'I think it's going to rain. Better keep it on.'

Gregory studied the scenery to either side. He could make no interesting compositions from it; there was an exhausted monotony about everything. Bracket fungus jutted from the trunks of trees and spongy moss grew across mulch. Sometimes the edges of the road had been carved into raw banks by heavy machinery, and spindly black roots of bracken protruded from these like dead feelers. High above the moor two buzzards circled slowly against a sky that had become so low and bruised that all of the colours bent towards a jaundiced yellow. It felt as if the world itself was running down.

'I'm tired and my boots hurt,' Alice said.

'For God's sake, you knew this wouldn't be a stroll in the park.'

The vigour of Gregory's response was surprising even to him. Irritation bled from his words as if they had been cut.

She did not respond. Gregory felt the shape of the urn against his back. He considered apologizing, but did not. To one side were a dozen or so trees that must have been toppled years before. Their grey roots were dry and brittle and their bark was sheathed in moss.

Maybe Cassie had been correct, Gregory thought. After all, in the past she had often been proved right. And his daughter had never expressed an opinion, or given advice, that had been in bad faith. There was only one reason that he was toiling up this bleak slope with a dead man's ashes on his back. If he had not been so obsessed by Alice Fell, he would have refused.

A piece of stone cracked beneath his boot. He was thirsty. The air had grown heavier and beneath his waterproof clothing he was clammy.

'Let's drink,' he said, taking a bottle of water from a rucksack pocket and opening the top. 'You first.'

Alice took it from him and tilted back her head to drink. The skin of her throat was an unblemished white. Gregory imagined her head thrown back in pleasure.

When she handed the bottle back he could see that she was thinking of Thomas.

'I know,' he said. 'Never set off without a supply of water.'

'You could tell I was thinking him. There's no need to underline it.'

Alice was ahead by several steps before he could return the bottle to his pack. Her boots crunched softly on the grit.

Gregory had no idea what kind of person Thomas Laidlaw had been. He could not know if Alice had spoken the truth about him. Probably, he thought, Cassie was right – Alice had encouraged Thomas to feel more for her than she had been able to feel for him. Maybe that was a pattern in her life. Alice courted the attention of men and encouraged their love. As soon as they were helpless, she lost interest. Maybe, Gregory brooded, she was more like him than he had ever been willing to admit.

And if Cassie were right about Alice, she was right that Gregory had been foolish in allowing himself to be captivated. The only hidden depth in Alice was one of ambition. The best thing to happen would be for them to share a bed for a night, maybe several nights, and then part. She would care nothing for him and he should care nothing for her. His fascination had been an error, an aberration. Cassie's insight was valid; as soon as he had slept with Alice the truth would become obvious. Satisfaction would generate clarity.

They stopped for a few moments while he consulted the map again. The only mark that Thomas had made on the land between the courses of the Calder and the Bleng was a thin box that he had drawn around his destination. Every other site that he had visited had a date and time noted beside it, but there was nothing beside Sampson's Bratfull.

'According to this we should come to a fork quite soon. When we do, we need to take the forestry road to the left. The other one eventually leads you out to the main road to Wasdale.'

'And Thomas's bridge?'

'Maybe another ten minutes after the fork. It's difficult to tell.'

They set off again. The ground had flattened now, and above the geometry of the conifer plantations they could see the high bare moor that separated the two rivers. Beneath their feet the road was still broken stone and gritty mud. A spine of bright green turf ran along its centre, untouched by the wheels of timber lorries and Land Rovers.

Alice resented Gregory taking control of the map. She could read city plans easily but was less confident with contours and bridleways; nevertheless she had come to the conclusion that she should have insisted on carrying and studying Thomas's map. She would have been happier if Gregory did not act as if they were on an expedition. And although Alice had initially been pleased that he had volunteered to carry the urn, she had begun to feel that that, in ways that she could not fully rationalize, it was she who should take it to the tumulus where the ashes would be scattered.

Perhaps Gregory had adopted the role of guide to ingratiate himself, or perhaps it was an extension of his need to control. He had never regarded her as a true equal. Instead he had been driven by his need; Alice had always found that obvious. And yet Gregory's desire had always been expressed through his professional activities. His compulsion to photograph lay like a grid across everything. She had asked him not to bring his camera now, and he had agreed; but would he have consented to leave it aside for a longer period? Gregory had always kept a distance from the world by studying it through a lens; was he even capable of living without a camera?

It was not so long ago that she had thought of warning him. Remembering the distress that she had caused past lovers, Alice had wanted to look hard into Gregory's eyes and tell him not to fall in love with her too deeply. If he had asked why, she would have been honest. Because, she would have said, I cause pain that no one ever expects to suffer.

But now Alice believed that she must have misjudged Gregory.

He would never suffer pain; it was not in his nature. His only reactions would be of inconvenience, irritation, and perhaps embarrassment. He was incapable of the anguish that Alice was secretly proud of causing. Gregory could shrug off his love for her, just as he must have shrugged off his affairs with countless other women who had been mercenary and vain enough to sleep with him.

They came to the fork. The road ahead continued across fields of recently planted trees, their tips only about six feet from the ground, towards a wall of mature woods several hundred yards away. From within it came the sounds of a motor, rising and falling in tone. It reminded Alice of how, sprawled on the pavement, she had heard the robbers' motorbike roar away from her.

'What's that?'

'Forestry workers must be logging up there, but that's not the way that we're going. This looks like the road we want.'

They stood in a turning circle of packed soil and shale, its far edge indented with the broken chevrons of tractor tyres. Another road led down from the circle, bending round the side of a turf bank and then dipping out of sight as it followed the valley contours back in the direction of the river.

Gregory adjusted the straps on his rucksack. 'The upper bridge can't be far now,' he said, setting off again.

The road became steeper. Streams draining from the moorland ran along narrow man-made channels on their right. To their left a broad area of logged-out plantation opened up. Hundreds of ragged stumps, bleached as if they had been submerged, stuck out of a slope strewn with decaying pine needles and lopped brushwood.

'Listen,' Alice said.

Gregory looked at her. He could still hear the chainsaw whine in the far distance.

'It's the river,' she told him.

It was true; the Bleng could be heard again as it rushed through its channel beyond the harvested trees.

'I felt we were getting near,' she said.

When the upper bridge came into view it was disappointingly bare and functional. Both Alice and Gregory had imagined that in some undefined way it must be distinctive. Instead the bridge was nothing more than a broad unadorned concrete slab laid down across abutments to link one drab section of road with the next.

'Are you sure this is it?'

'No doubt about it,' Gregory said. 'Look how the land rises on the far side. Sampson's Bratfull must be beyond the next plantation.'

They walked down the slope, its angle making them unconsciously gather pace. Alice's boots had begun to chafe and she was increasingly uncomfortable. The noise of the river grew ever louder.

When Gregory stepped onto the bridge it made a hard unyielding sound. He took a few paces forward and then stopped just short of the lip at the edge of the slab. Dry mud had thrown its shallow depressions and furrows into relief, so that he appeared to be standing on the dispersing outlines of a carpet. Beneath him the Bleng tumbled between steep banks and boulders before flowing out of sight behind the trees.

Now Gregory decided that if they could empty the urn within the next few minutes, without further thought or ceremony, the ashes would vanish immediately. He and Alice could stand together as if in prayer for a short while longer and then they could go back, never again to set foot in this bleak, forsaken place.

'He must have climbed down here,' he said, and pointed down the rake of earth and shale to his right. 'Look how narrow they cut that channel. You can imagine what this would have been like after all that rain. Any increase in volume would force water high up those sides.'

Alice walked uneasily towards the edge, but then stood back from it. The air was heavy and relentless.

She had expected to be emotional at the site of Thomas's death. She was ready to be stricken by feelings of sadness and waste, and had even thought that she might feel disabled by guilt. Instead there was a blankness inside her imagination, as if she had completed a journey to an oracle and now found that she no longer needed to hear it speak. When she looked down into the river it seemed to have little to do with Thomas. It had been deserted by the past. The water that had carried him away was long gone and part of an ocean by now.

'There's a kind of shelf there, towards the bottom of that slope,' Gregory went on. 'It's narrow but we could stand on it. Do you want to go down?'

Alice shook her head.

'It would be difficult, but we could do it. Probably that's where he fell.'

After she did not answer, Gregory took his chance.

'You once told me that Thomas was fascinated by rivers. We could even empty the urn down there. If you wanted to.'

'No,' she said quickly, 'I don't want to do that.'

The peaty water rushed and drummed and swirled beneath them. As if readying himself to wait for several minutes, Gregory folded his arms and stood with his legs further apart.

He was growing weary of the journey, and had no desire to trudge even further along such a featureless track. Sampson's Bratfull held no attraction for him. Wherever Alice chose to throw the ashes, he would be content for the act to be done as quickly as possible. Afterwards, they would be able to return to the safety of the car and then to the warmth and privacy of the hotel. That was the real reason why he was here.

He tried again. 'Or maybe it would be right to scatter him from here,' he said.

'From the bridge?'

'Yes. Why not?'

'Because I promised to scatter them where he wanted to go, that's why.'

'It's your decision,' Gregory said, knowing that he would persist.

For a few moments Alice began to consider the possibility that Thomas had not been meant to reach his destination, that it had somehow been decreed that he should drown here, that the river might have always been his natural end. Perhaps after all it would be fitting to return his ashes to water. But not this water.

And she had made a promise. In her life she had broken many promises, but this was one that it was easy to keep. She had a duty that she was determined to discharge. Besides, if some vestige of Thomas's consciousness still flickered somewhere, then the Bratfull would be where it would want to be left. There was a sense of completion about that, a justice. Her lover's ashes would be disposed of in a way that would fit his life's ambition like a key.

'Do we carry on,' Gregory asked, 'or do you think that the right thing would be to return him to the river and let him be carried along to the sea?'

'He would never reach the sea,' Alice said. 'He'd be dispersed and laid down along the banks with all those tiny particles of silt and mud and peat. Thomas wouldn't want that. He would want his ashes concentrated in part of a mound that's been there for thousands of years, a mound that must have been used for reasons we can only guess at – burials, rituals, communion with the gods. It's the right place.'

To Gregory this made little sense. Alice had stopped loving Thomas months ago. She was under no obligation to his memory. It would have been simpler just to scatter the ashes now. Thomas could not be aware of what was happening to his remains. He was no longer part of the world. It did not even make sense to say that he was oblivious or insensate; he had simply been expunged.

'If I was going to throw his ashes into a river,' Alice went on, 'I'd pick a different one to this.'

'I can see its appeal.'

'Really? Look at the colour of that water. It's like liquid manure.'

They stood in silence for a few more seconds before she spoke again.

'We should move away from here.'

Gregory decided that maybe after all it was best to complete the journey. He did not want Alice to be harried by conscience and decide, perhaps when they were naked and about to make love, that she had somehow betrayed Thomas by not ascending the remaining gradients of this desolate and unvisited moor.

'You're right,' he said briskly, 'it's too exposed. Look at that sky. We should get back to the car before it starts to rain.'

He was still pretending to be a leader, Alice thought.

They crossed the bridge and began to climb the long curve

of hill. In several places the road had decayed into patches of rubble that they stepped across or walked around. The way upwards was a slow, tedious drag that held no pleasure at all. Along the plantation edge to their left were trees that appeared to have exhausted the soil. Several had been marked in spray paint by forestry officials, and these small incomprehensible signs stood out like bright badges on the dull bark. One tree, Alice noticed, had been sundered in a way she could not understand, as a scorched black line ran upwards from the roots to encompass the top of the decapitated trunk.

After a while they came to an indistinct path that led across a patch of bright grass and then plunged down to their left between dark-green trees. Gregory spoke again.

'The other way back. We could have taken that if it hadn't been flooded.'

'Is it shorter?'

'According to the map. But I don't know if there's a way past the river.'

'We can try it. I don't mind getting my feet wet.'

Gregory nodded and pushed onward. He was happy to try the other route; the sooner they were back at the hotel, the better.

Alice remained a pace behind him. In her imagination the water still seethed and roared. She pictured Thomas inert and lifeless among rocks stained the colour of excrement, thrown onto land by the same river that Gregory had suggested he be cast into for a second time. A man who could make such a comment must have an atrophied sense of right, a skewed view of justice and little grasp of harmony. The only thing he really knew about was the balance of tones within an image.

Alice reached a decision. As soon as she had, it seemed that it had been quietly encroaching on her sensibility for days, perhaps weeks.

Whatever happened, she no longer wanted to sleep with Gregory. She did not even want to kiss him; no doubt she would find it unpleasant just to touch him. He was selfish and an irritant. Oh, he was superficially kind, and he had aroused her interest because he was so obviously fascinated by her. But Gregory Pharaoh was an arrogant, conceited man who would never be touched by grace. Alice believed that he must fuck women in the way that he took photographs – with detachment, and as if he were doing them a favour. And all the time he would flatter, lie, tell his subjects what he thought they wanted to hear, and which for much of the time they actually *did* want to hear. Wherever he claimed his heart to be, it was always in his work. He looked at the world through a lens. Every man that Alice had ever loved had also had his heart in his work, but her own heart was always eager to be grasped. It was not her fault that no man had yet been able to hold onto it.

Gregory unfolded the map to study Stockdale Moor again.

'How much further do we have to go?' she asked.

'Not far.'

Alice decided that there was nothing to distinguish Gregory from any of her other lovers. Even his profession was parasitic. It pretended to be an art form, but it was not. It exploited uncertainty and vanity. If it was creative then it was creation at a base level, and scarcely comparable with painting or literature or even theatre. The skills it required were either technical or to do with the optimal selection of already extant visual information. Anyone could easily be trained to be such a judge. The pursuit of the image attracted people of a certain kind; failures willing to reinvent themselves in an unregulated trade. For this they obtained rewards out of all proportion to the effort they were required to put in. Alice was as worthy of better things as she was worthy of a better lover.

And now she saw clearly that she had never been destined to sleep with Gregory. At first she had thought that the phone call to tell her of Thomas's death had meant only that the moment had been postponed. Now she realized that everything had stopped at that instant. It had been not a delay but a termination, not chance but providence. She had been saved.

They crossed a cattle grid with weeds choking the space beneath its bars. Immediately afterwards a stream ran down the hill and vanished into a pipe beneath the road. The land dipped towards where smoke rose from a farm and then rose again in a bleak hill. There was a momentary disturbance of the light beyond the hill, a kind of suffused whiteness that immediately vanished. Alice did not know if this had been an illusion. She waited for it to happen again, but all was unchanged.

Gregory looked at her and then nodded towards the bank of grass and reeds that rose to their right. 'It must be up here,' he said. 'If we keep to the far side of the stream we'll find it easily.'

The boggy turf was scattered with the shiny black droppings of sheep. The flock had trampled areas of exposed mud bordering the stream. For several minutes there was no sign of any tumulus.

Gregory bent forward into the uneven slippery ascent. Sometimes his boots squelched in sodden grass, sometimes they clicked against pieces of rock. At one point he thoughtlessly grasped a handful of reeds and found them to be sharp and unbreakable. When he examined his hand he was relieved to see that it had not been cut. Gregory had a low tolerance of physical pain, and could not understand those who endured or even liked it. Once, one of his lovers had wanted him to hurt her and he had refused.

Quite suddenly he had a fantasy of making love to Alice here, now, in the middle of this barren, inhospitable place. He visualized the two of them, desperate with longing, grasping at each other's clothing to find zips or buttons to yank apart, their hands plunging to the base of each other's bellies, the noise of their agitated breathing pulsing like a beacon across the deserted moor.

It was all down to chance, Gregory believed. Life was random numbers and thrown dice. If the call had not come when he was photographing Alice nude, if she had ignored her phone and if they had been able to consummate their passion among the shrouds of that hushed cell of a room, then an urgent partial coupling on the moor might have been possible. Oblivious to the outside world, clothes only slightly disarranged, they could have masturbated each other into a shuddering frenzy. Perhaps, if she had been willing to kneel on the drenched turf, Alice could even have brought him off with her mouth.

Such wild imaginings excited him and he strode quickly ahead as she followed a few steps behind. As his fantasies deepened and took tighter hold, Gregory found that he was smiling at their energetic variety. Why, he wondered, had he sometimes considered the advantages of relationships with women that were rooted in comradeship rather than sex? Any benefits would be spurious. He was getting old, he no longer possessed the energy he had once had, and in another few years he would no longer be able to seduce his models with confidence and ease. He should make the most of whatever opportunities might remain. There would not be many. There was no time for hesitation or conscience. His personal winter was moving ever closer.

'This must be it,' Alice said.

Gregory looked up. Ahead was a heap of dirty white stone. It resembled a tall broad wall that was slowly collapsing into a low mound. He had almost walked onto it without realizing. He stopped and surveyed the area.

'Sampson's Bratfull,' he announced.

'It's not much to look at,' Alice said, and glanced away for a few seconds as if she did not want to study the tumulus too closely.

She must be disappointed, Gregory thought. No doubt she had imagined something imposing, and not this almost formless heap of rubble. He would understand if Alice felt cheated and became angry.

The bleak, dull moor stretched away around them, its only points of light infrequent gleams from water droplets clinging to moss and reeds. The bruised sky seemed low enough to touch.

'We should walk round it,' Alice said.

'It's going to look the same wherever we stand.'

'A circular walk is better. I don't know why, but it seems the right thing to do.'

Together they paced the edge of the tumulus, threading their way through dark spears of grass that rose in clumps at the edges of the mound. At its far side they paused and fell silent.

Alice put her fingers to her mouth and pulled her bottom lip fractionally downwards before releasing it. She did this without thinking, and then remembered it was a habit she had formed as a child, lost in her adolescence and had not repeated for years.

'Is this what you expected?' Gregory asked.

He wondered if his voice carried any of the amused cynicism

that he felt. They had come this far to find an object that was uninspiring and unremarkable. Even the singularity of the name was inaccurate; Sampson's Bratfull was nothing more than a ragged plurality of rocks.

But something puzzled Alice. 'It's odd,' she said, 'but it seems that there's something not quite right.'

'Considering what we had to do to get here, I wouldn't call it odd. Misguided, maybe. Or foolish. We've treated this hike as if it were a pilgrimage.'

'Duty isn't an emotion that you know much about, is it?'

The remark did not sting and Gregory did not respond.

'All the way round,' Alice insisted.

They continued to circle the mound until they reached the point where they had first stopped in front of it.

Gregory shucked the rucksack from his back and set it on the jumble of stones at the edge of the Bratfull. He pushed it down slightly so that it lodged more securely.

'Time for you to do that duty,' he told her.

Alice took a step back from the edge. The earth gave a damp sigh beneath her weight. She clasped her arms around herself apprehensively. The sickly light made her face bloodless. Gregory unfastened the rucksack.

'I mean it,' she insisted.

'Mean what?'

'I just feel that there's something wrong. I don't know why. If I knew I would tell you.'

Gregory was dismissive. 'Nerves,' he said. 'It's understandable. After all, you shared your life with this man and now you have to get rid of him in the most basic of ways. I wouldn't worry. It'll only take a few seconds.'

He drew the urn from the rucksack. It, too, was unprepossessing, a plastic flask with a moulded handle, looking almost as if it had been picked from a supermarket shelf. The brown plastic body was as dark as loam, the screw top the colour of cinders.

For all the baroque ritual of a funeral service, Gregory thought, the end point of every ceremony was remarkably trivial. Pouring ashes from a container like this would be an action that was almost domestic in its lack of resonance. The final disposal of Thomas Laidlaw would lack any overwhelming sense of meaning. It would be as easy and as thoughtless as pouring powder into a washing machine.

'Is it all right?' Alice asked.

As an answer, Gregory raised the flask in the air as though weighing it.

'Are you ready?' he asked.

Alice glanced round as if she expected another figure to suddenly join them. She could feel a tingling on the exposed parts of her skin, and when she touched the zip on her jacket it gave a tiny little snap, as if discharging static. Just as she had become determined never to sleep with Gregory, she now saw the impossibility of handling Thomas's ashes. In bringing them this far she had discharged her promise. She did not care what happened to them now.

Alice experienced a surge of relief. Thomas had held her sense of duty in his dead hands, but now they relaxed and her promise fell away. At long last he had become indistinguishable from all her other lovers. He had joined them in an irrecoverable and unvisited past.

'I can't do it,' she said.

Gregory put one foot on the bottom of the mound and turned to her like an instructor, his arms slightly spread. He spoke with amused disbelief.

'Of course you can.'

She shook her head. 'No. I can't.'

He unscrewed the top and held it away from the flask like a magician demonstrating a prop at the beginning of a trick.

'It's easy. You don't even have to climb up on the stones. Just stand here at the edge and tip out the contents. Look at the design of the neck – they'll pour out steadily and evenly.'

'You do it.'

Gregory faked a laugh. 'You said you wanted to.'

'I know I did. But I changed my mind.'

A gust of wind swept across them, bending the reeds, rustling their clothes, tangling Alice's hair, and then died around them as if the air would never move again. Gregory glanced at the sky and then looked back.

'You know what to do,' Alice said. 'You've done it before, with your wife.'

'That was different.'

One way or the other, he didn't care how Thomas's remains would be scattered. With Ruth he had been gentle, reverential, and had taken his time. Even though Gregory had no belief in an afterlife, and no conception of a divine presence in the world, he could in those moments have been mistaken for a scrupulous and devout believer.

'Please do it,' Alice said.

'You're sure?'

She nodded. Gregory tested the stability of the rock beneath his feet.

'Where do you think? So that the ashes will fall down and disappear inside the mound?'

'Yes. Yes, that's right.'

Gregory stepped onto the stones. They were uneven and unsafe beneath his feet, but he was confident that he could empty the flask in one smooth unbroken movement and then step back onto the ground. The air was motionless and oppressive. He held the flask as near to the uppermost stones and as far away from his body as he could. He did not want any of the ashes to drop on his clothes or his boots.

'Right,' he said.

The ashes fell smoothly. Their speckled and variegated grains cascaded between the stones. A fine dust drifted from them like a final offering. Within a few seconds all that remained of Thomas Laidlaw had vanished into the mound.

Gregory turned. His lips began to tingle unpleasantly with tiny needle-like shocks. He wanted to say 'That's it,' but unaccountably his mouth refused to open.

Around him the moor began to warp, as if he were viewing it from under water. There was a pressure beneath him that he felt could lift him free of the earth. Nothing was real and nothing could be understood.

His body was engulfed by a flame white as a furnace. Blindness fell like an avalanche into his eyes. He was transfixed within a roar or a silence and did not know which.

A woman's voice spoke not in his ear but inside his mind. 'Gregory,' the voice said, 'you do not need to live your life like this.' And he felt his soul pour upwards in a glowing unstoppable spume.

Alice was picked up bodily and hurled backwards through the

air. The tumulus burned as bright as magnesium. The sky deto-
nated, the noise exploding through her eardrums into her skull,
and everything collapsed inwards.

She could have been unconscious for seconds or for minutes;
she was never to know.

At first Alice did not know where she was; she was not even
certain *who* she was. Her face and hands were as raw as if she
had passed through fire, and her head was filled with unformed
images that hissed and sparked like severed connections. Gradually
she became aware that the back of her head was wet, that damp
was seeping into her clothes, and that she was lying on drenched
grass, spreadeagled and with her feet apart. Her entire body was
bruised and her nostrils and lungs had tightened as if she had
inhaled steam.

It was painful to sit up, and when she did it was in unclear
surroundings. An unequal blurring drifted across her visual field,
as if lenses of different focal lengths were passing before her eyes.

Alice put one hand to her face. It was tender and she flinched
at her own touch. Almost immediately she turned to one side
and retched. A thin stream of spittle ran across her lips and, as it
did so, she realized that they were dry and cracked. She struggled to get on to all fours and then she stared at the ground.
The blades of grass now appeared fascinatingly infinite and
welcoming, a sign that she was present in the world, that she was
still alive.

And now Alice remembered that she was on a remote, high
moor, next to a pile of ancient stones, that there had been a man
with her, and that the man's name was Gregory Pharaoh.

She could not see him and she could not see the mound. For
a few seconds she was perplexed, and then she realized that she

must have landed so that she was facing in the other direction. If she looked to her left she could see only the moor, dark as murk, but when she looked to her right she saw a mound of stones that now appeared white and shiny as cut marble.

A motionless figure was stretched out next to them.

When Alice called Gregory's name it was so muted that it could have been imagined, like a cry from the world of ghosts. She recognized that she had been deafened. Her dulled ears felt as though they had been stuffed and tamped with wadding.

She almost got to her feet but then fell painfully onto her knees. She waited for a few seconds and then got up again. Unsteadily she walked to where the figure lay face upwards on the grass. On the way she stumbled over a rucksack that was no longer in the place where she remembered it as having been left. Wispy smoke rose from the turf around the man's body. Some of the nearby reeds had been set alight and were burning like tapers with low flames that were dying one after the other.

For an incoherent moment Alice was not fully convinced that the man was Gregory. His eyebrows and the front of his hair had vanished. Across his forehead and cheeks were raw pink blisters and layers of peeled skin. His jaws were clamped together and the lips drawn back from the teeth. The tip of his nose and parts of his upper lip were burned raw.

Alice knelt beside him. 'Gregory,' she said again. It was like a name spoken through a bandage.

His half-closed eyelids were trembling as though a small electrical charge was being passed through them, but the eyes were distant and loose. His hands also shook, as did one bare foot that protruded from a ripped trouser leg. Nearby was a formless object that Alice could not recognize, but which appeared to have been turned inside out. She thought it could be the missing boot; only later did she begin to suspect that it might have been the urn.

Alice put her hands across her ears and then lifted them away three times, but it made no difference to her hearing. She bent close to Gregory and noticed that there was a ragged hole in one shoulder of his jacket. The hole was the size of a child's hand and its edges were scorched so that the cloth around it was the colour of charred paper.

She did not know what to do. She began to search for her phone, but when she found it the screen was a jumble of meaningless runes, and whatever she pressed did not work. Gregory's hands shook as if they were palsied. It was frightening just to watch them tremble so helplessly.

Alice did not want to touch him. She was possessed by a fear that his stricken condition could somehow be transferred to her. Then she forced herself to take one of those shivering hands between her own. There was a coating of mud across his fingers. Even though Alice squeezed hard she still could not stop the hand from shaking.

She tried to think of what she could say. She did not know if Gregory could hear, and if he could then she could think of nothing to say that would make sense. After a few seconds, still unable to think clearly, she lied.

'You'll be all right,' she said.

Her voice sounded as though it had come from another room. She waited for a few seconds and then repeated the phrase. This time it was even less convincing, even more trite.

Gregory's right hand stopped shaking. She stared at it for a moment and then looked at his left hand. That had stopped shaking, too. The exposed foot gave a final tremor and was still.

Until she looked at his eyes Alice thought that the worst had passed. The lids had become still and drawn back; the eyes stared up at the sky but did not see.

'God,' Alice said.

She placed the palm of her hand across his lips but could detect nothing. Then she told herself that even if Gregory breathed out she would probably still not be able to sense it. Desperately she tried to remember what she had been taught on a first aid course. She could remember where it was held, and the name of the tutor, and even the texture of the fake skin on the dummy she had to practise on, but she could remember nothing at all of what she had learned.

It began to rain.

Alice parted Gregory's jacket so that she could feel his chest. He was wearing a buttoned outdoor shirt with a T-shirt beneath. After a moment's hesitation she put her hands between the buttons to see if she could feel a heartbeat through the T-shirt. She could not. She put her fingers into the waistband of his trousers and pushed both shirts up over his ribcage. They bunched in an unmoving wave just above the heart.

The exposed skin was mottled and deathly pale. Alice was both repulsed and ashamed of her reaction. There was a layer of fat across his belly and several random hairs that he had let grow long. She realized with a shock that even though Gregory had studied every inch of her own body, she knew nothing of his apart from his head and his hands. Rain fell on the pale flesh and tricked it out with faint light.

Alice placed her hands together and pressed them down with as much force as she could muster above Gregory's heart. His flesh was slippery. She began to count, did not know when to stop, finished at thirteen and then tried again. She did this several times and then paused. She thought she could feel a beat, but her own heart was racing so strongly that she could have been mistaken.

Gregory's mouth opened slightly. Again Alice held her hand above it but could detect no outward breath. Maybe there was no point in going on. Her hand was shaking almost as much as his had been. Around them rain began to fall more heavily. A mist rose from the grass.

She took Gregory's chin between her hands so that she could steady his head. Then she put her lips to his, made the seal as airtight as she could, and exhaled steadily. His mouth tasted of blood and smoke. She lifted her head and searched for a response. Nothing came. She tried again. After she had done it a dozen times she put her ear to his mouth. Was that a shallow breath she could feel? Once again she could not be certain. Rain began to hiss against the mound.

They would both die, Alice thought. It was like this: Gregory could be dying or already dead, and if she did not get off the moor she would die too. She would perish from shock and exposure.

She got back to her feet. His body seemed to be lying in a slightly different position, but that could be an illusion. In the time that she stared at him he did not move, did not even twitch. In that posture, and with his clothing awry, he resembled photographs of battlefield corpses.

Mist rose higher from the moor. Within a very short time she would become disoriented and lost. Dozens of tiny clicks could be heard on the rocks; hail was falling with the rain.

She bent down and touched the side of Gregory's head with extended fingers. A tiny sliver of his skin became stuck to her hand and she dashed it away.

'Help,' she said in a croak, and then swallowed. 'I'll get help,' she went on.

He did not look as if he had heard. Maybe he had already gone beyond hearing. Alice turned away and began to walk as quickly as she could back to the road.

After several yards she began to tremble violently. Her limbs lost energy with each passing second, the moor sucked hungrily at her feet with each step, and the mist and rain grew ever thicker and more unforgiving. Maybe both she and Gregory were meant to lose their lives here, she thought. She had imagined that they had been drawn to the moor for a beneficial purpose, but perhaps all the time it had been destined to end this way, in deaths that were pointless and cruel.

She was still thinking this when she found herself standing on the road.

Reddish puddles of water were deepening on its surface and a stream was sluicing from the moor and down the hill. She had not expected to reach the road so soon. Now that she had, she was seized by a terrible uncertainty. She did not know what to do. Faint twin lights wavered on the road, their beams dissolving in the rain. Behind them a shape that was darker than the mist began to emerge from it. She fell onto her knees and did not feel the hurt.

Later, the driver of the Land Rover was to tell Alice that she had been almost invisible in the fog, and that his headlights had only picked her up when she was standing just a few yards in front of him. And that both he and his colleague could hardly believe what they were seeing.

12

Many of the prints are strikingly large – much larger than Gregory would have chosen. He would have filled the space with smaller, more numerous images. Cassie, however, had measured the walls, weighed up the sight lines and concluded that fewer photographs in larger formats would have a greater impact. Whenever she sees guests pause before the more dramatic compositions – the near-abstract depiction of numbered skulls, say, or a statuesque nude – she is satisfied that she has made the right choice.

Cassie has also ignored her father's decision not to give any clarifying detail. Instead she has described each print on information cards fastened to the walls alongside them. Portraits quote the name of the sitter and buildings are given a location, so that a bishop and a damaged church are clearly identified. Some other nomenclatures are deliberately brief. Three photographs of a dying woman are called *Ruth I–III*; various nudes, usually of different models, are simply called *Nude*, and numbered *I* to *XIV*. Each print is fine-grained and with subtle gradations of contrast, so that every image has a tactile quality – velvety jets, whites as glossy as albumen, greys like fine volcanic ash.

The occasional colour prints all use vivid primaries to focus attention.

Despite a clear statement in the catalogue that Gregory is alive and well, and despite a recording of him that she has arranged on a loop, Cassie believes that most of the guests will treat the exhibition as a summation, an ending, a coda to work that has ceased. Business associates now acknowledge that, although the name of Gregory Pharaoh continues, it is his daughter who will fulfil any contracts agreed with the company. Most are content with this arrangement, and only a few have compared her work unfavourably with her father's. Whenever clients have asked if Gregory will return, Cassie has truthfully answered that she does not know. If they have then gone on to ask if he will take up the business again if he does, she has smiled politely and replied that nothing is impossible.

Cassie has posted invitations not only to clients, subjects, reviewers and cultural commentators, but also to many of the other names that feature in her long list of contacts. On reflection she believes the potential guest numbers to be too high, but perhaps they are justified if this is to be Gregory's last exhibition. She has even sent an invitation to Alice Fell, although she does not expect her to accept it.

Since the accident on Sampson's Bratfull, Cassie and Alice have spoken on the phone several times. They have even found it necessary to meet – only once – so that Alice could recount exactly what had happened on the moor and Cassie could inform her of Gregory's present condition. They met at a café in the centre of town and sat at a table by the window so that each could turn away from the other and study the outside world as it passed by.

A spiky awareness replaced their mutual antagonism, but neither was prepared to give ground to the other. Alice wore dark glasses with large frames and a fashionable cap that she pulled low on her forehead. At first Cassie thought that these and the heavy make-up were part of a defence mechanism, but then Alice lifted the glasses and raised the cap to prove that she, too, had suffered flash burns.

'The dermatologist says I'll be fine in a couple of weeks,' she said. And then she added, tartly, 'I hope you're not disappointed.'

'You must be pleased,' Cassie said. 'I know that looks mean a lot to you.'

'More than they do to you, Cassandra.'

Cassie recognized that Alice was not unattractive, but she also saw that she possessed a certain worn, depressive quality. Alice's life had been full, but she had lived it without sufficient discrimination. Her smart but conventional clothes, her looks, the way she carried herself, all formed part of a guarded charm that would draw many men towards her. Men who were ageing, and whose sexual chances were lessening, would feel the magnetism more fiercely than others. They were the ones who would be willing to endanger their own peace of mind. For them, love would become a burden and a damnation.

Once again Alice described what had happened on the moor. In her previous phone conversations she had been sparing with detail. Now the presence of another woman, even one as unsympathetic as Cassie, gave her licence to speak much more extensively.

Afterwards Cassie described the accident as the last step on a path she had been unable to prevent her father from taking. The decision to scatter crematorium ashes on a remote moor had been made at Alice's whim. Who could doubt that if she had not persuaded Gregory to accompany her then he would not have been injured, not have been hospitalized, not have had to suffer the indignity of psychiatric examinations?

'Your father could have refused, but he didn't,' Alice told her. 'He could have altered the date and time of the visit, but he didn't. If he'd done that we would both have avoided the storm.'

It seemed the easiest thing to say. Alice did not wish to explain that the workings of fate were cruel and occult. Thomas was meant to die just as Gregory was meant to be on the moor at the moment of the storm. He was meant to be stricken just as Alice was meant to save him. If that was not true then the world was merely chaotic and without purpose or significance. More than that Alice was unable to see.

'I thought he was dead,' she admitted. 'I tried my best to save him. I really did. And if I hadn't been able to get to that road, and if the forestry people hadn't come along, he could still have died.'

'I know you did your best. I'm grateful for that. I have to be.'

They sat in silence for a while, each avoiding the other's gaze. And then Cassie spoke again.

'I was suspicious of you and I still am. But I see now that you have qualities that weren't obvious.'

Alice shook her head. 'I never wanted to come between your father and you. He just wanted to photograph me. That was it. It was never going to go any further than that.'

As soon as the words were spoken she wondered if Cassie had recognized they were a lie.

When the two women parted they shook hands formally. It was an acceptable compromise for them both. A departure without touching would have been insulting, an embrace impossible. As they walked away, each grew aware that they shared a disconcerting and unwanted comradeship.

Cassie does not register that Alice has arrived at the exhibition and is standing alongside others as they watch Gregory's
recorded message. The screen has been placed next to the table
with the catalogues so that as they enter the gallery everyone has
the chance to pause and watch him speak. Alice is confident,
ready to face anyone, and dressed in a tailored black suit that she
wore for her successful interview with a firm of business consultants. She has been working for them now for several months.

In his message Gregory appears distracted, as if he has only
reluctantly agreed to be filmed. There are no establishing shots
other than a few seconds of feed as he sits against a white background and fixes a lapel microphone to his heavy coat. When
the frame is almost entirely filled with a close-up of his face it
appears that his skin has undergone a change in pigmentation,
although many put this down to the inadequacy of the recording.
Gregory glances to one side for a few seconds and then speaks.
It is a short statement, its outline apparently jotted on a notepad
just out of camera range. Even so, his remarks are interrupted by
several pauses and at one point he appears to lose interest completely.

'Thank you for coming,' he begins. 'This has been planned for
more than a year and it will possibly be the last time my photographs are ever seen in an exhibition. My daughter Cassie –
Cassandra – has done all the hard work, including selecting what
she thinks are the best photographs to hang. If everything goes
well, it's thanks to her.'

Gregory stops and then looks aside for a few seconds before
starting again.

'Some of you will know I live in another country now, so I

can't be there with you. I'm not going to say I'm sorry because that's not true. I'm living where I want to be and this is where I'll stay. What will be on show in this gallery are the results of a former life, one that I don't have any interest in reviving. The images hanging on the walls are like archaeological finds. They have a certain value and some of you will speculate about their composition and their messages and their meaning. But you won't really know the answers, just as I don't really know the answers. Reality, true reality, lies outside those photographs, just as it lies outside of the world that we all inhabit, like it or not.'

Keen to finish, evidently bored, Gregory reaches forward to switch off the camera. He says nothing else. As he looms close to the lens his features are made distorted and bulbous before the image vanishes.

Alice turned away and began to walk around the gallery. A waiter offered drinks from a tray; she took a glass of white wine and held it high in front of her body.

The silvered prints were hung on white walls with overhead lights. Clusters of guests had gathered in front of particular exhibits that they wished to admire or criticize. Several had attended solely to network and they were holding discussions in tight inward-facing groups. Ready to leave soon if necessary, Alice strolled the perimeter of the room in a calculated saunter, as if she were so used to private views that they were becoming tedious. As she moved she registered fragments of comment about the content of each frame, the variation of shape and motif from object to object, and the calculated dynamism in every composition. Such arcane modes of communication reminded her of humourless gatherings of physicists or archaeologists, except that these conversations were even less rooted in measurable fact. They were merely opinions, quickly assembled as response and defence, but actually as billowingly insubstantial as cloud.

None of the work in the first room was familiar. There were landscapes, industrial scenes, portraits, groups, buildings. Some were close-ups of objects that Alice could not recognize until she read the accompanying note. Some had sold, most had not, and a few were marked as not available for sale. Dutifully she patrolled them all, and as she did so she watched Cassie Pharaoh out of the corner of her eye. Alice was certain that Cassie had now registered her presence, but so far she had shown no sign of recognition.

Cassie was talking animatedly to two guests. She was wearing a maroon velvet jacket with scalloped trims, wide lapels and a high neck. Alice believed that it must have been copied from a Regency original, possibly bought at a museum, and that although no other woman in the room was wearing anything similar, it made Cassie look frumpy.

Alice turned her back on Gregory's daughter and looked at the next exhibit. A formally robed bishop gazed stonily outwards. It was the photograph Gregory had taken on the day that her handbag had been stolen. Everything was pattern. It was just that patterns were usually difficult to make out.

She sauntered away from the bishop and stood in front of a panoramic shot of a partially destroyed church. She remembered Gregory telling her about the shoot. At the time, she had not considered it significant. In his composition he had included a standing figure to add depth and scale. The figure was almost in silhouette; behind it a broad diagonal of light fell across the nave.

Another guest was standing beside her. After a few seconds he spoke: 'It's still for sale. The church has bought his portrait of the bishop; it hasn't yet bought this.'

Alice had grown used to strange men trying to engage her in conversation. 'I didn't notice,' she answered neutrally, to let him know she was not interested. The man spoke again.

'The restoration is going well. His daughter is coming back to photograph its completion.'

Alice wondered why he was telling her this. It could only be that he was expecting to be recognized. She looked more closely at the print.

'It's you,' she said.

He nodded. 'That's why I was invited here, I suppose. I gave Pharaoh my business card so he could keep it in his records – I wanted to make sure they got my name right in the newspaper caption. This photograph isn't quite the same as the one they printed. And it doesn't even mention my name. The paper didn't, either. You knew him, too?'

Alice ignored the question. 'You must have a professional link with this church.'

'The church as a whole, not just that particular one. I assess damage and recommend action. The destruction here was an unusual case. Very dramatic. Most of the time I'm dealing with plain old-fashioned erosion, lack of maintenance and decay. My name is Adrian Wells, by the way.'

'I thought people who did that kind of thing would be very old,' Alice told him. 'I thought they would have worked as ministers for years and years.'

There was a momentary pause before the man answered. Alice realized that he had been expecting her to introduce herself, but today she did not want to give her name to anyone.

'Well, no, I'm not a minister. I have a PhD in church architecture. Although obviously I have to know a lot about liturgy
and how buildings were moulded to reflect and reinforce ortho-
doxies. It's all rather fascinating – to me, anyway. I'm afraid most
people find it very boring.'

'Most?'

'I think so. I have these theories, you see, about what should
be done.'

Ah, she thought, another man with a theory. Wells began to talk.

Alice had found that when they met an attractive woman most
men were far too eager to list what they thought or what they
had done. They did this automatically and without hesitation,
like peacocks unable to resist a display.

Wells spoke too rapidly, as if he had to cram as many facts as
possible into a strictly limited space. Belief systems, he claimed,
had been forced by modernity to take new shapes. Everyone knew
this to be true. There was a saying that the waterhole of each
scientific advance was surrounded by the corpses of theologians.
Knowledge could no longer be ignored. The heavy, ornate,
enclosed spaces of the traditional church were unequal to the
discoveries of cosmology and physics, to what we now knew of
the social constructs of reality, and to biblical archaeology and
textual scholarship. What the faithful needed was a solution that
was collective and inclusive. Worship, communion, call it what you
like, had to be open and accessible and not restricted by outmoded
forms.

Alice knew that if she did not stop him he would talk like
this for another five minutes.

'You mean like the communities that must have worshipped
at prehistoric circles and avenues and henges?'

She could see him considering what to say next. 'Perhaps. It really depends if people need a charismatic leader and a priest caste. I'd like to think not. Evidence seems to suggest that they do.' He paused for a moment. 'You know about pre-historic sites?'

'I used to visit them. It was a while ago.'

Wells nodded. Alice could see that he had begun to think differently about her. She could not resist impressing him further.

'Stonehenge, of course,' she said, 'but also Avebury, the Rollrights, Sampson's Bratfull.'

He was puzzled. 'I haven't heard of that one.'

'No,' she said, 'not many people have.'

'That's fascinating,' Wells said admiringly. 'It's not just the space, you see. It's alignment and illumination. Whatever religion you follow, light is always a sign for the eternal, for the numinous.'

Aware now that he had been too enthusiastic, he shrugged in self-deprecation.

'I talk too much, given the chance. I'm sorry if you're bored.'

'I'm not bored,' Alice said, but smiled to end the conversation. 'I have to go,' she said.

'Of course. You knew Pharaoh too, did you?'

'Yes, I knew him.'

'And did he take your portrait? Is it on these walls? Will I recognize you?'

'Oh, I don't think you should look for me here,' Alice said.

As Wells nodded in an attempt to demonstrate that he was an understanding listener, she turned away.

Like lovers parting after an argument, they moved off in opposite directions. Other conversations, other approaches grew and flourished in the widening gap between them.

A waiter appeared with a tray. Alice put her empty glass on it but did not pick up a replacement.

In the next section of the gallery she came across a print of the skulls in the crypt. It had been taken at an angle that made them resemble smooth and uniform boulders, steeply raked like shingle after a violent tide. Only the empty eye sockets showed that these were human remains, and their cumulative and remorseless fate was emphasized by the inked numbers on the craniums. Gregory had been right.

A woman spoke close to her ear.

'They're going to bury them all.'

Alice recognized the voice, but did not respond.

'The decision was made last week. They're going to be boxed up together and buried in consecrated ground. There will be a short service.'

She turned. Cassie was standing much nearer than she expected. Their faces were uncomfortably close together, but neither woman stepped back or averted her eyes or blinked.

'I didn't know if you'd come,' Cassie said.

'I didn't think I'd be asked.'

'It wouldn't have been right to exclude you.'

'But you didn't expect me?'

'I didn't say that. I thought you might see this as an opportunity to draw a line.'

'I'm going to keep out of your way from now on, if that's what you're asking. Your father and I have already gone our separate ways. But there again, he's gone his separate way from everyone. Even from you.'

Cassie glanced to one side and appeared to soften.

Alice decided that perhaps she had been too abrupt. After all, any stranger who looked at the two of them would be aware who was better equipped to live a full life. Alice thought that it must be obvious to every woman in the room that Cassie had not done herself justice, and that her hairstyle and dress and make-up were unflattering. Men would probably not notice such detail, but simply judge that Gregory's daughter looked too much in control to be approachable. Perhaps they would even conclude that she was indifferent to sexual intimacy. But women would speculate that there was a need in Cassie that had been denied for so long that it was no longer capable of expressing itself.

'Have you heard from him?' Alice asked. 'Recently, I mean?'

'Not since the video. Have you?'

'I've heard nothing. He must want to keep silent. Maybe because he realizes now that we're all just part of a pattern.'

'What pattern?'

A distant feeling of responsibility sang within Alice, like a slow sequence of musical notes that Cassie would never be able to hear.

'I used to think that I was the focus of it all,' she admitted. 'Until Sampson's Bratfull everything seemed to have been directed towards *me*, to my future, to my understanding. But I'm not the focus at all. I'm just an agent. An enabler.'

She stopped when she saw that Cassie's expression had remained neutral.

'You don't know what I'm talking about,' Alice said.

'Should I?'

'It doesn't matter. Just forget I said it.' Anxious to change the subject, Alice looked again at the rake of skulls. 'I helped at that shoot,' she said.

Cassie had suspected as much but had never asked, and Gregory had never volunteered to tell her.

'He was wrong to involve you,' she said. 'Dad never used his models as assistants before he met you. A lot of the decisions he made in those last few months were mistakes.'

'I'm ahead of you. You're going to tell me that I was the worst of those mistakes.'

'Weren't you?'

'No, I was good for him.' Alice leaned closer to Cassie and lowered her voice. 'I wasn't like the other women who modelled for your father and then slept with him. I was out of the ordinary. I was special. He saw things in me that other people can't. That will always be true.'

'I admit this, Alice. I never thought a woman would be able to *lead* him. But you did. You're probably the kind of person who feels proud of that. Who knows what he thinks of you now? I don't know what Dad thinks about the past. I wonder if he thinks about it at all.'

'Maybe he's happy.'

'If you can say that a person is happy at the feet of someone he used to think was either disturbed or a fraud.'

'I remember that photograph. Did you select it for this?'

'Along here.'

They threaded their way through the crowded gallery. Twice Cassie had to stop briefly and promise other guests that she would return to talk to them soon. On the second of these pauses Alice looked to one side and recognized, high on the wall, the image of a naked back spread as if in crucifixion, the deltoid muscles emphasized by the angle and intensity of light, the elegant neck ascending to a dark screen of elegantly styled hair.

'I've marked it not for sale,' Cassie murmured. 'I thought you would prefer not to be part of a market. You and I know that it's you. No one else does. That was the day he borrowed my necklace.'

'He took it away.'

'I told him it wouldn't work.'

'I knew that the necklace belonged to you. I felt bad about wearing it.'

'Didn't you know that I inherited it? It was my mother's. His wife's. Ruth's. That's why it's important to me.'

Alice felt the muscles of her belly become tight. 'I didn't know. He didn't tell me.'

'No, I can see that he wouldn't. For Dad, the image was all that mattered.'

'Like this one? He says on that video that you made all the choices for the exhibition. Is that right? Did you choose this?'

Cassie nodded.

'I look so muscular. It's the way that the light fell. Look at those shoulders.'

'That's why I chose it. They seem as though they could support wings.'

'Like an angel?'

'No, I don't think he ever saw you as an angel.'

Cassie had carefully studied each of Alice's picture files, had perused each image as if it held within it a code that would explain why her father had become so obsessed. Naked, Alice Fell was no great beauty, but her unembarrassed displays flaunted a physical confidence that Cassie would never have wanted to match. Secretly, however, she had found that she grudgingly admired that confidence and was perhaps even in awe of it.

'And the other shots of me that are stored in his library,'

Alice asked, 'the ones taken in a hotel room with dust covers?'

'I've kept his promise to you. That's why there are none on display here. Someday you'll change your mind and want to have them exhibited.'

'I don't think so.'

And Alice thought of the hours that she had spent looking at the pictures taken in that shrouded, paint-spattered room. It was the first time she had studied herself as a lengthy display of static images, and as her reactions had swung from uncertainty to fascination she had begun to have a clearer insight into what men found so exciting and so humbling about the nude female body.

She could not know what her reactions would have been if she had found an identifiable image of her naked self displayed on these walls. For the near future she would continue to insist that those photographs not be shown, and yet a part of her imagination relished the impact they would have. Gregory had been right about that, too. Alice had always thought of herself as special, but she had never assumed that a part of that singular nature could be expressed in explicit terms. And if Gregory had been able to find and exploit that pictorially, then it must also be possible that others could detect further aspects of her unique-ness and wish to express them in different ways.

Cassie and Alice walked further along the gallery to where an image of Little Maria was hung. They had to wait silently for a short while until other guests moved out of the way and they could see it clearly.

The photograph was slightly different from the one that Alice had seen when she had first visited Gregory's studio, but must have been taken within a few seconds of it. Little Maria's pinched, undernourished face displayed a kind of stunned suspicion. There was no sense of holiness, of being chosen, or of revelation. Instead she appeared to be trapped.

'This has been sold,' Cassie said. 'I didn't expect that. One of her future disciples, maybe.'

Alice read the descriptive card: *Girl Who Sees Visions*.

'People must ask,' she said.

'They do,' Cassie answered, 'and if they do, I tell them that's where Dad is living. But I don't talk about all those other misguided dreamers who camp out there as well.'

'Do you want him back?'

Cassie shrugged. 'Would he listen to me, or to you? No. That part of his life is all over. Whatever we think and whatever we do, we have no influence with him now.'

'I don't want influence, Cassie. Not any more.'

'That's a difference between us. I do.'

Little Maria's eyes were as impenetrable as glass. Just by looking at her, Alice began to feel the chill of renunciation.

'It may be all over,' Alice said, 'but in the end, you got what was due to you.'

'His business? That wasn't my due. We talked about it, but I didn't think it would happen. I wasn't even sure that I wanted to take over the Gregory Pharaoh company. But I carry it on, and fulfil his contracts, and I'm good at what I do. Someone had to pick up the pieces and it had to be me. I can't just walk away from responsibility.'

Alice knew what Cassie was thinking – that unlike her, Alice could easily walk away. That she had a history of walking away. But Cassie could have no idea of how difficult that was, and how each time it tore at her heart.

'A lot of people in this room would say that you got what you deserve,' she said.

'Maybe,' Cassie answered. 'But what have you got? Nothing?'

'I've got rights over a few photographs. That's all. I deserve more. I *always* deserve more.'

'You don't have any rights, Alice. You don't even have a veto.'

'He promised.'

'That means nothing. None of Dad's promises meant anything. He could never keep them. Oh, he wanted to – he made them in good faith. But if there was ever a good reason to break a promise, then he would break it. Surely you could see that?'

Alice did not answer. Cassie shook her head.

'That's why I never let him take my photograph. I would never know what he would do with it.'

'Are you saying that he would have released those hotel studies, no matter what I felt?'

'Of course he would. Maybe not for a while, but eventually ambition would overcome everything else. In a way, I agree with him. They're part of a portfolio that is too good to be hidden away for years in a digital file. They have to be published sometime. And if you were honest with yourself, you'd want them to be published, too. Otherwise you wouldn't have posed, would you?'

'Are we talking years?'

'I'm not sure. I need to think about it.'

'You'll consult me?'

Cassie considered for a few seconds. 'All right,' she said. 'When I decide, I'll ask your opinion. But that doesn't mean that I'll take it.'

Alice imagined gallery walls hung with life-size images of her body. She saw herself as sculpted, immediate, yet untouchable.

The vision brought a flush to the skin across the top of her ribcage. She hoped it was not visible.

'Before you leave,' Cassie said, 'there's another display I want you to look at – over there, on that far wall. None of these are available for sale. I couldn't bear it.'

She led Alice to the triptych of her mother.

Ruth had been seriously ill in the first photograph and was dramatically worse in the second. In the third she was shrunken, comatose, on the point of death itself. To look at them made Alice feel like a blundering intruder, as if she were a stranger who had opened the door onto a tragedy she could not fully understand. This was the woman who had dominated Gregory's life, and his daughter's too, and yet Alice knew nothing about her. Ruth had always been a blank, a cipher, and Alice had always had scant interest in her. Now she had been given a face and a fate and suffering. Alice became slightly dizzy with the knowledge, and with the unsettling realization that Gregory could take photographs of his wife as she was dying.

'I didn't want to see these,' she told Cassie. 'You shouldn't even have them on display.'

'I had to. Dad would have wanted it.' Cassie paused for a moment before she went on. 'Now you can see what he was willing to do.'

Alice looked away.

Cassie leaned closer to her. 'My mother was the only woman he ever truly loved,' she said quietly. 'I want you to know that. Everyone else was a substitute. Even you.'

'You know nothing about what we felt for each other,' Alice answered.

Cassie smiled, distant, aloof and superior. 'I know enough. You'd be surprised how much I know. And now I think you've seen everything here that you would have wanted to see.'

Suddenly, unexpectedly, she leaned forward, kissed Alice quickly on one cheek, and turned away before she could respond. Alice stood without moving as Cassie walked back towards the people she had promised to return to.

Alice stared again at the photographs of Ruth.

This was all that remained of love, she thought: a few images of a dying woman. At least Alice would leave a record. When it became available, as it would do sometime, men and women would find her image enticing, distinctive and erotic. She did not wish to be memorialized as objectively as Gregory's wife had been. That was a form of exploitation. But didn't all love eventually become a series of transactions strung like a web across foundations of exploitation, dissatisfaction and ambition?

She turned to make her way to the exit. At least part of what Cassie had said was correct: it was, indeed, all over. But Alice had known that for weeks. In visiting the exhibition, all she had done was settle accounts with a short period of her life. She had placed a seal on it. She had turned it into history.

A man edged his way through the crowd and stood in front of her. She did not even look at him. She would simply walk round him and leave.

'I hope you don't mind me talking to you again,' he said.

It was the architect. She shook her head and stepped to one side.

Wells began to talk quickly. 'Look, it's just that you seemed interested in what I had to say. And that you know more than I had assumed about archaeological sites. I misjudged you and I have to apologize for that. We have more in common than I thought. So, well, maybe we could take up those subjects at a different place – when we can both have a bit more time to talk about things.'

Alice looked into his face. Smug with his own forwardness, Wells held out a small rectangular card.

'You're interested in structures, I can tell that you are. Structures with a particular function. We could have an interesting discussions. I'm sure we could.'

She smiled faintly, but did not encourage him. He advanced the card a little closer and spoke again.

'If you'd like to meet sometime – if that appeals to you – well, we can have a drink or a meal or something. That's all that I mean. If you'd like to do that, well, just give me a call.'

Alice took the card without enthusiasm. She could always throw into the waste bin outside.

'Maybe,' she said, to avoid any further discussion.

'You'll think about it?'

'I'll think,' she said, and walked away.

Newly arrived guests were talking across each other in the space in front of the screen. As she walked past them Alice noticed that Gregory's message was still being played, but that someone had turned down the sound to a whisper. Isolated within the screen, he looked out from it without seeing and mouthed words that went unheard and unheeded. It was, Alice thought, probably the last time she would ever see him.

Outside it was cold. Drizzle gusted through the streetlights. She would get a taxi home. As she began to look for one coming along the road Alice began to consider how little she knew about architecture, or building restoration, or the rituals of the Church.

Or about how beliefs were expressed in vaults and buttresses and spires.

She put her hand around the card from Wells and held it firmly so it would not be lost.

★

He never rested soundly and always woke before dawn. Often his sleep was disturbed by the weather, but sometimes it was loud cries or the repetition of prayers that seemed as if they were being offered up just outside his door. Bad weather was the worst, and this winter was implacable. Gales harried the bare trees and pushed against the sides of the tiny caravan so that it seemed about to tilt across its moorings. As its frame creaked Gregory heard the overhead branches keen eerily, as if spirits were being driven from them. At other times hard rain would beat tattoos on the roof, or hailstones rattle the metal, or snow build up in a suffocating hush. The tiny heater was inadequate and every morning he lay within his blankets, fearful of the cold, while daylight broke in soft gradations through the ice layers that had formed on the inside of the windows. When he looked at his face in the tiny mirror on the wall he saw how he had aged. He was haggard, unkempt, and did not suit his ragged grey beard. Fortunately, appearance, either his own or anyone else's, was no longer important to him.

He put on the jacket he had worn to visit Sampson's Bratfull, laced his boots to the top eyelet, and opened the door. A fresh snowfall glared from the settlement roofs and lay in crumbled avalanches where it had slid from the sides of tents. A fox had prowled the length of the dwellings and its tracks punctuated the drifts.

On the mud path to the latrine the snow had already been

trodden into brown slush. Gregory carefully picked his way along it. The latrine was a canvas shelter with a small board hung outside with a crude marker to indicate whether or not it was occupied. Inside was a chemical lavatory that the users emptied by rote. He had developed the habit of not looking inside as he lifted the cover. Smells of shit and disinfectant rose round him, but back outside, a mere few yards away, the air was pure and cold enough that when he breathed through his nose he could feel the tiny hairs bristle inside his nostrils.

Back in his caravan he made a meal from a sachet of instant porridge while he waited for a knock on the door. Today was his special day; he had waited for it for weeks, and he could only hope that it would be the first of many. People who were not followers were incapable of understanding its importance. But there again, he thought, most people were forever denying themselves the offer of illumination.

Carla was living in a small hut nearer to the road, and had to walk a hundred metres to reach his door. When he opened it he saw that she was wearing her usual waterproof clothing with trousers whose legs were spattered with mud. A green woollen hat was pulled down over her ears. At the crown an incongruous group of loose ends had been gathered so that they stuck out from the top of her head like fronds. She nodded at Gregory and he opened the door wider to let her in. She scraped the slush from her boots on the metal steps and then stepped onto the coarse matting that he had put down at the entrance. Neither of them spoke.

By the time that Gregory arrived Carla had been living in the camp for three months. Almost immediately she had asked why it had taken him so long to decide that he must come back to this place. She had not acknowledged that they had once slept together, and neither had he. Although it had not been obvious to Gregory at the time, it was clear to him now that when they had made love Carla must already have been succumbing to the mystery that was unfolding on this bleak remote hill.

Now she sat on his thin divan, her hat between her hands as she picked idly at the fronds. Her face was as lined and tired as his own, Gregory thought. He was grateful to Carla. She had helped him adjust, although recently she had seemed less committed to remaining in the settlement. And perhaps sooner or later one of them would admit they had once been intimate, but that they recognized that this had been part of a past that had often been tinged with unacknowledged shame. As for now, as though in preparation for a life of abstinence, they followed an unspoken rule and never actually touched each other.

Gregory put his jacket back on. He had not repaired the charred hole that had been blasted through its shoulder; he was as proud of that as any badge.

Carla spoke for the first time.

'I hope you will not be disappointed if she speaks to you in simple words. Maybe she will tell you that we do not realize how much we need simplicity. Most probably she will say that only you can solve your own—' For a moment she sought the apposite word. 'Predicament,' she said.

'I understand. And I'm grateful for the translation.'

She nodded. 'I do the best that I can.'

They stepped back outside. Sunlight was brightening the camp. It reflected upwards from the drifts, illuminated the stubby icicles hanging in friezes from the protruding edges of roofs, and shone on the dirty pathways, patches of soiled snow and caravans with flat tyres, flaking chrome and warped panels. A woman they did not know, and who never greeted anyone, was on her knees by her caravan door, her hands raised and her eyes half closed. Her lips moved rapidly in prayer. She looked emaciated, cold and desperately ill, but would never be stopped from doing what she believed was demanded of her.

When Gregory and Carla reached the road they found they were able to follow it upwards along trails of compressed snow that had been formed by car tyres. Others had gone before them and left footprints across the tracks. A hundred metres ahead a small group of people laboriously pushed a wheelchair uphill. They took turns at the handles. Sometimes the occupant, an elderly woman, shouted out as if in pain. The wheelchair scored thin wavering marks across the tyre indentations. Powdery snow drifted liked spume from conifer branches and fell across the road in a glittering mist.

'Are you nervous?' Carla asked.

'No,' Gregory answered, 'I'm looking forward to it.'

'Other followers are still waiting. You are favoured. She remembers you, I think. You were different then.'

'We both were.'

'Yes. We both were.'

The snow crunched or slithered beneath their steps. The wheelchair slipped and would have begun to slide backwards had its movement not been blocked. The people around it began to argue among themselves. Gregory could not understand what they said. The face of the woman in the chair was full of anger and fear.

Carla talked to them for a minute and then turned back to Gregory.

'They do not want our help.'

'They refuse?'

'Yes. We go on.'

The group reformed around the wheelchair and once more began to push it uphill. Their breathing was as noisy as the breathing of animals. By the time the shouts started again Gregory and Carla had left them far behind. He thought that if he had still been a photographer he could have turned and taken their picture. It would have been an evocative image.

'We could have helped,' he said.

'No,' Carla explained, 'they see it as a trial they must under-take. We cannot interfere with that.'

They trudged past a line of deserted cars blinded with layers of frozen snow. Gregory often wondered how soon after his first visit they had been abandoned. The engine of the broken-down tractor was sheathed in a block of dull ice. Nearby the nail heads on the cross no longer shone, but had rusted into the wood.

A wall of roughly mortared blocks had now been built like a palisade on either side of the road. In front of it was parked a four-wheel-drive police car, recently arrived and with only a light dusting of snow across its bonnet. Beyond the wall was an open courtyard that was partly roofed by canopies of corrugated plastic. Sheltering beneath these were a number of stalls, all gaudy with the tacky paraphernalia of worship – crucifixes, rosaries, statuettes, portraits, pottery, trinkets, postcards, choral CDs.

Further up the incline two armed policemen in heavy coats and fur hats were talking to men who had the look of officials. Gregory realized that one was the priest he had photographed on his first visit. The priest showed no sign of recognition until Carla spoke to him, and then he grasped Gregory's hand in exag-gerated greeting.

'Welcome,' he said in English, and then, too emphatically, '*welcome.*'

When Gregory tried to pull away his hand the priest resisted. Through the gloves his fingers felt stiff and badly articulated, like those of an automaton.

'Perhaps a donation,' Carla said. 'Donations are needed to help protect this place.'

She had already suggested to Gregory how much he should give, and he handed over the notes without complaint. The priest put the payment into his pocket and ushered Carla and Gregory forward.

'Will they really use it for that?' he asked under his breath.

'They need charity. Also it guarantees that you will be given an audience.'

Not for the first time, he noticed a sceptical edge in Carla's voice.

The site of Little Maria's vision no longer stood on its own. Instead it was surrounded by other buildings, all of them assembled hastily and without thought to anything other than worship and shelter. Everyone knew that the broken-roofed cowshed was now a sacred place that none but Little Maria could enter.

Two guards stood by the door of a new building with a wooden balcony. It was here that Little Maria would stand, once a week and for only five minutes, while pilgrims fell to their knees in prayer. Sometimes she spoke a few sentences; often she was silent. For many, that was enough. They gave their money to officials threading through the gathering and afterwards talked of the halo they had seen around her head, or the words that had come unbidden into their minds, or the profound sense of peace that had settled within their souls.

The guards stopped Gregory and Carla from going any further. Carla produced a document that they took a long time to peruse. Eventually they nodded and motioned that she and Gregory should stand where they were. The door was heavy and functional and set into a blank whitewashed wall. It was closed. A bright metal crucifix had been screwed to the wood.

Carla spoke in a low voice. 'Some want to cover over the site of the vision with a transparent glass dome. And there are others who want gold cloths, incense, lamps, sacred music played through speakers. Little Maria has said no. She says that true holiness is never honoured by riches. She says the Holy Mother of God chose this place because it was like the stable in which she gave birth to the Christ.'

Gregory began to shiver. He was not sure what was going to happen.

'Are you cold?' Carla asked.

He did not have time to answer. The door was opened from the inside and a middle-aged man came out. The man held one hand cradled within the other and he walked downhill past them with a curious shuffling gait. Distant light shone in his eyes, as if he had gazed for too long into a vivid sunset.

The door was opened further and a dark-haired young man beckoned them inside. They stood in a vestibule with three seats of moulded plastic and a divan that they could leave their coats on. Carla had to produce her document again. The young man checked it as though it were a passport, stared hard at Gregory, and then nodded and led them forward through another door.

'This is where she is,' Carla explained in a murmur.

They stood in a small and sparsely furnished room. It had bare walls, a table, and one tiny window with a white plastic

Madonna on the sill. A portable heater threw out fumes that made the room airless. Gregory felt his eyes begin to smart. The tabletop was partly covered by offerings that included Bibles, dolls, bracelets, and bars of chocolate. Carla stood one pace behind Gregory and a little to one side.

At the head of the room the girl who saw visions sat on her own in a comfortable chair.

Carla drew a small, neatly wrapped package of expensive tea from her pocket and left it alongside the other gifts, and then she spoke for about fifteen seconds. Gregory only knew a few words of the language, but he recognized that Carla was reminding Little Maria that he was a photographer, and that they had met before.

The girl appeared much taller than when Gregory had seen her last. Her face had filled out and her hair had been restyled simply but effectively. After a few seconds he noticed that she wore a gold ring on her little finger. Her blue eyes never left his face and never blinked. He felt that she was looking deep into him and finding nothing there.

When Carla had finished speaking Little Maria remained silent. After a few seconds Gregory began to feel uncomfortable. He did not know what to say or do.

'You must speak now,' Carla said softly, and Gregory cleared his throat.

'My name is Gregory Pharaoh.'

Immediately he felt guilty, and that he had been caught out in a lie. Little Maria stared at him as if waiting for the truth.

'But I invented that name. I was born George Farrar. I was a photographer.'

He felt something lift within him, as if he had walked out of a shadow.

'I took your portrait last year. It was printed in a newspaper. Maybe now it is hanging in an exhibition of my work at a gallery. I was happy and proud because I thought it was a good photograph – it *is* a good photograph.'

As Carla translated he looked to see if there was a change in Little Maria's expression. There was none.

'It's good because it lets people know what you look like. But it can't tell the world what you have seen – *who* you have seen. Any photograph is just . . . surface. It's like a sign. A magazine or a book or a print on a wall, they're all a kind of maze of surfaces. I didn't understand that for years, but I do now. I lived in a world where all that mattered was what could be seen. Surface was all there was. That's why I'm here. I have left behind me a folly of signs.'

Carla finished her translation so quickly that he wondered if she had omitted some of his explanation. Maybe he had been too ambitious in speaking to Little Maria like this. Perhaps he had confused her enlightenment with an ability to understand. She said nothing as she stared at him.

And now Gregory believed that he stood within Little Maria's changeless gaze as if it were a searchlight that was illuminating all his lies, all his ambition and all his vanity.

'I based my life on the look of things,' he said weakly. 'Only one of the five senses informed my work and that was the sense of sight.'

Gregory paused. Nothing in the room had changed; perhaps the light coming through the single window was a little stronger, that was all. He remembered standing in the crypt with light from a solitary window fading across skulls and bones. In the end everyone was reduced to bones, to dust, to ash. There had to be more to life than a heap of ash.

Little Maria spoke. Although her voice was plain and unquestioning, Carla's translation was hesitant and slightly tremulous.

'The Holy Mother understands and forgives. She is the way to our salvation.'

'I heard a voice,' Gregory confessed. 'A woman's voice.'

There was no response.

'It spoke to me when I was imprisoned by light and unable to move and unable to think. I had a . . . revelation. It was like something out of the scriptures. I don't know who said them but they were the words you said to me.'

Little Maria paused for a long time before speaking again.

'And what did I say?'

She could not have forgotten, Gregory decided. Her question was not simple; it was deep. Little Maria was asking him to measure his behaviour and his belief against what she had told him.

'You said that I need not live my life in the way that I was living it.'

Gregory felt suddenly alone, as if he stood at the edge of something that others shared but that he could not enter. He did not know what this was; he only knew that it existed.

'I don't know what to do,' he admitted weakly.

Little Maria could have nodded her head slightly; he was unable to decide.

Gregory went on. Every word he said felt as if others could also have spoken it. His plight ceased to be individual and became common.

'I believed that when I came here I would find the answer,' he said.

She appeared to be waiting for him to say more. He spread his hands helplessly.

'I'm here because I was sent.'

Little Maria answered. At the end of each sentence she paused and waited for the translation to end. Carla struggled to find the right words. They came at Gregory like bursts of code.

'The Holy Mother knows and understands. The Holy Mother gave me the gift to see into your soul. You lived with avarice, with lust, with ambition. You can live now as you have been living or you can change. You made the right decision. The Holy Mother will smile on you. You may not be able to see her face, but I can promise you it will be smiling. But the Holy Mother cannot cure you. The answer lies within. You must heal yourself.'

Abruptly, Little Maria fell silent. It was as though she had discharged all that she had wanted to say. Cold sunlight, building across the window glass, touched her face to give it the look of marble.

'What must I do?' Gregory asked.

Little Maria's head inclined slightly. At first Gregory did not understand that this was a signal.

The young man who had let them enter the room appeared alongside him. He reached out and held Gregory's elbow in a light but firm grasp. Gregory had not realized that the man had been standing behind them all the time, ready to end the audience when he was told. They had only been in the room for a few minutes.

'Our time is up,' Carla said in low voice.

Little Maria remained impassive.

'I don't know what to do,' Gregory pleaded, but Carla did not translate.

The young men reached his other arm in front of Gregory and tugged slightly so that he would turn and face the door. As though in reflex, Gregory obeyed. Carla had already turned. He wanted to look back and call out to Little Maria, but he knew that if he did he would not be answered, and that if he were judged to have misbehaved then he would never again be allowed an audience with the girl who saw visions.

As they were escorted to the door the young man murmured soothing, incomprehensible words. The door closed like a judgement behind them. In the vestibule Carla talked to the man while she and Gregory put on their coats.

'I told him you want to come back,' she explained. 'He says you are welcome but that you must wait your turn.'

'And that could take weeks,' Gregory replied. It was not a question.

Carla shrugged. 'There are many who want an audience. And some are far, far richer than you.'

Within less than a minute they were back outside with the cold air clearing Gregory's head and singing in his ears. Standing in front of the door were the people with the wheelchair. They had cramped, desperate faces. The woman in the chair was swaddled with scarves so that only a pair of bright, hunted eyes showed as they glanced rapidly from side to side. The people said nothing as Gregory and Carla set off down the incline. Concerned only with lighting their cigarettes, the two guards also ignored them as they passed.

'You do not want any of these mementoes?' Carla asked as they walked between the stalls of crucifixes, statuettes and souvenirs.

Gregory shook his head vigorously. He was not sure if she was asking ironically.

They were silent for a while as they made their way past the roadside cars and the tall wooden crucifix and back down the snowy road. Sunlight illuminated the tops of the conifers; soft plates of snow tumbled from the high green branches and disintegrated against the lower ones.

After several minutes an old car laboured up the hill, its worn tyres making it slide alarmingly across the hissing surface. Gregory and Carla were forced to stand aside until it had passed.

'And what about you?' he asked. 'Will you stay?'

'What she said to you,' Carla said after several seconds, 'it was almost exactly the same as what she said to me.'

'So?'

'It's probably what she tells everyone.'

'Perhaps that's because we all have the same faults and need to be told the same thing.'

'Perhaps.'

'Just because it's repeated doesn't mean it's without worth. When I was a photographer my work didn't lose anything by being reproduced. It still had the same point, still had the same value. But it reached more people.'

'You may be right,' Carla said neutrally, making it apparent that she did not wish to argue.

Soon, ready to part, they stood together at the settlement's edge. Someone had lit a wood fire and its smoke drifted across the site. The kneeling woman still prayed from within her closed world. A touring coach with tinted windows and bright lettering drove up the hill, snow exploding from its wheels.

Gregory stared at Carla. Unapologetic, she looked back at him.

'You haven't found anything here,' he said flatly.

'I tried. I really tried.'

'I always thought you believed in her.'

'I did. She's not a liar. I'm sure that she saw the Virgin. But I do not think she sees her any more. Visions like that don't survive in this world. They are like creatures taken out of water – they die because they can no longer breathe.'

Gregory's feet were cold. He shifted his weight from one foot to the other.

'You haven't told me if you'll stay,' he said.

'This place is only a stage in life. It's not an end.'

'That's what you think. I'm different. You're here out of interest, but it was destiny that brought me back. There's an answer for me somewhere. I have to stay.'

'Gregory – are you still Gregory? Or are you George?'

'Maybe now I'm more like George than Gregory.'

'Whatever you call yourself, I have never known a person who has changed so much. You never believed in Little Maria. You said her visions were absurd and you joked about them with that reporter. You thought that I was crazy for giving her the benefit of the doubt.'

'You're right. But I was forced into change. I almost died. Maybe I *did* die. And a man lost his life so that I could stand in the right place at the right time.'

'That is cruel. I cannot believe that God acts like that.'

'Little Maria would tell us that we can never know God's purpose. All I can say is that when I look back on the last few months everything falls into place. Who I met, what I did, what happened. For me there was no such thing as coincidence.'

Carla stared at him like a doubting inquisitor.

'I was *chosen*,' Gregory insisted.

She looked from side to side, as though wary of being over-heard.

'We were lovers,' she murmured.

'Just for one night,' he said, as if she needed to be corrected.

Gregory had no reliable memory of their lovemaking. He could recall almost nothing. Recently, whenever he was tempted by the memory of sexual pleasure, or its promise, it was with an image of Alice Fell standing naked and untouched in a room with crumpled sheets that had been spotted with paint.

'But it was a night that we shared,' Carla insisted. 'Was that part of your destiny, too?'

'Yes. I didn't know it at the time, but I was being given a comparison.'

Carla pulled the hood of her coat up around the lower part of her face. Hurt still showed in her eyes.

'I believed that you had picked me for myself,' she said, bitterness seeping from the words. 'I did not suspect that you had been compelled. If we made use of each other it was because we were both searching for pleasure. It was not because I was part of some divine plan.'

Gregory shrugged.

To him the conversation had become almost pointless. Carla would never accept his conviction that destiny was at work in his life, nor that others would have to suffer because of that. For Carla the world was still a puzzling, contradictory and impenetrable place. For Gregory, it was beginning to take a locatable shape. He did not know why he had been selected to shuffle so awkwardly towards an understanding, an enlightenment; he only knew that it lay somewhere ahead of him, in space, in time, or perhaps only at the moment of his death.

They said a perfunctory goodbye and Carla walked away from him through the trodden snow. Gregory wondered if she expected him to follow or to call her back. He did neither. All he thought was how ridiculous her hat looked, with its crown of bobbing fronds.

And then he thought how ridiculous *he* would look to Cassie, how shambling, how morally dependent, how pathetic. Uncertainty passed over him like the shadow of a whirled cloak, and in that instant Gregory knew that he was destined eventually to return to the life he had believed he had given up forever.

Some hours later, when he least expected it, a vision came to him. Even though he was the only person in the caravan there seemed to have been a change in the light, as if something bulky yet furtive had paused in front of his mirror. A prickling sensation tingled at the corners of his eyes. Gregory had experienced this before, a week ago, but it had subsided. Now he felt that something was about to happen that he must witness but not necessarily understand. He put down his Bible and stared into the mirror.

At first he thought that the glass was lying, as he could see the back of a naked man's shoulders and head. As he stared, the man slowly turned and rose, as if his feet had lifted free of the ground. Gregory saw he was looking at himself. And then, quite suddenly, the reflection became edged and defined by a white halo of light that radiated outwards for several seconds before dissipating to leave no trace behind.

Gregory stared at his new self in the mirror. The surface of his skin became translucent and within the bars of his ribcage there pulsed a gigantic heart. It almost filled the entire chest cavity, and it glowed a fierce blinding crimson with each un-yielding beat.

Outside on the caravan roof, across the settlement, and over Little Maria's broken-roofed cowshed at the top of the hill, snow began to fall – quiet, deep and relentless.